PRAISE FOR THE (

"A fast-paced, heartfelt, and fun read!"

—Lauren Blakely, *New York Times* bestselling author

"Violet Duke made me laugh and cry in this incredible romance. One of the best I've read this year. Emotionally charged with wonderful characters, I just couldn't stop reading!"

—J. S. Scott, *New York Times* bestselling author

"A unique series that will take you on a roller coaster of emotions. I couldn't put these books down!"

—Carly Phillips, *New York Times* bestselling author

"Sexy, heart-melting and guaranteed to make you laugh and cry, Violet Duke writes the loveliest romances ever."

—Sawyer Bennett, *New York Times* bestselling author

"Stellar collection of stories with unforgettable characters and a truly unique plot . . . will leave you wrecked and elated."

—*Guilty Pleasures Book Reviews*

PRAISE FOR THE FOURTH DOWN
SERIES

"Violet Duke's writing just jumps off the page and grabs you from the first sentence."

—Bella Andre, *New York Times* bestselling author

"Hot, sweet, and filled with tender moments, Violet Duke writes heroes who make me swoon!"

—Kendall Ryan, *New York Times* bestselling author

"From the giant men getting schooled to the happily ever after, I was enthralled! Violet Duke has a touchdown with *Jackson's Trust*!"
—Melody Anne, *New York Times* bestselling author

Praise for the Cactus Creek
Series

"A contemporary romance star! Violet Duke is a must-read for guaranteed feel-good, heart-tripping romance with *true heroes*, *sassy heroines* and *delicious journeys* to *happily-ever-after*."
—Erin Nicholas, *New York Times* bestselling author

All There Is

OTHER TITLES BY VIOLET DUKE

Can't Resist Series

Resisting the Bad Boy

Falling for the Good Guy

Choosing the Right Man

Finding the Right Girl

Cactus Creek Series

Love, Chocolate, and Beer

Love, Diamonds, and Spades

Love, Tussles, and Takedowns

Love, Exes, and Ohs

Fourth Down Series

Jackson's Trust

JUNIPER HILLS SERIES

All There Is

VIOLET DUKE

 Montlake
Romance

Text copyright © 2017 by Violet Duke
All rights reserved.

Published by Montlake Romance, Seattle

www.apub.com

Amazon, the Amazon logo, and Montlake Romance are trademarks of Amazon.com, Inc., or its affiliates.

ISBN-13: 9781477848326
ISBN-10: 1477848320

Cover design by Janet Perr

Chapter One

"C'mon, have you at least *considered* opening up a shop in the city instead? This place is in the middle of nowhere. I mean, there isn't even a Starbucks around here. It's a hick town, Emma. No offense."

Plenty taken.

Emma Stevens plated up a fresh chocolate croissant and sat down with a sigh, while Bill—her latest proof that the online dating app her sister had signed her up for was profoundly and disturbingly flawed—took a messy bite out of the flaky pastry he'd requested she have waiting for him when he came by this morning before work. Exactly an hour before her bakery opened, which, as she'd told him on numerous occasions, was her craziest time of day.

All because he wanted to give her "a chance to wish me good luck" over the big real estate investment he was going to land today.

Seriously.

And, of course, he didn't even *pretend* to offer to pay for the croissant. Not that she'd really expected him to. Emma had been out on only two dates with the guy, yet somehow he'd managed to stop by her bakery for free pastries and desserts nearly a dozen times. The last had been for an entire cheesecake for his office a few days ago.

Mathematically speaking, this relationship was not doing so hot.

Now to add insult to injury, here he was disparaging her amazing little town, the only place that had felt like home for her in a really long time.

Never had the three-strikes rule in dating seemed so painfully overgenerous.

Since, per usual, he'd proceeded to simply bulldoze right along without waiting for an actual answer from her to his question, she took the opportunity to study him for a bit . . . as an anthropologist would when encountering a possible *Homo jerkus*, a male species of ego-vore, originating from Putzland.

Currently the subject was displaying his pompous plumes, sitting there with his power tie thrown over one shoulder—now officially her newest pet peeve—while belittling her neighbors' businesses as he scarfed down his free pastry.

Huh, Megan's right, he does kind of look like a Tyrannosaurus rex *when he eats things with his hands.*

Her sister, Megan, had first witnessed him in here eating the other week with his elbows held out like outstretched wings while holding his free glazed-blueberry scone with two hands, pinkies and ring fingers in the air, as if he were eating a royal hamburger with the queen of England.

Since then, the subject's eating habits had been a frequent topic of analysis. Apparently it was all about his arm placement. According to Megan, when he had his elbows tucked in at the ribs like he was doing now, *bam*, T. rex arms.

The resemblance was really quite uncanny.

As he took his next big bite, Emma tried channeling some *Jurassic Park*–worthy sound effects in her head—*rawr, snarfle, chomp, chomp*—and nearly burst out laughing.

Misunderstanding the giggle that seeped out of her in a way that only he could, Bill went on to then reassure her with a firm hand squeeze. "Don't laugh. With my help, this *is* possible. You could be

2

making some real money if you took this little hobby of yours seriously. We're talking distribution to big grocery chains, even franchising. You'd just need a few investors, a commercial space probably in a mall for visibility, and a strong commercial campaign to really get your name out there. I'd be willing to take one percent off my usual commission to help you find that perfect business space to lease."

Emma had stopped being amused the moment he'd called her business a hobby. Now the T. rex growling that she was hearing was accompanied by the visual of her taking a big bite out of Bill's overinflated, condescending head.

"That's not the kind of bakery I want to run. I love it here. I love my regulars and all the town visitors. And I make a good living."

The polite, patronizing scoff from Bill had Emma's back teeth grinding. "Look, Bill, I need to finish up an anniversary cake and get ready for the morning crowd, so why don't we just catch up later."

Bill brushed all the crumbs from the pastry onto her formerly freshly swept floor as Emma looked on in disbelief.

"You're right—I better get going. Coming out here was so far out of my way." He patted her on the arm, and she only barely stopped herself from recoiling. Balling up his napkin and pushing it toward her on the empty plate, he asked distractedly, "So are we still on for dinner tonight? At that place I told you about?"

Emma groaned silently. It wasn't that Bill was a bad guy per se. In fact, he was a catch in comparison with the last two dates the demented dating app had paired her with. She figured she should probably give the guy at least one more shot. Wasn't there something to that whole opposites-attract theory?

"Do you want to just come back over here for dinner instead?" she offered. "They have some great specials at Sally's Diner this week. And we could maybe catch an early movie afterward or just walk around town."

Bill frowned. "But what about the new gastropub in Shawnee? I already made reservations. And there's also this great nightclub I wanted to take you to. Give you a chance to ditch the apron for a bit—you know, get dolled up with a hot dress and some sexy heels."

Oy, the man didn't know her at all.

Some girls loved their designer shoes and handbags; Emma much preferred her soft cotton pj's and fuzzy slippers. "I'm sorry, but my mornings here start really early." As she'd told him for the past few weeks. Repeatedly. "So that wouldn't work for me."

"Oh." He pouted in disappointment. "I guess we could go out another night then."

Translation: he was going to find another chick for his pub-and-club plans tonight.

"What about next weekend?" he asked, making a not-so-subtle visual scan of her legs and chest while licking his lips. *Gross.*

Clearly he still wasn't understanding. She was getting ready to bust out a sock-puppet show with a catchy cartoon jingle to get through to him. "I have early mornings every morning, Bill. Sort of goes along with the whole running-a-bakery-seven-days-a-week thing. That's why I'm usually in bed by eleven p.m."

"You mean *every night*?"

Eureka, he finally got it . . . and now he was giving her a look as if she'd just broken out in warts.

Before Emma could propose a quick and merciful end to their clearly doomed relationship, a loud metallic crack suddenly boomed from the ceiling.

What the . . . ?

An ominous thunk and hiss resounded a few seconds later. She went racing to the back of the bakery to find bursts of pipe water already starting to spray in every direction and waterfall out of the seams of the ceiling panels and lighting fixtures.

"The cake!"

She ran forward to grab the beautiful cake she'd made for Mr. and Mrs. Johnson's forty-seventh anniversary, only just barely managing to slip it into the nearest fridge before her ceiling basically exploded.

Two ceiling panels above her display cases came crashing down, freeing a deluge of rushing water so strong, it nearly knocked over her register. And judging by the screech from Bill, he'd gotten splashed by some water in the front, as well.

Not good. The place would be flooded in no time at this rate. Grabbing a big baking pan from the counter to hold over her head in case more ceiling panels came falling down around her, she made a run for the back door, snagging a wrench from her utility drawer in case the main water valve outside was rusted shut.

"Bill, can you run under the stairs and shut off the electrical breaker?" she shouted as she propped open the back door. The water was pooling on the floor. If the water level rose to the electrical outlets, she was in big trouble. "I'm going to try to shut the water off!"

Sure enough, the valve outside was nearly frozen solid with rust. She was practically horizontal with the wall in a super-Spidey crawl trying to torque the wrench when, finally, the valve began turning, at a micromillimeter pace.

With it no longer sounding like the base of Niagara Falls in the bakery, Emma slumped over in relief, feeling every muscle in her body burning over the exertion and adrenaline. A striking contrast to the icy-cold water that had drenched her from head to toe. Thank goodness the spring snowmelt had started the other week, or else she'd be a numb Popsicle by now.

Just as she was thinking she needed to go break out the thermal underwear again before she dealt with the mess inside, however, she witnessed something that had her blood heating up to an angry boil.

"Where are you going?" she shouted to Bill's retreating back as she saw him sneaking off to his little silver coupe parked across the street.

He hesitated and then turned to give her a helpless shrug. "Sorry, babe. I couldn't find the electrical panel thing you were talking about. Plus all that pipe water got on my suit! Hopefully it didn't ruin it. I need to rush home to change before my big meeting. I've got a lot riding on this. I need to look sharp."

"Are you freaking kidding me?" Her entire bakery was now submerged in ankle-deep water, and he was complaining about his suit getting a little damp.

"I promise I'll call to check on you later."

That was a total lie, and they both knew it.

"Un. Believable."

She continued to glare at him for exactly one second—while he was swiping at the water splotches on his suit pants and cradling his suit jacket like a Fabergé football—before she stomped over to her butcher-block island and grabbed the nearest ruined cupcake.

If he was going to dry-clean the damn thing anyway . . .

She took aim, and launched the cupcake.

"You bitch!"

Nailed him right in the ass.

Looks like those middle school summers playing district league sports really *had* taught her valuable life skills.

She took out her camera phone and zoomed in on the cupcake sticking to Bill's slacks like a snowy-white rabbit tail puff. Folks didn't call her buttercream frosting the thickest and richest in the county for nothing. That sweet lil' treat was good and stuck.

Say cheese!

As she pocketed her phone and headed back into the bakery to shut off the electrical panel, Emma made a mental note to add "excellent aim with projectile baked goods" to her online dating profile . . . along with this spiffy new photo for her profile pic. The site *did* say to choose one that best represented her, after all.

She couldn't stand when folks weren't honest on stuff like that.

Chapter Two

At the sound of his ringing cell phone disrupting an otherwise peaceful morning, Jake Rowan didn't even have to check the caller ID to know who'd be calling on this specific day, at this specific hour.

It had all started once upon a time. When his father had told him that serving a short stint in juvenile corrections would allow him to walk away from the worst night of his life.

Turns out, fathers lie . . . sometimes enough to have repercussions for their kids even years later.

About a ring or two before his voice mail normally kicked in, instead of offering a standard hello or any similar pleasantries, Jake answered the call from his brother Carter with a question he was genuinely curious about. "So tell me the truth—do you pencil me in for these fun phone chats, or did your tech folks create an app for that?"

"Good morning to you, too, Jake."

Yeah, that was Carter. *Always* bothering with the pleasantries. Just one of the many ways they were like oil and water. Jake being the more flammable of the liquids, definitely.

"To answer your question, I do, in fact, have a scheduling app for my calls with you."

Of course he did. Now that his curiosity on that matter was satisfied, Jake proceeded to do what he always did during his brother's bimonthly calls.

Absolutely nothing.

Though always civil, Jake had stopped making an effort to be overly cordial to Carter a long while ago. Fourteen years to be exact. Sometime between the judge's gavel slamming down in the courtroom and the first time Jake had gotten pounded to a pulp in juvie . . . where he'd been sentenced for the crime that *Carter* should've gone to jail for.

The latter factoid being one that only three people in the world knew about.

In all fairness, none of it had been Carter's idea. Nope, their winner of a father deserved all the credit for that one. Which was precisely why Jake was able to be so civil during these awkward-as-hell brotherly bonding times.

Cue his whistling the *Jeopardy* tune to fill the silence.

And the resulting tired, near-silent sigh on the other end of the phone line.

Instantly he felt like a jackass. Okay, so maybe his definition of *civil* needed some calibration. Lord knows on even a good day, Jake wasn't exactly Mr. Rogers in the neighborhood.

Expelling his own weary sigh, Jake supposed he *could* engage in some small talk for a change. Ask how the weather was today in California or something. Maybe banter a bit more about that app again . . .

But before Jake could fully talk himself into attempting his magnanimous gesture, Carter went and asked the one question that never failed to just *piss* him the hell off.

"So . . . you doing anything today?"

Now Jake was back to *wanting* to be the douchiest of all douches.

Logically he knew Carter wasn't trying to imply anything by asking if he had plans to be a functional member of society on a regular workday like the rest of the nonloser population in the world with things to do on a Monday morning. But hearing that innocuous question every two weeks for years on end was still damn effective at unmanning him all the same.

With the added bonus of reminding him of everything absent from his life.

Namely, the girl.

If he could add up every visceral memory from his childhood triggered by one of his five senses—every sweet victory that could compel a smile out of thin air, and every song lyric burned in his brain where algebra and history never took—the combined impact would still weigh in at just a fraction of the emotions he got hit with over a single, fleeting memory of *her*.

The girl next door he'd fallen half in love with before even learning her name.

Falling the rest of the way had happened just as easily.

Strangely, the older he got, the more frequently the flashbacks came. Fragmented memories of their daily talks every morning and every afternoon for nearly the entire month of June before his junior year, through the wooden fence separating their houses.

The flashbacks didn't seem to care if he was in bed with another woman before striking. He could be fighting his nightly insomnia with one of the casual bar-bunny hookups he allowed himself once in a blue moon, and he'd be seized by the vivid memories of a cute-as-hell smile made sweeter by an infectious laugh he could *almost* hear in his memories whenever the nights got real muggy and quiet.

That he thought about her the most in the summers wasn't a big surprise. God knew he'd dreamed of having her in his arms countless times that summer his family had moved into the house next to hers seemingly a lifetime ago.

But only the cruel and twisted universe knew why it had decided to be a real son of a bitch to him in the design of *how* it dictated that reality would finally come about.

The night he'd held his dream girl tight in his arms as he'd carried her out of her burning home—leaving her trapped, screaming, and scared little nine-year-old stepbrother behind to die—still haunted him to the core.

Still throat-punched him when he was least expecting it.

Still ripped him awake at night by hijacking the air from his lungs.

Still filled his chest with quick-dry cement whenever he saw a scruffy redheaded boy being doted on by his big sis . . . the same way *she* used to. God, she'd adored that kid.

Damn cruel, twisted universe.

He remembered the guys back in juvie who would take part in the religious programs the ministry folks ran twice a week. Jake used to envy them. Those dudes all *knew* they still wanted to be considered for heaven, for redemption. Whether they deserved it or not.

If only they'd had a Purgatory 101 class for the guys like him . . .

"Is it just me, or did I catch you before your second pot of coffee?" called out the voice in his ear, nearly identical but about ten times more refined than his own clipped, just-this-side-of-a-growl charm.

For most, that would be a teasing gibe. Not for Jake. "It's just you. I'm actually starting my third pot." He dragged himself out of his memories and poured another piping-hot mug of ulcer-inducing goodness before going back to sitting in silence to pointedly ignore Carter's other rude-ass question altogether.

Not that he had any grand illusions it would get Carter to drop the interrogation. The man was more persistent than a bill collector on the topic of Jake's current state of work. And about ten times more difficult to shake. To give credit where it was due, though, the pricklike sense of style Carter managed to infuse in his tenacity was, at times, rather impressive to behold.

Take this past holiday season, for example. Since it had been his leanest winter finance-wise in years, Jake had just plain dodged Carter's call after Thanksgiving with a curt "traveling out of the country" voice mail recording. Seeing as how they both knew Jake didn't possess a passport, let alone a remote desire to travel outside the Midwest, it was a blatantly transparent cover story to drive his point home that he didn't want to talk about it.

Of course, the freaking paragon of patience just played along.

First came the jolly-ass Christmas e-card with a snowman in Jamaica in Jake's in-box.

A week later? Daily e-gifts of language-translating apps for basically every European language imaginable, *with* follow-up e-mails written *in* those foreign languages.

The best one, however, was the vacation hold Carter later filled out online with the post office to stop all Jake's mail temporarily. That one was actually pretty frickin' funny.

After a month of Carter's subtle guerrilla attacks on his sanity, Jake finally "returned" to town and started answering the tireless bastard's calls again.

"Well, I have to say, your phone stalker breathing has gotten really good. You've been practicing—I can tell," broke in Carter once more, prompting an almost-smile from Jake then. He'd already been partway there at the reminder of what a pain in the ass it'd been to unsubscribe from the mountain of travel magazines—to the most obscure countries he'd never heard of—that had been awaiting him at the post office when he'd gone to pick up his held mail.

This time Carter was the one whistling the *Jeopardy* tune in the silence.

Smart-ass. "Okay, I think that's all the fun we have time for this week, folks. Sorry to cut your call short, but I'm pretty busy today." He really was. The Burtons' new doghouse wasn't going to build itself.

The long pause on the other end of the line called him on his lie. "You're home at nine a.m., Jake. We both know that means you're in between jobs again."

"I'm between *contracts*," Jake growled back, annoyed that he cared one way or another what his brother thought. He knew Carter wasn't trying to make him sound like an unemployed deadbeat. It still nettled.

While Jake loved being a carpenter, money wasn't always steady. Which was depressing seeing as how he was damn good at custom woodwork. Catalog-worthy residential built-ins, along with intricate custom doors and creative artistic furniture, were his specialties, while the imagination-beating kids' room pieces he created every chance he could felt more like a calling.

Sadly, though, he hardly got to do anything beyond rough carpentry and home repair jobs anymore. After having to strike out on his own after the mentor he'd worked with for years died a little while back, things had gone downhill fast. Thanks in large part to one home owner's vilifying online post in a popular home improvement forum informing anyone who had access to a search engine that Rowan Carpentry was run by a man who'd once been found guilty of arson, and was thus probably a pyro waiting to strike again on their unsuspecting houses.

The cost of his always being 100 percent candid about his past.

Unlike a bunch of other guys he knew in the same boat, Jake never swept his time in juvie under the rug. It had been the worst eighteen months of his life for a reason. Not because he hadn't been able to cut it or was overly scarred by it.

But because it hadn't been *enough*.

Nothing Jake had gone through in that hellhole had felt like a bad enough, *fair* enough punishment for the reason he had been put in there. The fact that he hadn't been the actual guilty party didn't block the guilt. There was no justice served. And gaining freedom the minute he'd become an adult hadn't felt like a pardon so much as the beginning of a new life sentence he still felt unworthy to be getting to live out.

So, yes, if it was important enough for a person to ask, if his reply regarding whether he'd ever been convicted of a crime was going to be *the* deciding factor on whether they trusted him enough to want to pay him, he figured they deserved an honest answer.

Unfortunately, bigger freelance work became practically nonexistent after that single inflammatory online comment. Power of the Internet.

Over the past few years, he'd thus been living off small, subcontracted on-call work with meager checks and cash jobs with general contractors who took the lion's share and threw him a few under-the-table scraps.

Not that he was complaining. He had a roof over his head and a top-of-the-line king-size bed he'd splurged on—the only marginally extravagant thing he owned . . . one of the few material things he used to dream about back in juvie.

And food was never a problem. Most of the neighborhood folks he did odd jobs for paid him well with home-cooked meals he kept his freezer stocked with.

Admittedly, though, some months did get rough. That feeling of not knowing if the ATM was going to laugh in his face? Most de-balling gut kick ever.

To his knowledge, his brother had never once experienced that feeling.

Not that he resented Carter for that fact. Truly he didn't. His brother worked hard for his wealth, and he was honestly a pretty decent guy. In fact, he'd offered to move Jake to California and line up some carpentry jobs with some of his rich friends. A bunch of times.

Truth was, if it had been their other brother, Daryn, asking, or even their baby sister, Haley, Jake probably would've said yes by now. He definitely could use the work.

But coming from Carter, it felt like overdue, guilt-laden restitution. For everything their father had screwed up between them. And that was the last thing Jake wanted from him. Especially since their old man had probably been . . . well, not "right" but at least smart in doing what he did.

Carter was a big deal now—cofounder of a cutting-edge company, exactly as their father had always forecast. And Jake had found a way to land on his feet, again, exactly as their father used to muster up as his biggest compliment of what Jake had going for him. Carter the success and Jake the survivor—the chips had fallen just as their dad intended.

Per usual, whenever he allowed himself to think any wayward thoughts about their dad's expectations and hopes for his two oldest sons, Jake wondered how different their lives would be if he had been the older brother who had set off the fireworks that night, and Carter had been the one their father wanted to take the fall for it. Would Jake have ended up even a tenth as successful as Carter today? Or would a sacrifice like that for him have been a waste?

Truthfully he wasn't sure.

One thing he did know, however, was that if their situations were reversed, he sure as hell wouldn't call the guy on the fifteenth and thirtieth of every month. That was just overbearing big brothering at its most ruthless.

Sure, Carter never made the mistake of asking Jake outright if he needed money to tide him over to his next paycheck—the last and only time Carter had done that, Jake's quiet promise of violence had been a clear-cut answer.

Still Carter was intentional in timing his calls when he did; Jake was certain of it. That was Carter's style. To push in the way only family could . . . with brutal kindness.

Well intentioned or not, it was still sort of a dick move.

And, oddly, *that* was the only reason Jake continued to take these calls.

Every other thing about Carter was perfect. Annoyingly so. So the idea that his brother was capable of being a bit of a jerk was actually kind of nice. Heartwarming even.

Yes, their relationship was all kinds of unhealthy.

"Look, Carter, I need to get going. Why don't we catch up some other—"

"I have a carpentry job lined up for you in Kansas," cut in Carter.

Aaand it looked as though they weren't anywhere near healthier horizons.

"No bullshit, Jake, this one is a hundred percent for me. A business purchase that I really need you to work on. You can start this week."

Well, that was different. And the choice of Kansas for the dangling carrot this time was new, too. "I'm touched that you've branched out your little hire-an-ex-con outreach program, dude. Really. But last I checked, you didn't have any SME Enterprises holdings out here." California, New York, and Boston, yes. But not the Midwest. Not that Jake was keeping track like a proud brother or anything. "What possible business could you have in my state?"

"I bought a library."

Sure, the go-to investment choice for every successful business guy in their early thirties.

"Why in the hell did you buy a *library*?"

"Is this you caring about my life, Jake? Because if so, I have to say, a little weird, bro. I draw the line at singing 'Kumbaya' in front of a fire—just saying."

Jake wasn't stupid; he knew Carter's uncanny impersonation of something he would say was just a distraction. But holy hell was it effective. Jake dropped his question. Then he said shortly, "You know I don't take commercial jobs. And besides, even if I did, nothing I build would fit in some big, stuffy university library that you slapped your name on anyhow."

"It's not a college library. It's a small one in the town of Juniper Hills just a few hours south of you between Elk Falls and Flint Hills. I told the general contractor I hired that I wanted a modern rustic colonial renovation."

Shit. That was *exactly* the kind of stuff Jake liked to create, and Carter clearly knew it.

"The contractor said none of the guys he subcontracts in the area were a good fit."

Jake was fairly sure that was a lie, but seeing as how his fingers were itching to work with wood, and his mind was already coming up with designs he'd be flat-out pissed if he couldn't get to build, he let the lie go. "I don't know if your contractor would want to hire me." Most weren't bad about hiring ex-cons, but some tended to steer clear, especially when it came to finish carpentry, which required a lot of independent work without the general contractor or foreman on-site.

"Then it's good you know the guy who *is* doing the hiring," replied Carter matter-of-factly. "I won't have you do a commercial employment form with that 'ever been convicted of a crime' box you're so friggin' fond of checking 'yes' to even though you don't have to legally."

Jeez, the man was swinging for the fences today. And did he really say *friggin'* just now? Jake was pleased as punch to see he was rubbing off on the guy.

"Before you say no, just go see the library, man. I'll text you the address. Call me later today with your decision. Whether you take the job or not, it's going to get done. This isn't a charity offer. The library is important to me. You'll see why when you get over there."

Click.

Jake stared at the address that appeared on his phone screen a moment later . . . sent with a GPS link that had a damned adorable little town in the image preview.

Ballsy ass.

Now for the big question—was this a fair ball or foul ball? Umpire's ruling?

He grabbed the keys to his truck along with his coat.

This was a home freaking run, and they both knew it.

Chapter Three

Three hours later Jake was following his GPS through hands down *the* most unique town he'd ever seen. He parked his pickup next to a converted cottage straight out of "Hansel and Gretel." The hand-painted LIBRARY sign out front? Quite possibly done by a three-year-old.

Cripes. This wasn't going to be a fair fight at all.

As far as little-town libraries went, with its all-original circular windows, storybook-shaped roof covered in ivy, and early-spring flower buds starting to sprout from its brick walls, the place was a hobbit house in the making. It was that darn cute. There was even an old round-top door weather distressed with so much character that Jake finally got what folks meant by the term *wood porn.* Seriously. The whole library was a carpenter's historical restoration jackpot.

Right down to the hand-chopped and age-smoothed log benches in the courtyard. All constructed out of salvaged tree trunks in honor of the town's namesake, of course.

Juniper Hills. He shook his head in wonder. Definitely a fitting description. He'd never seen so many Eastern redcedar trees and shrubs in one populated area before, at least not in the prairie regions, where controlled fires were set precisely to stop this sort of thing. As the only evergreen native to Kansas, the cedarlike juniper tree was common across the state. But since they were an ecosystem threat and a big wildfire hazard in flat grassland areas, lots of ranchers used prescribed blazes to burn down and control excessive growth on their pastures.

The town of Juniper Hills, on the other hand? Its citizens seemed to be in the "if you can't beat 'em, go nuts" camp with all the juniper. Likely because the local geography didn't necessitate its control. Or because they just *really* liked being different.

Sure, there were the familiar stretches of agricultural farms bordering the western edge of town, and, of course, tallgrass prairieland as far as the eye could see, but it was all draped over actual rolling hills and valleys, with earthy mineral boulders unlike the variety usually found in these parts, and pockets of equally atypical springs and shallow waterfalls.

Hell, he hadn't even accepted the job yet and already he was thinking of a dozen ways to showcase these great town differences—from a pergola built entirely out of driftwood for the book-return box near the entrance, to arched juniper branches over the dirt walkway circling the building to mimic the effect of walking through a forest.

Okay, *maybe* that latter feature was his soul talking, and not necessarily the library.

Though Jake was a proud midwestern boy to the core, sometimes he wondered if he hadn't been a mountain man in a past life. There were only a few rural and streamside forests in the state, and, after juvie, he'd made it his mission to visit every single one. Over the years they'd become his refuge whenever the ghosts from his past threatened to yank the ground out from under him and drag him through quicksand. Truth be told, those solo trips out into nature were the only times he'd ever felt a bone-deep comfort and connection to his surroundings.

Until now.

Looking around, he couldn't put his finger on what exactly it was he liked so much about the cozy town, but all he knew was that if his brother had bought this library with the intention of changing the feel of the place, or messing with any of its historic country charm and untamed rustic bones, Jake was prepared to fight hard to keep it all intact.

Dammit, he was getting invested in the project.

Frickin' Carter.

"Hey, you must be Jake," called out a man who could've easily passed for a tall big brother of the red-bearded Viking-looking dwarf from Lord of the Rings as he walked over, tool belt slung over one shoulder and clipboard in hand. "Name's Paul. Thanks for coming down."

"Good to meet you." Jake shook the man's Hulk-size hand, feeling a touch of nostalgia over the striking resemblance between the friendly Nordic giant and his former mentor, Erik, who he'd always thought sounded *exactly* like that growly dwarf from Middle-earth.

Jake still missed hearing that curmudgeonly grump's thunderous bark keeping every worker on his crew on their toes from sunup to sundown.

Speaking of. Jake looked around, surprised at how quiet the job site was. "Did I get here too early?" There was only a handful of guys working as far as he could see.

"Nah, I just sent some of my guys down to check on a friend of ours a few blocks over. Poor thing, her bakery flooded this morning. Heard there was some pretty heavy damage. The boys have been there helping out with the heavy lifting for the past hour, but they're on their way back so you can get a chance to meet 'em."

Paul gave Jake a hearty pat on the shoulder then that would've shaken a few teeth loose on a smaller guy. "Boy am I glad you're coming on board on this; we could use your expertise. Frankly, most of the things on these project plans seem like overkill for our little library if you ask me. But it's your buddy's dime, so who am I to say how the guy wants to spend it?" He held up the unusually thick project clipboard he was carrying and shook his head. "Never seen such detailed preconstruction plans like these. You two been friends long? He always been this, err, *exacting* about stuff?"

Jake snorted. *Exacting*. A nice way to say bullheaded. *Um, yep. All my life.*

"He does have a tendency to go big when he gets an idea in his head," he replied, choosing to address only the second question. He wasn't sure why it bugged him that the foreman hadn't been informed that Carter was his brother, but he shook off the aberrant, mildly hypocritical feeling and pointed at the clipboard in Paul's hands. "Could I take a look at the job details? Carter didn't give me a whole lot of info. Just heard about it today, in fact."

"Doesn't surprise me. The sale just closed a few weeks ago. Came home the night the deal finalized to find a message that the new corporate owner, SME Enterprises, wanted me to handle the job ASAP, no expenses spared as long as I could restore it just so. Truthfully, when I'd first heard that a big ol' company wanted to buy our little library, I thought for sure they were going to bulldoze it and make some fancy spa or a tucked-away country inn for the rich and famous or something that they could turn around and sell off."

Jake shook his head. "That's not SME's style. They usually work with top national brands that have big in-house creative teams or tech companies and labs. Sometimes universities and private academies. I've never known them to work on anything like a spa or an inn."

Or a small-town library, for that matter.

"Huh. No kidding. You don't see that kind of hands-on attention to detail with most of these corporate owners. Hell, after my bid for the library got accepted, he actually called me directly and kept me on the phone for three hours discussing things. Then he e-mailed me a shitload of photos that looked like he'd downloaded every Pinterest page out there with small-town libraries from around the world."

And some not even of this world, from what Jake could see. He was pretty sure a lot of the photos were artistic renderings of mythical libraries. All pretty radical, and a touch extreme, but nothing too far removed from the realm of possibilities, carpentry-wise.

Well, for him, anyway. Christ, he really wanted to work on this project.

Incredibly, each page of rough plan notes was more involved than the last. To the point where he began seriously questioning why on earth his brother had taken this library on. True, he didn't have the fancy degrees Carter did, but even Jake could tell these plans couldn't possibly be typical of a sensible SME acquisition.

The most damning evidence being, of course, the budget.

He let out a low whistle over the grand tally on the last page.

Paul nodded. "I know. Biggest damn budget I've ever seen for a project this small."

That was the final clue pointing to this being anything *but* a business project for Carter.

Which meant Paul was no doubt being very diplomatic in describing Carter as "hands-on"—as opposed to "more intrusive than a hemorrhoid."

"Let me guess. Carter's arranged for you to have an engineer and an architect at your beck and call 24-7, along with a magical fast track on all the permits. Am I right?"

"Never seen anything like it. Approvals were coming in faster than I could ask for them." Paul tapped on the thick manila envelope under the clipboard. "Gotta tell you one thing, though—the guy does everything aboveboard. He may be greasing some folks to get things moving, but he definitely isn't cutting any corners or breaking any rules. I respect that."

Jake had to smile over that tidbit. Yep, his brother was nothing if not a color-in-the-lines kind of guy. "Well, I'm definitely interested in the contract. Count me in. Do you need me for building framing and rough carpentry, as well, or just finish work?"

"To be honest, I have a full crew who I'd normally have handle the whole thing, rough to finish, but they're not experienced on this specific kind of design, and only a few of 'em have done historic restorations.

I've got a few ideas, but nothing on the level of what Carter wants. That's why I agreed to Carter's stipulation to bring you in separate as basically a specialist."

Paul flipped back to the renovation plan and pointed out different points in the timeline. "So my guys will handle all the initial construction, but then it'll basically be your show from there since I've got a big residential job coming up in a few weeks. I'd usually leave just my newbies with you to do grunt work and finish trims, but I want my main journeymen and some of the older kids to get some training on this stuff. At least for a few weeks. They're good; you can put them to work while you're training them. With them helping you, I think we should be able to meet the four-month time frame Carter's given us to complete the project."

Jake nodded, liking that he was going to be able to do some teaching, which he always enjoyed. "Sounds good. With these tight deadlines, I could use all the guys you can spare." Checking the list of work and the rough computer sketches again, he did some quick calculations. "So we're looking at me getting started here in about three weeks then?"

"As long as the weather holds up, yeah, that sounds about right. But I want to work faster to get us some cushion—you never know what we'll run into with these older constructions. I'll keep you updated, and we can meet about the design a few times, but, yeah, if all goes as planned, you can probably start ordering supplies in about two weeks."

Suddenly Paul stepped back and eyed him for a bit, sizing him up. "Say, you got another big job scheduled before then?"

Granted, the Burtons' doghouse was going to be the size of a MINI Coop to effectively house their mammoth mutt, but he wouldn't consider it a big job. He decided to be straight with the guy. "Got a few things lined up that I can move to the weekends. Man to man, I could use some bigger work during the week. You need another hand on deck?"

"Carter sent me a portfolio of your work from the past few years, and I was pretty blown away. If my crew wasn't already full-up, I'd hire you in a heartbeat."

Jake nodded in understanding, although mentally he was still back at that whole part about the portfolio of his carpentry work. *How the hell . . . ?* Anyone that knew Jake knew he wasn't a snap-a-selfie-on-the-job kind of guy. The camera on his current cell phone had broken within the first week (they really should make those things less sensitive—he couldn't be the only one who'd accidentally dropped a two-by-four on his phone before). Plus, little-known story, the *one* time he'd made the effort to stick an old camera in his toolbox two or three years ago with grand plans for a website, he'd been shocked to find that stores didn't sell film anymore.

That had seemed like some sort of sign from the universe at the time.

"Would you be willing to work nonunion?" ventured Paul, pulling Jake away from the perturbing image of Carter waving a magic wand over his life like a meddling fairy godfather.

"Nonunion works for me. I go where the work is."

"Perfect. I was actually going to ask if you could head over and put in an estimate at that bakery I told you about. The owner is going to have a shit ton of repairs. I don't want to leave her in a bind, but I need my guys here, and I don't want anyone from outside overcharging her."

Sadly, that happened way too often. It always pissed Jake off to hear about contractors price gouging business owners in a tough spot.

"Plus, the bakery is sort of . . . eclectic. Outside the box. Right in your wheelhouse."

Jake took that as a compliment. "You know if anyone else has bid on the repairs yet?"

"I doubt it. Most of the guys I'd vouch for are booked solid with the weather warming up. Told her as much this morning on the phone. So she might even hire you on the spot if you tell her I sent you." His voice turned a touch menacing then, eyes narrowed something fierce. "She's a sweet girl—damn near like a big sister to everyone in town.

Carter gave me his word that you're good people, so don't go making him a liar. You best not even put in a bid at the bakery if you're not a hundred percent sure you can do right by her."

Huh, they certainly were a protective bunch here. It was nice. "I stand by my work, Paul. And my customers always say my estimates are the lowest. Considering I need the work, I can go a bit lower than usual for your bakery friend to make this happen."

"Nah, no need to go overboard. Just be fair." Paul fished his card out of his wallet. "Here's my number in case you need to get in contact with me. Let me know how it goes. Either way, though, check in with me in about two weeks for a status update on the library job. Carter already gave us your résumé, so I have all your info."

Of course he did. Why would Cinder-freaking-ella have a portfolio without a résumé?

Clearly Carter didn't mess around with meddling half-ass.

Jake pocketed Paul's card. "Sounds like a plan. And thanks for the heads-up about the bakery. I'll drive over now and put in a bid."

"Good. Remember, we're all watching you. That bakery owner is beloved in this town. If you screw her over, I promise you, you'll have to sleep with one eye open because we'll hunt you down. And as soon as we find a cesspool vile enough for the likes of you, we'll be dumping you in it." He gave Jake a toothy grin and a friendly, bone-bruising double shoulder pat totally at odds with his descriptive threat. "By the way, welcome to Juniper Hills."

Yep, it was official. Jake was really starting to like this town.

Holy shit.

Jake did a double take as he walked into the colorful little bakery on the north end of town. The place looked as if a massive water bomb had exploded in it.

This was easily the worst case of pipe flood damage he'd ever seen. Not only were the bakery and kitchen a mess; from what he could see through the exposed holes in the ceiling, and judging by the size of the commercial water pipes that had burst, the apartment above had also taken a small beating and would likely need fixing, as well.

There had to be a few weeks of work here at the very least, which he knew was going to be tough news to break to the owner. As he walked around, he did a quick assessment to get a better ballpark budget and timeline. Ceiling, drywall, floor, cabinets—all pretty straightforward repairs and restorations. Luckily the major pipe joints affected hadn't been directly over any of the pricey appliances; they'd managed to dodge a bullet there. Unfortunately, though, he could tell a lot of the decor had gotten waterlogged badly enough to require replacing, along with some framed photos and personal effects on one of the display walls.

Pity. Broken things could be fixed. Good memories were irreplaceable. And the ones meaningful enough to keep close by on a daily basis were always the hardest to part with.

Wonder if she was able to salvage any photos from the fire.

He stilled to a dead halt. Just like he always did when those random thoughts about her were triggered.

The ironic parallels between past and present were never subtle when they hit him out of the blue and yanked him back to that night. Fists clenched, muscles locked, he didn't dare move because he knew what came next—the deluge of flashbacks that would slash and slice like visual shards in a mosaic of pain and devastation. One after another. Always in shattered fragments.

This time the mental image they all pieced together to form was from *after* the fire for a change. A pile of charred rubble where a house full of irreplaceable memories had once stood.

The remaining air in his lungs bled out of him.

To hope that anyone would be able to recover *anything* good from a wreckage like that . . .

His fault for wondering.

Deep breaths. *Get your shit together, man. You need this job.*

It took a while. Longer than usual for some strange reason. But, eventually, he was able to claw his way back to the here and now.

His vision slowly blurred back into focus. And immediately, he had to squint to dim the effect of all the bright colors in the bakery registering full-force on his retinas again.

"Eclectic," Paul had called it . . . apparently using the same thesaurus that had supplied his earlier description of Carter as merely "hands-on."

For what it was worth, Paul had been right about this being in Jake's wheelhouse. He dug everything about the bakery. It had style. And *life*. Like Juniper Hills, there was something about it he liked that he just couldn't put his finger on . . .

"Hey, you!" called out a low, muffled voice from the kitchen. "Think you can give me a hand for a sec?"

Jake headed on back to the kitchen, where a plumber on a ladder was elbow-deep in pipes up above the ceiling tiles. "These damn galvanized pipes are working my last nerve. Could you hand me that red pipe press by my tool bucket? The shortest one."

Jake went over to grab the smallest of the big hedge-clipper-looking clamps, along with the tallest stool he could find to stand on so he could hand it to him. Professional unwritten rule—climbing up another man's ladder face-to-ass with him while he worked being just an accident waiting to happen and all.

"Thanks, man. With the foundation settling on this lot, it was just a matter of time before these old pipes burst. Could've been a lot worse if no one had been here when it blew." The plumber proceeded to grunt and curse and clang away with his pipe press and wrench. "You here to give an estimate on the repairs?"

"I'm hoping to. Have you seen the owner around?"

Suddenly a woman's soft voice pierced through the air from behind him to answer. "*I'm* the owner." Her quietly charged words hit him like a Taser, with fifty thousand volts of pure, ungrounded emotions as she added, "So you can take this as a request from management when I say, please get out of my bakery. Now."

Chapter Four

It was *him.*

Of all the bakeries, in all the towns, in all the world, he walks into mine.

It didn't matter that she hadn't seen the guy in more than fourteen years; Emma had no doubt in her mind that the man standing before her in her bakery right now was Jake Carmichael, literally the boy next door she'd had a crush on from the day he and his family had moved into the house next to hers back before her junior year in high school.

The summer her nine-year-old brother Peyton's house-fire death had ripped her family apart.

"Emma Stevens."

It wasn't a question. And even through his thick beard, she could see he wasn't uttering that nonquestion with a smile.

She hated that she cared, that she noticed how much lower and grittier his voice had become over the years . . . and how much it still sounded the same.

Everyone always says the best defense is a strong offense, right? Well screw "strong"; she was going straight to a DEFCON 6, downright *jugular* offense. "What part of my request did you not understand, Jake?" She turned her back on him and headed to the front of the bakery, index finger helpfully pointing out the door to him. "I asked you to leave."

Whatever you do, don't look at him again, Emma.

Of course, he didn't make it that easy on her. She heard him approach her from behind, and she spun around to stop him from coming any closer.

Arms crossed like a shield, emotions kept ruthlessly in check, and all facial expressions wiped clean, she looked him straight in the eye . . . only to find that, shockingly, he was meeting her gaze head-on. After all these years, Emma wasn't sure what she'd expected Jake's reaction to be if their paths ever crossed again—it'd be a lie to say she hadn't thought about this moment more times than she could count.

But, safe to say, not once had she imagined it going like this. With Jake looking back at her, eyes as bleak and tormented as they were right now, blinking as if he expected her to vanish like a mirage. He said her name again in a ghostlike whisper. A rough rasp this time, tattered around the edges with such visceral, exposed emotion that it pained her to hear it.

And just as she couldn't unhear him, she couldn't unsee him, either—the teenage boy some had called a hero because of the way he'd saved her and her sister Megan from the burning house that night. Others had called him a criminal for having set off the aerial fireworks that had resulted in the fire in the first place. The same boy that her stepmother had outright called a murderer for taking her Peyton from them.

Fourteen long years had left only a few traces of the Jake she'd first met that summer.

Back then he'd been an effortlessly irresistible, laid-back, corn-fed farm boy if ever there was one. Classic all-American looks and charm, with a smile in his voice just for her that she had always been able to hear clear as day. Warmed by the sun and as carefree as the wind.

That boy, who still existed in her memories regardless of how hard she'd tried to purge him, and this hardened, stoic man in front of her now were like two completely different people.

Strangely, even though it was the teen version of him who'd once broken her without intending to, somehow she just knew that *this* man here with her now had the capacity to be infinitely more dangerous to her heart.

Not because he'd grown up to become gruffly, *devastatingly* more handsome than she'd imagined, but because without saying a word, or even trying, inexplicably he was making that once-dormant organ in her chest *feel* something again.

Pain, mostly. Along with other emotions she simply wasn't equipped to handle.

After the fire, her grief counselor had told her it was a coping mechanism. The way she'd closed her heart off to memories of that night, to emotions she refused to let see the light of day. The woman had gone on and on about the dangers of putting hearts behind walls like that.

Emma still recalled the crack she'd put in the seasoned therapist's composure when she'd told her plainly, "I'm not putting walls around my heart; I'm burying it in a casket. Alongside my baby brother. The one I didn't save. And nothing you say will make me open that grave."

The woman had stopped being her therapist that day.

In retrospect maybe if she'd let the well-meaning shrink try to "heal" her back then, it wouldn't feel like there was a raw, open wound in her chest right now. *Live and learn.* Now all she could do was hope to find some stronger nails to keep the coffin closed as soon as Jake left.

Only he didn't leave.

Instead he stared at her for several long moments, eyes never wavering from her face. Even though she was treating him like an eclipse and not looking directly at him, she *felt* his gaze on her, drinking her in. Which somehow made *her* throat feel parched as a result.

Because she wanted to do the same to him.

She *wanted* to secretly trail her eyes over that granite-hard square jaw of his, just like she used to back when they'd both find themselves in their respective backyards at the same time. Which, coincidentally, had been every day through the month of June. Right before sunset.

She still remembered how he used to drape his arms over that old wooden fence between their houses and just plain light up the rest of her night by simply smiling at her.

Though it made absolutely no sense at all, right now, looking at this haunted grown-up Jake, more than anything else she wanted to see him smile at her that way again.

And that *wasn't* okay.

Not knowing what else to do, she turned her back to him to sever the connection.

"I didn't know this was your bakery," he said softly.

Well, that answered her biggest burning question.

"I wouldn't have come in here if I'd known."

Aaand that answered the question she hadn't known she'd been looking for an answer to.

Just 998 or so more burning questions to go. But considering his last admission was making her feel lost without any semblance of gravity for her emotions, she didn't want him sticking around to actually answer any more. "So now that you know it's my bakery, are you going to leave anytime soon?"

"No."

Emma turned back in surprise and blinked at him slowly, sure she'd misheard him.

Jake looked nearly as surprised as she felt. But he recovered quicker. "I'm a carpenter now. A good one. Your friend Paul sent me over here."

That was major breaking news. Her worlds were now officially colliding. *Mayday, Mayday.* No exaggeration, she felt like a ship about to capsize.

"Emma, I do good work—I swear. Let me help you with these repairs."

"No." She didn't mean to throw that one-word reply back at him, but, honestly, it reflected exactly what was going through her head. She didn't have an eloquent explanation for her feelings. All she knew was, no, she just . . . couldn't accept his help. Not now. Not here.

Here in Juniper Hills, she and Megan had been able to start over. Here, no one even knew the story of the Stevenses' house burning to the ground over in Riverside. No one stared at poor Megan Stevens's scars anymore—at least not when either of them were looking. No one whispered about the teenage neighbor that poor Emma Stevens had had a crush on before he got sent to juvie after little Peyton Stevens had been killed that night.

Theirs lives weren't tragic here. They'd moved on.

So just . . . no. She couldn't have Jake come back into her life.

Before she could attempt to explain all this to Jake, or even analyze it better herself, however, the plumber she'd hired that morning came out of the kitchen with a friendly, outstretched hand. For Jake. "Hey, how's it going? Sorry I didn't get a chance to come off the ladder and introduce myself. I'm Marco. Marco Moretti. Thanks for the assist earlier."

"Jake Rowan. Glad I could help."

Emma did a double take at the unfamiliar last name.

Not going to ask. *None of my business.* The man's new last name was of no concern of hers. It's not as if she wanted to know more about him and his life for the past fourteen years.

Nope, no sirree. That said, she did find herself making a completely uninvolved passing observation about how much better *Rowan* seemed to fit him than *Carmichael* ever did. And that's all the thought she was going to put into the matter.

Still not going to ask.

As if hearing her inner struggles loud and clear, Jake turned and took another step closer to her after Marco left to go on a supply run. "Rowan is my mom's maiden name. She and my dad got divorced, and she got sole custody of me, my brother, and my sister." Then he just stood there in silence and studied her for a beat, gazing at her with those intense brindled-green eyes of his that seemed to burrow straight into her soul.

Where all her secrets and boxed-up feelings about him still remained.

Emma told herself she didn't want to hear any more. Didn't want to know how long after the fire his dad had left them. If it had happened after Jake had been sent to . . .

No. She wasn't going to wonder. Or worse, *care.*

"Their divorce finalized after I was already in juvie."

Damn mind reader. She recalled now how he'd always been able to read her like an open book. For some reason, the fact that he still could had her jumbled up on the inside.

"My younger siblings, Daryn and Haley—I don't know if you remember them—got their names changed to Rowan after all the divorce settlement paperwork cleared." He looked away, his voice detaching as he stated matter-of-factly, "But mine was legally changed before. Before I got sentenced, in fact."

God, she really didn't like thinking about him in juvie.

His eyes softened in response to some tell on her traitorous face. "My father 'requested' that I take my mom's name before my sentencing was fully on record. Moved mountains to get the lawyers to make that change in time. That way I officially entered juvie as a Rowan, not a Carmichael." His jaw tightened. "Never heard from him again after that."

Emma flinched. That was just awful. Cold, cruel, and just deplorable. No child deserved to be returned like that, discarded like damaged goods. "I'm so sorry, Jake."

This time it was Jake who flinched. Or recoiled, rather. As if he'd been shot.

She hadn't intended for her apology to be a verbal bullet, but there it was, lodged somewhere she couldn't see, making him hemorrhage pain right before her eyes.

She wanted to comfort him. Wanted to tell him how her parents had split up, too. How she understood. How she knew exactly what it felt like to have one of your parents blame *you* for the destruction of their marriage, their family . . . of a young, innocent life.

How she knew exactly what if felt like to blame *yourself* for the same.

But instead she called on her inner Tin Man to help her pivot away from him again. Maybe if she ignored him, he would go away, reasoned her inner Scarecrow and inner Cowardly Lion in unison.

She stifled a sigh. First *Casablanca*, and now *The Wizard of Oz*. See, the man was already making her bonkers. He needed to leave.

Maintaining military silence, she grabbed the broom and proceeded to sweep residual floodwater toward the back door as if Jake weren't standing ten feet away from her.

Finally, after a good solid minute or so, she heard him quietly exit her bakery.

A part of her felt an inexplicable, irrational sense of loss.

Which went away a minute later when Jake trudged back in, this time with his tool belt clipped on. "Just give me a few minutes to survey the flood damage so I can give you a full written estimate."

Emma couldn't do anything but gape at him as he flipped open a composition notebook, like the kind they used to have in school, and headed over to her kitchen to start his assessments.

Stop staring at him, Emma.

Way easier said than done.

Earlier he'd been wearing one of those woodsy corduroy jackets with the gray jersey fabric hoods that you simply *had* to be rugged to pull off. Had to. Now, without his jacket on, he was still lumberjack rugged, but in a much more, errr, *obvious* way.

Jesus Christ, that body.

Through his plain white T-shirt, she could practically count each of the shredded muscles carved into his back because he was one of *those* guys. The kind who had the sort of physique that casual, loose-fitting T-shirts molded and clung to, contrary to the laws of physics.

When she eventually managed to tear her eyes away from the mesmerizing dance of the rippling muscles, she gave herself a mental slap and stomped after him. "You are *not* doing an estimate," she maintained hotly, keeping her eyes on a spot on the wall, a few inches above his shoulder. Mostly because the front view of his T-shirt was even more distracting than the back.

He dignified her command with a single impertinent eyebrow raise. "Hate to break it to you, honey, but I'm not working for free."

Just like that, drunken butterflies began banging around in her chest. All over a simple word. *Honey.* Logically she knew that wasn't an actual endearment, but her stupid heart didn't seem to know the difference.

That was when she made the mistake of *un*-diverting her attention and really seeing him.

First off, the man was definitely due for a haircut.

But, unfairly, he was all the more gorgeous for it.

He still had the chiseled features and the dark, almost black, wavy hair that had always made him look so dreamy, like those old Hollywood heroes. Except now he had this ridiculously masculine beard that just brought out his deep, prismatic green eyes even more.

"Hey, you mind if I move this big shelf to check the wall behind it?" he asked before just plain doing it anyway. With an impressive one-handed shove.

Good lord he was burly.

And far sexier in a tool belt than a mortal man had any right to be.

When he turned to a blank notebook page to crunch some figures—by hand—she finally managed to shake herself out of her stupor. *Why doesn't he just use his phone's calculator?* The realization that she'd spent enough time looking at the bulge in his pocket to figure out it was a phone simply proved her biggest worry. "Jake, you can't *possibly* think this is a good idea."

That's when his eyes did that thing again, where they flickered through a dozen different emotions, all the while pulling her in for the turbulent ride. "I want to help you, Emma. *Let me* help you." He put his number two pencil behind his ear—seriously, how did he manage to make *that* hot?—before leveling with her. "Look, bottom line is that there's a lot of damage here, and you won't be able to beat my rates. All of this should take about two to three weeks, tops. After that, I'll be working on the library way over on the other side of town so I'll be out of your hair."

Whoa, time-out. Her entire world suddenly tilted on its axis.

Feeling her stomach down somewhere around her feet, she barely managed to articulate the words that would confirm her fears, "*You're* going to work on the library remodel?"

She watched him carry the seven in another penciled-in equation, and then multiply the total with another number before replying. "Yup. Just talked to the site foreman today. I'm only hired to do the custom finishes, though, so they don't need me for a few more weeks—"

"You know what?" she interrupted. "I will hire you for the bakery repairs, after all."

"Really?" He gave her a dubious look. "Just like that?"

"Uh-huh, you can start tomorrow morning, bright and early . . . on one condition."

His brows lowered warily. "And what would that condition be?"

She dug deep to gather up her ice-cold conviction and her best no-nonsense voice to assert firmly, "That you turn down the library job."

His reaction was swift. A combination of disappointment and resigned sadness. "Do you really hate me *that* bad? Enough that you want me to turn down a huge job that could be great for me? A job I need right now just to make ends meet?"

Well, when he put it that way. *Dammit.* Now she felt like a complete jerk.

"Emma, be reasonable. I want to help your bakery, but I'm not turning down the library contract. The job's a huge opportunity for me, and *exactly* the kind of work I love to do."

It was the look in his eyes over that last statement that made time stop and stand still for a moment. Made her runaway emotions come to a jarring halt.

That look in his eyes. It was the same one Megan had whenever Emma caught her running her fingers lovingly across the spines of the books in her library. It was probably the same look Emma herself had whenever she was in the kitchen experimenting with new recipes or out in front watching customers eating her creations.

She couldn't possibly live with herself for extinguishing the grounding passion responsible for that look. In anyone. Even the man responsible for the worst night of her life.

But. If it meant protecting her sister, she would do everything *just* short of that.

"I promise, Jake, I'll spend every waking minute helping you find another job that'll involve the kind of work you love and will cover your bills." She gripped his forearm and did her damnedest to smother back a gasp at the jolt of electricity from the brief contact.

Based on the scorching flash of heat in his gaze, he'd felt it, too.

With a shaky voice now thick with emotion, Emma finally laid all her cards on the table. "My sister, Megan, is the head librarian here, Jake. Megan. You remember her? The little girl you carried out of the house with burns over a third of her body? Well she's all grown up. And that library is like her second home, her sanctuary."

Her breath broke on a heavy shudder weighted down by years of rough memories. "We've worked so hard to move forward from our past, Jake. This town, that library . . . there isn't much in our lives the fire you caused didn't manage to incinerate somehow. I had to move my baby sister several counties away from Riverside just to escape it. Me, I can handle you working on my bakery." *Wow, that sounded almost believable.* "But I didn't go through everything Megan went through. So for her sake, I'm asking you to please turn down the library job. Not because I hate you, but because she deserves that much. She should be able to have one special thing in her life that's still completely untouched from any reminders of that fire."

The shock on his face lasted only a second. Before stark, bleak shadows flooded his features like an overflowing tide of grief and torment.

Emma froze. The only time she'd ever seen anguish like that was . . .

In the mirror. *"Jake."*

He didn't meet her gaze, but he did respond. "I'll call the foreman and turn the library job down." Then he hesitated for a brief moment before tearing a page out of the notebook he'd been writing in and handing it to her. "If you're still interested."

She slammed her eyes shut for a beat to mentally prepare herself for the final verdict. This bakery wasn't just her livelihood; it was her *life.* She was insured, of course, but her policy covered only so much. And based on her calls to her claims department, with the never-ending paperwork, the hoops to jump, and loophole-filled "qualifying claims," not to mention drawn-out processing times, it didn't sound as though she'd be getting a check for a few months at least.

And since staying closed longer than a few weeks would set her too far back, her only option was to start draining her savings. Which meant that the number on this piece of paper would tell her if she'd soon be getting "account overdrawn" love letters from the bank like she used to when she'd first moved to Juniper Hills. *Oh, just stop stalling and look already!*

Only one eye cooperated when she forced herself to peer down at the paper.

The total circled at the bottom had her jaw dropping in disbelief. And relief. Or whatever emotion was a thousand times stronger than relief.

"That's my rate to do the repairs here. Take it or leave it. If you don't want to accept my bid, tell me right now. Otherwise I'll be back at seven in the morning to start."

Emma studied the calculations again, amazed to see figures she could actually afford. Honestly, she didn't just feel relieved, she felt *saved*. It was an unnerving sensation. One she hadn't felt in years. Needing someone like this. *Counting* on someone like this.

"Jake, are you sure you can—"

When she looked up, she discovered she was alone in the room.

Looking out at his retreating figure walking across the street to a beat-up work truck, she found herself worrying over what tomorrow would bring. Would she be ready to admit to Jake, and herself, that if anyone was going to help her try to repair all this damage, she *wanted* it to be him? What would happen if they uncovered even more problems, hidden ones, deep in the foundation? And, scariest of all, what would she do if things didn't just bounce back afterward?

As she asked herself these impossible questions, she surveyed her bakery, turning in a slow circle to take in everything around her to help her find the answers.

It wasn't until she'd spun full circle that she realized she wouldn't find any answers that way. Because deep down, she knew.

The damage and the repairs she was really, truly worried about where Jake was concerned didn't have anything to do with her bakery at all.

Chapter Five

He's gone—you can stop staring now.

Emma pushed herself away from the front window just as Jake's truck turned the corner and disappeared. Instantly her brain picked up the slack and began playing a highlight reel of everything Jake had said and done while he'd been here. Just hearing that deep, raspy voice of his in her head was enough to make her corneas steam up a little.

"So who's the sexy lumberjack?"

"Holy crap!" she yelped, spinning around to find Megan standing right behind her, peering out the window, as well. "How long have you been here?"

"Long enough to know some of the flooding on the floor is from you drooling over burly Mr. Fix It. Seriously, if not for all those authentic carpentry tools in his truck, I would've pegged him as an in-character stripper with a mighty big tool belt sent to cheer you up today."

There were so many things wrong with that statement. First and foremost: "Who the heck would send me a *male stripper?*"

"Are you kidding? Have you not met the salacious old biddies in this town? Most of 'em would welcome any excuse to bring in a male stripper. Or have we already forgotten about the ladies' night party they threw at the bar in celebration of the last leap year?"

Until just this very moment, yes. Emma had in fact banished the memory of the stripper show that had brought a whole new meaning to the game leapfrog. "He's not a stripper."

Great. Now it was all she could do to *not* imagine him stripping out of his tool belt.

This was so not good.

Megan picked up the business card Jake had left on the counter. "Rowan Carpentry. Huh. Why does that sound so familiar?" Then with a tickled-pink expression, she pulled out her phone to look something up. "It is the same guy! Your carpenter is going to be working on the library, too. Oh my gosh, Emma. You have to see his work. The man is a genius." She clapped excitedly. "I already know he's going to do an amazing job on the library remodel."

Crap. Crapcrapcrap. "Um, Megan, did you get a good look at him before he left?"

Megan frowned. "Sort of. I walked past his truck while he was putting stuff away, but there were at least half a dozen ogling women blocking my view."

A flash of jealousy smacked her in the face. *Holy hell. What in the world?* It wasn't any of her business if women wanted to ogle the man. "Half a dozen, really?"

"Oh please, don't pretend you didn't notice how gorgeous he was."

Emma blinked in surprise. Her sister had never commented on a man's looks before.

Megan turned bright crimson. "I'm not blind. I wasn't panting after him like the others, but he had a handsome face, though a little on the intense side. And holy cow, his eyes—"

"It's Jake," Emma blurted out, ripping the Band-Aid off. "You remember . . . *Jake.*"

"From State Farm?" Megan asked slowly, with a teasing grin. "Em, aside from that guy wearing khakis on the commercial, I don't know any Jakes. Except—" Her eyes shot out to the street and then back at Emma. "That's not . . ."

Unsure what to say, Emma just nodded to confirm.

Megan's gaze flew back to the street again. "I didn't recognize him. Why didn't you call me? I would've come down sooner if I'd known."

This wasn't going at all how she'd imagined. "Why would you have come down?"

"To see how he's doing. To thank him for saving my life. To see how his brother and sister are doing. I don't know. Why? Did you think I wouldn't want to see him or something?"

"Can you blame me for thinking that? He was the one responsible for your scars, Meg. Of course I thought you'd never want to see the man again for as long as you lived."

"Well you were wrong."

Whoa. Emma had never seen her sister this upset before. "Is this because . . . are you attracted to Jake?" Because really, that would just be the icing on a completely messed-up cake.

"What? *No.* He's all yours, no worries there."

This time Emma was the one with the Hypercolor cheeks. "That was a high school crush. He's fair game. Honest."

Megan raised a single eyebrow. "Really? Okay then. I'll be sure to spread the word."

At that now-what're-you-going-to-do head tilt, Emma took a startled step back. And smiled, "Why hello, Miss Lioness. Never seen you here before. You just visiting, or are you planning on sticking around for good?"

Her sister's token timidness peeked its head out again then. "Too much? I've been working on being bolder and more take-charge. Did I sound bitchy just now?"

Emma yanked her into a hug. "I kind of think you sounded like me. So that would be a no to the bitchy question, of course." Grinning, she shook her head. "So what's gotten into you? Why the fierceness—which I love, by the way—all of a sudden?"

"I want to get a tattoo."

That was without a doubt the last thing she'd ever expected to hear out of Megan's mouth. Emma gazed at her sweet, *normally* shy sister, who most thought of as a porcelain doll in both beauty and demeanor. "Any particular tattoo in mind?"

"At first I was thinking of something like the flowers on your pendants."

Emma hand immediately rose up to touch the three different floral pendants in question.

"But," continued Megan with a reassuring hand squeeze, "I know those have special, hidden meanings for you, so I didn't want to muck with that."

Even though Emma would never object to Megan adopting any of the three flowers as her own talismans of sorts in a tattoo design, a part of her breathed a sigh of relief that she'd get to keep the flowers as hers and hers alone. Not that she was surprised at Megan's sensitivity regarding the pendants. A few years back, Megan had given Emma a floral pendant that would've actually grouped nicely with the other three. But Emma never wore it. At least not when she wore the others. She'd thought she'd been doing a good job of cycling the pendants so as not to hurt Megan's feelings. But one day she looked in her jewelry box and found the pendant from Megan was no longer a pendant. Megan had taken it and turned it into a gorgeous anklet instead. They didn't have an overly emotional conversation about it all, but Emma did essentially tackle-hug her sister for knowing exactly how to be an amazing sister. Now rarely a day went by when Emma didn't wear the anklet.

"So the short answer is that I don't know yet what kind of tattoo I'm going to get. Figured I shouldn't rush the decision."

"That's smart. You are going to have this on your skin forever, after all."

Megan nodded and said softly, "I know how that goes."

Empathy—never sympathy—prompted Emma to reach for Megan's scar-covered hand. "So back to this new ferocious you. I take it this is a combo package with the tattoo."

"Yep. Figured I better start being more badass to match my tattoo."

God, she loved seeing her sister so happy. "I think you have that backward, babe. Personally, I can't wait to see the tattoo you pick to match the badass that's been in you all along, just itching to get out."

Megan beamed.

Emma hopped up and headed to the only small fridge she still had plugged in. "I wasn't able to salvage everything, but I did make sure to get your favorite cupcakes to safety." She pulled out the box she'd had waiting for Megan all morning.

"You are too good to me."

"Right back at you." Emma headed over to the register. "With the flood and all, I didn't get a chance to thank you for these flowers. How late did you drop them off last night?"

She picked up the beautiful basket of spring flowers to show Megan they'd survived the flood unharmed.

"Emma, no! *Wait!*"

Too late. As soon as she lifted the basket high enough, Emma got sprayed good and proper with a face full of water, thanks to a big ol' clown squirt flower that was hidden in the arrangement.

Sputtering and wiping water from her eyes, Emma spun around and gaped at Megan.

"Erm . . . it'll make more sense if you read the card," whispered Megan, who looked torn between horror and laughter.

Emma flipped open the card.

April Fools!

"Surprise," said Megan weakly, backing away with her cupcakes. "Now I realize that in light of today's flooding, this is just the worst practical joke ever. *But*, remember, I dropped the flowers off last night."

Instead of responding, Emma studied how Megan had rigged the flower's water pump to activate by pulling on the attached string, which was taped to the bakery counter. *Nice.*

Megan inched closer to the door, looking all but ready to make a run for it.

Finally Emma broke. She dropped the flowers and burst out laughing.

If possible, Megan appeared even more alarmed now. That just made Emma laugh even harder. "You actually did it. You finally did your first April Fools' prank."

A cautious smile twitched across Megan's lips. "Did I do good?"

"I think the evidence speaks for itself." Emma wiped the tears of laughter from her eyes.

Megan was in full-grin mode now, looking pretty darn proud of herself. "I can't believe I went through with it. Last year I chickened out the day of."

Emma shot her an affectionate smile. "I know. I actually saw you prepping for it the week before. But heck, you came out swinging this year. I just did not see this coming."

"That's what Dad always said was the most important part of the prank. Making sure it came straight out of left field." Megan shook her head appreciatively. "I still remember how you and Dad used to have the most epic prank wars. My favorite was the exploding soda bottle with the Mentos candy one you did on him."

Ah, a classic. "It was a proportionate payback for the time he refilled my entire ChapStick tube with a column of butter . . . the same day I just happened to loan my ChapStick to a friend." If memory served correctly, they didn't stay friends for long after that. *C'est la vie.*

"I actually helped him with that," admitted Megan.

"You know what? I'm actually not surprised." While Emma definitely inherited all the rascally rabbit genes from their dad, who used to be the king of hilarious pranks, she'd always thought there may be a few recessive traits in Megan that would've developed had the fire not happened. Lying dormant. Sure, Emma was the one the kids in town came to when they wanted ideas for fabulously extravagant, but totally harmless, practical jokes to do on their friends. But there had been a few occasions when Megan would shyly suggest something so awesomely crazy that the kids would be in awe. "See what I mean about the inner badass?"

Megan shook her head. "This, I didn't actually do for me. I did it for you."

Emma did a double take. "What do you mean?"

"After the fire"—her voice wobbled—"you and Dad never did another practical joke or April Fools' prank again. In fact, I rarely ever heard you two laugh the way you used to, either."

"Things were different after the fire, hon."

"But I didn't want things to be. Thanks to me and my stupid burned body, you two were chained to the hospital and missing out on April Fools'. I ruined the trend, and you guys never picked it back up. Neither of you ever laughed or had fun like that again. All because of me."

Emma rushed over and wrapped her arms around Megan. "Oh my God. Is that what you've thought all these years? Meg, you've got it all wrong. Our reasons for not doing pranks anymore were because of your injuries, yes, but not in the way you're thinking. We only stopped doing them because we were waiting on you to get better so you could do them with us."

Megan stared in disbelief. "What?"

"We didn't give up the fun and the laughter, honey. Far from it. We'd actually talked about how, as soon as your body was strong enough, we were each going to have you be our sidekick to play an epic practical joke on the other."

She used her sweater sleeve to wipe away Megan's tears. "But with Dad getting sick around when you were finally healed, we just weren't able to follow through is all. I swear your injuries didn't ruin anything.

Trust me—if the universe hadn't gone and taken Dad from us, you would've seen something real special. Pranks born of years of patience and prep." Emma looked up at the ceiling. "You're lucky, old man. I had some doozies planned for you."

Megan giggled.

Emma squeezed her again. "Dad would have been so impressed with that prank."

"You think?"

"Oh, I know. Even when I was a kid, I *never* fell for the clown squirt flower. I bet he's up there right now beaming with pride."

Megan's expression sobered a bit. "I bet Peyton is, too. He and I had made a pact to join forces and do a prank together, you know. On the next April Fools', on both you and Dad."

Emma's smile fell apart altogether. "I never knew." Yet another thing Peyton didn't get to live to do. The list was never ending. She should know. She was constantly adding things to that list. Every day, seemed like.

"Lemon-face," murmured Megan softly.

Instantly Emma felt the tears prickle her eyes. "Is that the face I'm making?"

"Yep. But you're doing it wrong. Not nearly sour enough. Peyton would have a fit."

That he would. "I have to say, of all the proverbial sayings he used to put his own funny spin on, that one was my favorite."

Megan nodded. "Mine, too. That stepbrother of ours was a wise one. I can't tell you how many times I'd be in the middle of a crappy day, and his little matter-of-fact voice would echo in my ears, 'When life gives you lemons, make lemon-face.'"

"And would you make the puckered face exactly how he showed us?"

Megan proceeded to make the sourest puckered face ever.

Emma chuckled. "That's the lemon-face all right."

And just like it always had back then, it made them laugh.

"I miss him. Every day." The prickly tears finally broke free. "With Jake here, I think it's going to be harder than usual. I don't know if I'm going to be able to do it, Megan." She felt almost ashamed to say it out loud. Especially since Megan was clearly not having the same trouble with the situation that she was. "I don't know if I'm going to be able to have Jake in here every day without dragging everything from our past in here along with him."

Seeing the question marks in Megan's eyes, Emma expected her to ask if she was going to go through with having Jake work on the bakery.

But instead she asked a question that collided her new uncharred world right into the one she'd thought she'd left behind with the fire.

"Do you miss him, too?" queried Megan gently. "Jake, I mean. You don't have to tell me the answer, but at least be honest with yourself. I know you miss Peyton. But you didn't just lose Peyton after that fire. You lost Jake, too. So the question is, do you miss *Jake*, as well?"

Megan nodded pointedly at Emma's floral pendants. "I know it's not the same thing, but it's something most folks don't get. Things we lose usually stay lost. Folks we miss, we typically don't ever get a chance to stop missing. Now, Peyton's never going to walk back into our lives again, but *Jake just did*. So if you miss Jake like I suspect you do, you now have a chance to close up that hole he left in your heart after the fire . . . one way or another."

One way or another.

That was the scariest part of it all.

Because she truly didn't know which way she wanted her heart to heal.

Chapter Six

Jake dialed Carter's phone number and—surprise, surprise—got his voice mail.

Again.

If not for the commitment he'd made to start Emma's repairs this morning, Jake would've used all the bonus miles he possessed to be on the first plane out to California . . . so he could personally deliver the guy a well-deserved ass kicking.

In the absence of that possibility, Jake had to settle for the next best thing: leaving a voice mail strapped with some terrifying verbal shrapnel. "If you don't quit dodging my calls within the next forty-eight hours so we can discuss whatever the hell possessed you to buy *Megan's* library, swear to God, I'll sic Haley on you."

That was a damn serious threat, and they both knew it. Haley was the baby of the family, who never hesitated to guilt her three big brothers to within an inch of their sanity whenever she deemed it necessary. Typically when one or all three of them were being stubborn asses to one another, as only brothers can. Come to think of it, if memory served, *she* was the one who first got Jake to start taking Carter's bimonthly calls to begin with, way back when she'd still been a kid in high school.

Her powers had only grown since.

Truthfully Jake had half a mind to sic Haley on Carter anyway. Especially after the lovely chat he'd had with Paul last night when he'd tried to turn down the library job, as he'd promised Emma he would. Not only had the amused foreman been expecting the call from Jake; he'd had a Carter-supplied response already prepared. Evidently unless the directive came straight from SME Enterprises, Paul was instructed to expect Jake to show up to start the library project no matter what.

When Jake next called Carter's office to raise some hell over that, the similarly amused assistant had informed him that regrettably, he was "out of the country," in search of a "snowman in Jamaica." It was abundantly clear Carter had told his assistant to use air quotes in her reply.

The jackass.

If Jake weren't annoyed enough to spit nails right now, he'd be grudgingly impressed that Carter was upping his game to professional dickhead level. Jake had no doubt that the reggae jingle Carter had replaced the voice mail greeting of his personal phone number with was going to be stuck in his head all day long.

As if today weren't going to be difficult enough.

Jake tossed his cell phone onto the dashboard and dropped his head against the steering wheel, noting a distinct irony here, what with his taking this job at Emma's bakery and all. In his own defense, he'd always been inexplicably *unbridled* where she was concerned.

Some things never change.

Emma certainly hadn't. She was just as much of a force to be reckoned with as he remembered. Strong and opinionated. Captivating. And still as sweet as ever. Hell, seeing her big, bleeding heart peek through when he'd briefly mentioned his time in juvie and his parents splitting up had been like seeing a damn gorgeous ray of sunshine after a storm.

Jake understood now why Paul's threat yesterday had been cesspool-serious. If anyone could get an entire town to love and want to protect her, it'd be Emma Stevens. She'd always had as much beauty on the inside as she did on the outside, not to mention all the smarts, creativity, and grit that he'd known would take her far in life.

Seeing her now as the stunning adult she'd grown into, he wasn't at all surprised she was running her own thriving business. Kicking ass and taking names.

And, Jesus, she was still the prettiest female he'd ever laid eyes on.

The quintessential girl next door, Emma had that bewitching mix of an angel's face with the smile of an unapologetic imp. Along with expressive, laughing blue eyes he recalled her describing as "light-denim blue" once, which had prompted a debate between Jake and Haley, and extensive research with Haley's giant 120-count Crayola box.

They'd eventually landed on the shade of cornflower blue as the closest fit to Emma's eyes. After that, all summer, whenever he'd see Haley coloring with that particular shade, he'd immediately think of Emma and get all smiley and distracted beyond saving. At least according to his brother Daryn's relentless teasing that Jake was in *looove*.

In all fairness, honestly, how could a guy *not* smile when thinking about her? Between those mischievously animated eyes and that sun-streaked golden-brown hair she always wore in a long ponytail or French braid down her back, Emma had been the very definition of the spunky midwestern farm girl, complete with the lovable charm that could tempt any red-blooded guy to grow country roots right alongside hers.

Jake was man enough to admit that he'd spent most of last night thinking about her and the now-foreign idea of roots of any sort where his future was involved. Hadn't been able to get a wink of sleep as a result. And as a guy who needed at least a few solid hours of shut-eye to be functional, he was paying for it this morning. Brain-fuzzed and tired, he wasn't so much drinking his a.m. coffee as he was pouring it down his gullet midyawn.

At least he'd come well prepared on that front. Having left his house at 2:00 a.m. to get here, he'd brought three travel mugs of coffee for the drive over, and that was in addition to his usual monster thermos he never went a day without. The rugged Antarctica-worthy thermos was nearly as big as a paper towel roll, and a legit revolution in coffee drinking as far as he was concerned. With an old-school cap-as-a-mug design and new-school space technology, the thermos bottle was a serious piece of engineering that Carter had gotten as a joke for Jake a few Christmases ago—the first and only Christmas that Haley had managed to get all four siblings together to exchange presents.

True story: Jake had nearly wept when he'd unwrapped it. Even went batshit crazy enough to semihug Carter, if the rumors, and damning photographic evidence from Daryn's phone, were to be believed.

Now Jake never left his house without it. Normally he needed only his two pots of coffee in the morning before he headed out and that trusty thermos to help him survive the day. But today was not most mornings. Hence the additional travel mugs.

Not wanting to be late, not being able to stay away, not trusting himself to spend an entire night dreaming about the woman—take your pick. They were all applicable reasons why he'd arrived two hours before the 7:00 a.m. start time he'd told Emma, and why he'd been parked outside the bakery slowly emptying first his travel mugs and then his thermos ever since.

It was still only a little after six, and, although the thermos usually lasted him at least until nine, he was down to his last capful. *Damn.*

"You're going to burn a hole in your stomach lining at this rate," groused a sharp voice from just outside his truck.

"Holy shit!" Jake quickly counted his blessings that the heat in his truck had been barely functional this morning. Because if it had been working, he wouldn't have been wearing his late winter coat. And the testicle-scalding cup of coffee he'd managed to spill in his lap would've done some real damage.

He rolled down the window and practically came nose to nose with Emma. "You did that on purpose."

She didn't back down one iota. "You betcha. I always offer intestine-preserving advice to the creeps who park outside my home in silence for hours." In a very put-upon you're-*welcome* tone, she added, "I would've used my bullhorn if not for the early hour."

Despite wearing a full cup of coffee he really could've used, he found himself fighting a smile of his own. "Still as sassy as I remember." When she proceeded to look damned proud over that observation, he forgot all about the two areas of conversation he'd told himself to stick to for the next few weeks—carpentry and the weather—and asked curiously, "Are you planning to make my life a living hell the entire time I'm here?"

"Only if you don't keel over drinking that tar you call coffee." She shoved a to-go cup of something hot in his hands. "Door's open. I'll see you inside when you finish that."

With that, she headed back to the bakery with a walk that was classic Emma all the way. There was no hip swinging or anything seductive about her strut, but she may as well have shimmied and shook her way across the street for the instant effect it had on him . . . or, more specifically, certain coffee-warmed parts of him, which, again, made him thankful he was wearing a coat.

Hell's bells, Emma had for damn sure wreaked havoc on his teen hormones back before she'd developed the gentle hourglass figure he'd somehow missed the full impact of yesterday. Seeing it in all its glory today, paired with the hot-as-Hades poise of the strong woman she'd become, she was now easily the sexiest thing he'd ever seen.

And criminy, could the woman wear the holy hell out of an apron.

Good lord, don't go there. This entire line of thinking was twenty different kinds of wrong. Listening to NFL-Sunday-game-day-coverage-during-church kind of wrong.

Before he had a chance to tar and feather himself over that, however, he glanced up—yes, up, meaning his eyes had still been on her long, honey-brown ponytail swishing from side to side against all those soft curves. What he found was her peeking back at him over her shoulder, with the corner of her mouth twitching up in a crooked grin.

An actual full grin. He took a mental snapshot just in case it was one of those freak occurrences destined to never happen again.

Only she didn't stop smiling.

Frankly he hadn't come prepared for such a thing. The foot-stomping, tell-it-like-it-is woman he'd locked horns with yesterday was who he'd expected to find today. Who he'd thought he knew what to expect from, at least.

This Emma, on the other hand, was a wild card he didn't have the first clue what to do with. With her criminally sexy apron and soft, mysterious smiles, this Emma reminded him of those tempting, sweetly charming cigar girls in old Hollywood films from the Roaring Twenties. But in a far more wholesome way. Like an insanely pretty milkmaid. God help him.

What on earth had happened between yesterday and today to cause *this* big of a change?

Right. Like he had enough blood flow going up north to be able to do something as involved as thinking right now. Hoping the coffee she'd just handed him was fresh enough to scald some sense back into him, he lifted the cup to his lips with every intention of downing the whole thing in one swig.

But he stopped himself just in time.

Jake eyed the drink in his hand warily. He'd *almost* forgotten that included in Emma's many charms was her wicked sense of humor, which she sometimes used for evil and not good. The harmless but still epically hilarious pranks she and her dad used to help the neighborhood kids plan had been the stuff of legends.

For all he knew, she could've just handed him a steaming hot cup of laxatives.

Given their history, it was entirely possible.

That said, a part of him had faith that the woman watching him right now from the bakery was still the sweet girl he'd once seen try to cheer up a sad puppy she'd been dog-sitting for a family friend. She'd attempted everything from pretending to be a fellow puppy to doing a hysterical dog-and-cat sock-puppet show complete with all-original canine and feline music.

The one thing that had finally worked?

Her climbing up a big ol' tree in her backyard and bouncing on a bunch of branches to shake out as many leaves as she could, which she'd raked up to make a summer version of a giant autumn leaf pile so she and the puppy could take turns running and leaping onto it.

That had probably been the day Jake began falling head over heels for the girl, as she kept raking up the pile and flinging herself onto it in tandem with the grinning puppy.

Fast-forward to today—it wasn't possible that his sweet puppy-cheerer-upper had matured into a woman who'd give him a freshly brewed mug of laxatives, was it?

Here goes nothing.

He took a deep breath, then swallowed a trusting gulp.

And immediately began sputtering in disbelief.

Decaf? She'd given him decaf?

With milk and what tasted like ten tablespoons of sugar, from what he could gather when he popped the top off and looked at the offensive concoction.

Decaf coffee with milk and sugar wasn't very far behind boiling laxatives in his book.

And somehow the chuckling wildcat in the bakery had figured that out. Whether by Sherlock deduction because of his bounty of coffee containers or pure witchcraft, he wasn't sure.

All he knew was that it was *on*. Messing with a man's coffee was just plain mean.

Hooking and holding her simpering gaze, he manned up and proceeded to guzzle down the entire cup. Every last drop. Stood his ground and drank that heinous drink as if it weren't a violation of everything he knew to be good in this caffeinated world.

The entire time Emma just stood there sassing him in silence with her innocently blinking smile and a hot mug of coffee of her own, which she raised to him in a toast.

He'd bet dollars to doughnuts she wasn't drinking *decaf.*

Dammit, this little stunt of hers may have been more successful than the leaf-raking thing at jump-starting his rusty, dusty heart.

Chapter Seven

After rummaging around his glove box for a pack of gum to kill the taste of the milky, sugary decaf, Jake quickly made his way over to the bakery. "'Morning," he called out as he pushed open the jangling front door.

Emma's wholly entertained blue eyes dropped down to his gum-chewing mouth for a second before smiling at him over the top of the mug she was holding to her lips. "Good morning, Jake," she replied before taking a long, slow sip.

Sweet baby Jesus, what the woman could do with an innocent cup a joe.

"Thanks for the coffee earlier. It was great." Said it with a straight face and everything.

"Oh, good." Her eyes twinkled. "I wasn't sure how you liked your coffee. But now that I do, I'll make sure to have a mug ready for you when you come in the mornings."

He mentally dry-heaved in dismay. Lordy, this was going to become a thing, wasn't it?

Her eyebrows quirked up as if confirming his horrified thoughts.

"Yum," he finally managed weakly.

At that she flashed him a truly radiant smile, the likes of which he hadn't seen since they were teens, and he felt the warming effects all the way down to his bone marrow. Hell, he'd happily drink a whole pot of the stuff if she served it with that smile every morning.

Something in his reaction must have relayed that same message because a touch of color stained her cheeks shortly before the wattage of the smile lessened to merely polite and friendly.

Shame.

"So," she began. "I just wanted to say that I know we sort of got off to a rough start yesterday, what with me telling you to get out and everything. That was out of line for me. I was just shocked to see you. And with all our history, clearly, I didn't handle it well . . ."

She was apologizing to him again. Not in so many words, but there was an apology in there, and he didn't like it one bit. Never should *Emma Stevens* have to apologize to *him*.

That sobered him like little else could. "Don't do that. Nothing you could ever say to me would *ever* be out of line, Emma." When that came out far gruffer than he'd intended, he added, in a far less affected tone, "Your reaction to seeing me was completely warranted."

"Maybe, maybe not. All I know is that I'm not proud of myself for how I spoke to you. That wasn't me. True, we have a difficult past. But it was a long time ago."

A heavy emotional fog settled around them, making it nearly impossible for him to see where this was going. She looked as though she had more to say, but she remained silent as she reached up to grip one of the three floral pendants that hung from the dainty gold necklaces he'd noticed her wearing yesterday. After a long, steadying breath, she asked quietly, "Do you know what important, complicated, and rather surprising discovery I made last night?"

"What?" His voice was barely louder than hers.

"I discovered that I'm not nearly as evolved or as grounded, or even as *reasonable* as I thought I was. Not in terms of the past." Her breathing hitched just the slightest bit. "Or you."

Now he was the one wanting to say something but holding back.

Shaking her head, she expelled a gusty, frame-sagging sigh, and admitted further, "I also came to the awful realization that try as I might, I don't think I'm going to evolve, or get grounded, or even become any more reasonable during the time it'll take to fix up this bakery."

The regret in her gaze said it all.

Well, that's that. Jake nodded gently and picked up his tool belt to head back out. He didn't blame her. Not in the least. "I know a few guys who owe me some favors. I'll ask them to come down here and do the repairs at a price near what I quoted you—"

"Don't go."

He stopped. Couldn't lift either foot one more step if he tried. And every long, silent second that followed was the equivalent of hope pouring more cement in his concrete shoes.

"I think . . ." She lifted her eyes back up to meet his. "I think we could make this all work if we . . . started over again. Left the past in the past and sort of treat today as a starting line. A new beginning between two strangers: Jake Rowan the carpenter and Emma Stevens the baker."

That he hadn't been expecting.

She chewed on her lower lip nervously. "What do you think?"

He thought she was a saint was what he thought. A mildly crazy one. "You want us to pretend we're meeting for the first time?"

"Yes."

"Why?" And just as important: "Why now?"

"Because you're here now. You're not the ghost buried in my past that I never thought I'd see again. And unfortunately, fair or not, I can't untangle you from all the painful memories I've done my damnedest to forget, or separate you from the nightmares I can't seem to get rid of. I can't look at you or be around you without ending up feeling battered and broken on the inside."

Jake sucked in a harsh breath.

Her face paled. "I'm sorry—"

"*Stop* apologizing to me," he growled. "I can't take it. Won't stand for it. So just stop. Please, Emma. I know I don't deserve to ask you for anything—"

"I'll stop." The two words hung in the air between them, shaking like wobbly leaves in a windstorm. Dammit, *she* was shaking just as bad, and seemingly seconds from falling.

Son of a bitch. He should just hightail it out of town and never look back. Emma was hurting, and he was responsible for that. Again.

"Don't go." This time she said it with even more conviction than the last. "You look ready to bolt. And I swear, that's not what I want."

"For chrissakes, you just said I make you feel *battered and broken*, Emma." Even repeating it was a sucker punch to the gut.

"B-but it's not you, Jake. Really."

Jake took another deep breath to try to calm the hell down. His neighbors a few years ago, a young couple, had had a horribly toxic relationship, which ultimately devolved to the asshole actually *hitting* his girlfriend. Hearing her cries for help, Jake had broken down their door and pulled the poor woman out of there. But not long after the cops came to arrest her boyfriend, she'd started crying hysterically and saying it wasn't his fault that he hit her. Most heartbreaking thing ever to watch. That was the point Jake had stepped back to have a professional help her.

Of course, this wasn't the same situation, not by a long shot, but hell if it didn't make his insides burn to hear Emma saying such similar things. This was on him, and they were going to square things right the hell now. "Emma, it kills me to hear any of this 'it's not your fault' line of thinking, especially from you. You're way too strong for that. Always have been."

She stared at him as if he'd grown an extra eyeball or two. *"What?"*

With an ache in his chest over her lost expression, he attempted a less subtle tactic. "If a man, *any* man—even me—is hurting you, whether he means to or not, it's *never* your fault, sweetheart. Don't you let any sorry sack of shit make you feel that way. Call me to kick his ass if you don't feel strong enough to. I'll beat the living daylights out of him like he deserves." He paused. Then added awkwardly, "Again, even if that sack of shit is unintentionally, well, me." *Reel it in, buddy.* This was going down as the strangest intervention talk in the history of time.

A look of understanding dawned on her features, and a gentle hand squeezed his forearm. "Jake, that's not what I meant." She laced her fingers with his to stop him from interrupting her. "Jeez, I forgot what an amazing person you are." With an affectionate head shake, she said quietly, "Thank you for saying all of that. I know it couldn't have been easy or remotely comfortable." Another hand squeeze. "But, Jake, when I said 'It's not you' earlier, I meant that literally. As in you, the man standing before me, isn't the one causing me to feel . . . what I said. It's the Jake from fourteen years ago. The one who was there with me when Peyton died. *He's* the one I can't disentangle from all the pain of the past. Not you."

He frowned. "But he and I are the same person." Funny how this conversation came up so many times. With his siblings, with his former mentor. He was constantly reminding folks that he took accountability for his past. It had made him who he was today. Defined him.

"No, you two are most definitely *not* the same person." She gave him a look that was as empathetic as it was unyielding. "You are not a product or some repentant evolution of your mistakes. I don't care what the court system, or your parents, say. Trust me—I know."

This was the second time she'd alluded to being blamed for something that had happened that night. And he had to know why. "Honey, talk to me. What happened with your stepmom?"

Just like that her expression turned to stone, and a mile of dense brick and mortar now stood between them. "Let's just say I know what it's like to have someone equate you with the worst thing you ever did . . . look at you and see only the person who took a loved one from them."

He clenched his jaw so hard he may have cracked a few molars. "Emma—"

"No. No feeling sorry for me. My stepmom and I haven't spoken since Peyton's funeral. It's better that way." She transformed then, right before his eyes. Her voice got stronger, her coloring less pallid. "I know you and I aren't in the same boat; heck, we're not even in the same harbor. But Jake and Emma from Riverside share an anchor to a tragic past that Jake and Emma from Juniper Hills *don't have to*." She looked . . . *freed* just from that notion alone. "I know it sounds crazy, Jake, but in the same way that I know in my heart that my stepmom and I would probably be such great friends if we met for the first time today—you remember how close we used to be—I know in my soul that you and I could, as well. Be friends, that is—"

"If we met for the first time today, too," he finished for her.

"*Yes.*" A tremulous smile broke over her lips. "If Megan has taught me anything, it's that leaving one foot behind in the past will just keep us stuck somewhere we don't want to be." She gave him a slow, what-more-can-we-do single shoulder lift. "I just want to unstick our feet from our pasts. Or at least try. But only if you want to. Have a fresh start, that is."

The blow to his solar plexus came so swiftly, he wasn't able to brace for it.

"Jake, juvie will just be a short blip in your life. Barely anything worth remembering. You can have a fresh start afterward; walk away from this mess and have a clean slate."

With his father's dead-wrong words echoing in his ears so loudly he couldn't breathe, Jake found himself forcibly shaking his head to get the looped playback to stop.

Emma's face went from stricken to sad. "Oh . . . okay. I shouldn't have assumed—"

Shit. "Emma, no. I wasn't shaking my head over what you said. Of course I'd want us to try to have . . . a fresh start if we could. If it were possible." *And not just fiction fathers tell.*

Ah, bloody hell. The spark of hope lighting her eyes pretty much sealed his fate. There was a very good chance he was going to agree to this ill-advised plan of hers.

"I tried it last night," she confessed, breaking into his brain's long list of objections on the topic. "I tried thinking of you, Jake Rowan, as this man I'd just met yesterday. And it worked. It was actually easy not to associate you with the Jake Carmichael from my memories. I didn't have a single triggered nightmare last night. Actually, on the contrary, I . . ."

She blushed, fast and fierce.

"What?" He frowned. "What were you about to say?"

"Nothing," she replied quickly.

Yeah, that was all kinds of suspicious. "Tell me."

"No." Her chin lifted mulishly. "You know, you're more demanding than I remember."

"And you're more evasive. Tell me what was supposed to come at the end of that."

She flushed a deeper crimson and muttered something about his ironic choice of words.

He was completely lost. But not ready to give in. Stewing in the silence, he replayed the entire conversation for one more maddening second. Then another. Until . . . *Holy sin on a saddle.* Every male atom in his body woke up and howled when he finally got it.

"Stop reading my mind," she huffed.

Damnations, he probably wasn't hiding his thoughts well. Though he highly doubted any jury of his peers would blame him. The woman had basically just said that last night she—

"I can already see you're making this way dirtier than it was!"

Now who was the mind reader? Man alive, she was a sight to see with red-hot cheeks and daggers in her eyes. Both for him. "To be fair, honey, if you don't tell me something I can compare my thoughts to, how am I supposed to—"

She whacked him good and hard on the arm. "You're not just bossier—you're also pervier than you used to be."

He grinned. "Right back atcha, babe."

Whoa. If looks could kill, he'd be worm food right now. This was way too fun. How in the hell did they even get here? He rubbed the back of his neck, surprised he wasn't feeling evidence of whiplash.

Suddenly her expression shifted to surprise. Which led to satisfaction. Then finally unfiltered triumph.

Never a dull moment with this one. "What's the impish smile for, sugar?"

She gave him a big told-you-so brow quirk. "You just proved my point."

Aw, hell. "No, I didn't."

"Yes, you did. The adult versions of us get along great. We have chemistry. And fun."

"What we *have* is a past you want us to ignore."

Her lips turned down at the corners, then transformed into the very definition of a sad smile. He never got that description until now. All at once, he wanted to go back to the playful banter. Between Jake the carpenter and Emma the baker. Maybe she was right about this.

"Do you want to know what I think about sometimes, even though I know it's silly and probably more damaging than good?" she asked, her voice at a confessional decibel.

Knowing she was getting to the closing argument of her case, he just buckled down and nodded for her to continue.

"Every once in a while, I wonder what it would have been like for us if that night had never happened, if Peyton hadn't died. I wonder sometimes if you and I would've ended up together. If we'd have grown up to become one of those disgustingly happy high school sweethearts with the fairy-tale wedding, successful careers, and the house-dog-and-kid combo. With proud parents to babysit for us." She peered into his eyes as if he had an answer.

He didn't. God knows he'd wondered the same things countless times over the years.

"That night interrupted a happy road we were headed down, I think," she said softly, slowly, as if trying to describe an image no one had ever really seen before. "We can't go back on that road now. It's done, destroyed. But we *can* start a new one. Can't we? Why can't we?"

Hell if he knew. Right now he wasn't sure he knew anything. "So you want us to literally put our past behind us to see if we'd end up on a happy road together again?"

"Not exactly."

He'd honestly never been more mentally exhausted in his life.

Her lips twitched to the side. "I don't mean to frustrate you. When I said no, I was clarifying that I'm not completely insane. I know we can't actually ditch our past altogether. Not really. But I thought, at least for the next few weeks, we could travel to an . . . alternate reality. Just for a bit. One where we can start over. Be friendly. Explore the chemistry. And have *fun* for a change." She sighed. "I can't remember the last time I had fun like Jake and Emma from Riverside used to have. Can you?"

Sure he could. It was the day of the fire. When they'd had one of their marathon talks over the fence, then somehow ended up having a friendly water fight with their respective garden hoses. She'd started it, of course. His having riled her to that point being wholly irrelevant.

Instead of bringing them back to that memory, though, he asked a question he was fairly sure he could guess the answer to. "What happens after the bakery's all done, sweetheart?"

She flinched but replied without missing a beat. "We return to reality. To our real lives."

And there it was. That right there was exactly why this was a god-awful idea. There was no way in the world he'd be able to do this without getting burned.

Wholly inappropriate pun intended.

He sighed, unable to do anything but stare at her guileless, hopeful face for a beat.

Finally he held out his hand. "Pleasure to meet you, Ms. Stevens. I'm Jake Rowan. Grouch. Obstinate hater of decaf. Carpenter extraordinaire. At your service."

Her slow-growing smile plain shook the ground under him even before reaching full wattage. "Pleasure's all mine, Mr. Rowan. I'm Emma Stevens. Determined work in progress. Wholehearted fan of the uncomplicated. Baker badass. Ready to make you work."

The moment their hands touched, he watched her eyes widen and those shiny pink lips of hers part on a telltale hitched breath.

His own reaction wasn't that far off. *Jaysus.* Would this happen every time they touched?

Don't kick over that rock, man.

She quickly took back her hand. "So, yes. Anyway, nice meeting you, too. Thanks again for bidding on these repairs. Guess I'll just leave you to it. I'll be upstairs in my apartment working out a plan so I don't go bankrupt while the bakery is shut down the next few weeks."

While her tone was light and airy, he could hear the genuine worry there. "Emma, if I can find ways to save on costs, I promise I'll try." He'd already given her a rock-bottom price, but if it would take away some of that anxiety in her eyes, he'd do his best to make the impossible possible. "I don't know. Maybe I can figure out a plan so I can get done quicker."

"Really?" She gazed up at him as if he'd just invented a way to replace the holes in Swiss cheese. And just that easily, he was halfway to offering to work 24-7. For free.

But then she went and said something to make him stop thinking about work altogether.

"Holy Christmas nuts, I'll name my firstborn after you if you're able to finish earlier."

He tensed. And very nearly growled.

Well, that was damn primitive. Who knew he was the kind of guy who would get all testosterone pumped at the prospect of procreation? To be fair, it was probably mostly because of the woman bringing up the topic. Still. *Down, boy.*

"Or I could bake you some cookies," she swiftly amended, worrying her lower lip with her teeth in response to whatever she saw in his expression. "I, uh, make great cookies."

"I remember," he rasped in a voice two sandpaper grades away from a rough scrape.

Only a few minutes into their agreement, and already he was breaking character. But no way was he going to pretend she hadn't once baked him the best cookies he'd ever tasted.

"Okay, cookies it is," she rushed out, her lightly freckled ears looking nearly sunburned as she took a few steps back. "Just holler if you need anything down here." Her sentence had barely gone airborne before she was spinning around and running off to the stairwell near the front of the bakery that led up to her apartment at the top of the landing.

Christ almighty. Jake let out a shuddering breath. He'd heard that every man had his inner Neanderthal just walking around inside him, but he'd never actually met his until he saw Emma backing away from him.

Something in him had wanted to prowl after her something fierce. And take over biting that lower lip for her so he could taste for himself if she'd in fact been drinking fully caffeinated coffee earlier or not.

Get your head out of your ass, man. Just grab your sledgehammer and do some demo work. It'll take your mind off that walking temptation upstairs.

Best piece of advice he'd given himself all day. He went straight over to the biggest area of damage in the kitchen with every intention of doing just that. Until he looked up through the gaping hole in the ceiling . . . right into Emma's apartment above.

Now, it was one thing to know she lived up there; it was another to *see* her up there, just going about her business outside work—an aspect of her life he wasn't an invited part of.

But absolutely wanted access to.

One day. If this whole Jake and Emma 2.0 plan didn't completely combust in their faces.

Emma halted in the middle of sitting down at her dining table when their gazes collided. She waved down at him, chuckling. "Guess you won't have to holler too loudly. I forgot the plumber had to pull up the floors in this section of my apartment to do some of the pipe repairs."

"I'll fix those, too," he offered. "No charge. It's a small area. I've got extra plywood with me, so I can come up and replace your subfloor right now if you want. Give you back your privacy. Plus, that'll keep all the construction dust from getting up into your apartment."

"That'll be great, actually. If you can take care of that for me, I can lay the hardwood floor over it later. I know I have extra planks from when I first installed 'em."

Lordy, that was hot. Where Jake was concerned, a DIY girl was a damn sexy one.

Hell, would nothing about the woman turn him off?

He got his answer two seconds later when he saw her reach over to pull out some simple hardware-store flooring essentials from a nearby drawer . . . and he was forced to get creative in covering up his immediate reaction to seeing her with tools in hand.

Scrubbing a calloused hand over his face, he glanced over his shoulder to make sure Paul or any other men from his crew weren't outside checking on him. Thankfully the street was deserted for the time being.

Last thing he needed was to have to explain to a bunch of construction guys he'd soon be working with why he was presently wearing his tool belt sideways like a loincloth.

Chapter Eight

Luckily Jake was able to get Emma out of his head long enough to make a big dent in the repairs. At the midday mark, he was actually ahead of schedule, thanks in part to Emma having done a bunch of grunt work he hadn't expected. From pulling saturated baseboards to drilling air holes into the toe kicks of all the cabinets, she'd done her flood-fix homework for sure.

Not just that but she'd even left Post-its everywhere, mentioning things like which walls housed junction boxes she knew about, or where the dedicated electrical circuits were. Seeing as how there were dozens of notes on the walls for him, it was safe to say she'd worked all night checking building blueprints and crawling behind appliances to match outlets with breaker box switches, essentially mapping out the circuits to make his life loads easier.

It was hard not to become a little taken with a woman like that. Ask any guy in the trades. A girl willing to get some dirt and sawdust on her hands for them was a keeper.

A theory she proved indisputably a little later when she plopped a generator at his feet.

Though using bigger construction equipment after a flood was never totally safe, typically as long as the water levels didn't get too high, most building owners didn't bother with the added expense of a portable generator for contractors to plug into for repairs. But Emma did.

With a romantic little Post-it Note to boot:

Don't get electrocuted.

A downright love sonnet as far as he was concerned.

So really, by the time he found the homemade Reuben sandwich she left on his toolbox come lunchtime, it was like seeing a bow-tied bouquet of power tools for him; he was smitten.

Of course, the Reuben turned out to be the absolute best he'd ever had. He expected nothing less from the goddess. For lack of a strong enough description, it was *pornographically* good. Sex-noises-while-you-eat good.

That's when the woman really went and blew his simple, simple mind.

Emma, being Emma, made it crystal clear that his illicit alone time with the Reuben and the downright scandalous sounds he was making between bites weren't going unheard. Not by teasing him or anything overt. Nope. She referenced it in style. By slipping out and returning bearing gifts in a brown paper bag, which she left next to his plate before he started the second half of his sandwich.

Inside the bag?

A pack of bubblegum cigarettes.

And condoms.

He burst out laughing. Seeing that she'd gone out of her way to provide a variety of condom sizes, from extralarge *all* the way down to extraslim fit, had him nearly busting a gut. God, he loved her sass. Grinning, he pocketed them all—even the pint-size pecker protector—for safekeeping. Not because he intended to find out how quickly the minicondom, which was apparently half the standard size, according to the picture on the box, could cut off his blood flow and make him pass out. But because that was a thrown gauntlet if ever he'd seen one.

Far be it from him to ignore a dare like that. Whether the feisty woman realized it or not, she'd just started a *very* interesting game between them. *Oh, the possibilities.*

At that point even he had to concede that so far this Jake and Emma 2.0 experiment was off to a promising start.

Which grinded to a halt not three hours later, when his repair work led him to a wall with a cluster of framed family photos.

Just that quickly they were back to this plan being all kinds of wrong.

Of the many things Jake had prepared himself to face today, seeing a photo of Peyton—and acting as if he didn't recognize him—definitely hadn't been one of them. He supposed it helped that this was the first photo he'd ever seen of Peyton. Since the family hadn't approved the release of any pictures to the media following the fire, all Jake had had to remember his young neighbor by over the years were fond memories of a fun, rambunctious boy who was quick to tell anyone who asked that he loved baseball, hot dogs, ice-cream sundaes, and riding his bike. But not as much as he loved his stepsisters. Especially his big sis, Emma.

That little guy used to think the sun rose and set with her . . . a mutual adoration, from what Jake remembered of Emma's doting ways when it came to her stepbrother.

Silence blanketed the bakery as he felt Emma walk up and stand beside him. Together they stared at the photo he was holding: a laughing Peyton holding a trout in each hand.

"Cute kid," he finally managed to comment in the most casual voice he could muster.

"That was the first time we took him fishing," she explained softly. "My stepmom's first husband had never been the outdoorsy type, so she and Peyton had never even gone camping before we took them.

Ironically, he took to fishing way better than Megan or I did. Used to practice fishing in his kiddie pool and everything."

Ah, that explained why Peyton had once asked Jake to help him cut a bunch of sponges into fish shapes and then squeeze weighted ball bearings into the sponge holes.

Hell, Jake really hated having to shove down good memories like this of Peyton. It was a rare occurrence to have any not linked to the fire. But with Emma holding her breath as if expecting an ice-cold plunge with his next words, he knew he had to stay the course. "You heading out?" he segued smoothly, nodding at her purse and jacket. "I can wrap things up now if you need, or just lock up when I leave. Either way works. I'm almost done for the day."

A long, relieved breath whooshed past Emma's lips. "No rush—take your time. If you could just lock up the front, that'll be great. I'll go out the back."

"Will do. I'll be in at the same time tomorrow."

Polite and professional. A perfect exchange between Jake and Emma 2.0.

And dammit did it suck.

Emma gave him a friendly wave and headed to the back. Halfway there, she stopped and, without turning around, murmured quietly, "Thank you, Jake."

The emotions vibrating below the surface of that single sentence was neither polite nor professional. But they were well hidden. He sighed. "Have a good night, Emma."

Jake kept working for another hour, needing the extra time with his power tools to gather his thoughts, work shit out emotionally. Though hammering and sawing away at things didn't perform miracles, it did give him a chance to get to know the grown-up version of Emma a little better, via her bakery.

There were traces of her all over the place—from the bright, bold palette of colors to the array of warm, comfy mismatched furniture. The entire space was Emma in a complex nutshell.

Jake never would've thought the papier-mâché piñatas, in seemingly every color made by Crayola, hanging as art pieces over the wide window benches in the front would look fun and trendy as opposed to gaudy or childish. Likewise on the modern wicker poolside patio sofas along the walls of the seating areas—first time he'd ever seen them used *inside* a business, but, oddly enough, they looked really good. Especially with the distressed wooden crates serving as cocktail tables and the wrought-iron standing bar tables dispersed throughout, which he'd never seen outside a bar or pub before. Even the unlikely pairing of shockingly cheerful bohemian-patterned pillows next to the country whitewashed shelves lined with mason jars of plastic utensils for the customers, and the surprisingly homey baskets of rustic balls of yarn everywhere worked well together. In a unique, unexpected way.

Not unlike its owner.

Taking it all in was therapeutic. So much so that by the time sunset rolled around, he was almost okay with the situation again. As he locked up his tools in his truck bed and stretched out the welcome ache in all his muscles from a hard day's work, about a dozen folks greeted him on the sidewalk as if he'd stepped into a family TV show from the 1950s.

Soon he felt something thawing inside his chest—which led to him deciding to walk around town instead of hopping in his truck and driving off right away. The traffic home would be a congested beast this time of day anyway.

That was his excuse, and he was sticking to it.

It was not because this cozy little town somehow felt more like home than his own apartment did. *Nope.* And his walking into the lively little joint called Sally's Diner clear on the other end of town had nothing to do with the bologna sandwich, canned soup, and nuked ear of frozen corn on the cob that was originally going to be his sad dinner for the night. *Nuh-uh.*

This was all about the traffic.

"Hey, you must be the carpenter working on Emma's bakery," a smiling, silver-haired waitress greeted him as she plopped down a glass of water and a hot mug of what looked like double-black coffee, or something darn close.

When he clutched the mug like a wild animal getting ready to devour his prey, she chuckled. "Took a shot in the dark. You looked like you could use a mug of our trucker special," she explained with a wink.

Clearly she was some sort of psychic soothsayer or powerful wizard sent to undo the damage Emma's decaf had done on his body's caffeine balance. He drank the black-as-night coffee gratefully, downing half the mug on one swig, practically feeling his woodsman beard get denser as a result. "Damn that's good coffee. I'm not even kidding—you can just set the whole coffeepot on my table and put that order pad away."

Barb, according to her bedazzled name tag, tipped her head back and laughed. "As much as my boss Sally will love hearing the compliment on her special 'burly-man brew,' she'll come out here personally and start piling food on this table if you don't order something to eat."

He grinned, knowing right then and there that he and this town were going to get along just fine. With Barb refusing to budge until he ordered some food, Jake looked around at what everyone else was eating to make his choice. Seeing everything from pot roast to enchiladas to lasagna, however, soon had him almost whimpering in starved indecision.

Barb quickly took pity on him and pointed up at three plates displayed on the wall. "No worries—Sally also has a mess-hall-style 'flat rate for the plate' ordering, where you can get however many different things you can fit on one of those three plates."

He looked up and found the prices unbelievably affordable, considering the three sizes ranged from a standard dinner plate to what looked like a twenty-pound-turkey platter.

"The biggest size is usually for folks here on a date. Inspired by Sally's all-time favorite cartoon movie, *Lady and the Tramp*. One massive platter, two forks. Romance guaranteed."

Man, this town was so wonderfully weird. Chuckling, he selected the first dinner-plate size, and asked Barb to pile it high with all her favorites, certain he wouldn't be disappointed.

Sure enough, the food was delicious.

Surprisingly, the company it came with was also.

All through his meal, diners kept stopping by to introduce themselves, catapulting right past small talk to third-date-type crazy-town stories, usually starring someone within earshot, who would, of course, retaliate with an even zanier story that would have him in stitches.

He'd never met a more colorful, mismatched blend of folks.

Their ability to coexist in utterly paradoxical symbiosis reminded him of Emma's bakery decor. Which explained why he liked 'em so much. And probably why they appeared to like him, too. If the number of people who brought their food over to his table to eat and chitchat away was any indication, no one here was even distantly aware that "cantankerous, growly bear" was the default setting for his personality. On the contrary, he suspected the townsfolk were operating on inaccurate intel painting him as more teddy than grizzly as far as bears went.

Case in point, five minutes into his meal, a trio of sweet old biddies descended on him to make sure he kept space open on his dance card for them at the spring square dance during next month's bonfire block party. Yeah . . . he'd had about as much luck politely declining that invite as he had the berry-picking field trip little Cassie's preschool class needed chaperones for later in the summer. Don't even get him started on the fall hayride festival that got snuck in there in the blur somehow. And their annual holiday production of *A Charlie Brown Christmas*?

Hell, he'd apparently been nominated—and was already rumored as the favored nominee—to go out and "lumberjack" the iconic little tree from the story. Town vote pending, of course.

For a man who'd gotten used to living a solitary lifestyle without much in the way of future plans, Jake was surprisingly disappointed over the sad reality that he wouldn't actually be around to attend any of these functions. *Remember, this is just temporary—you and Emma are going to go back to your "real lives" after these few weeks are up.*

Just as he was clubbing himself over the head with that hard-to-swallow fact, however, two tiny hands perched up on the edge of his table, followed by the long-lashed doe eyes and button nose they belonged to.

"Well, hello again, Miss Cassie. What can I do for you?"

"I need your finger," she replied with all the boldness of a four-year-old who knew what she wanted in life.

"Yes, ma'am." He held up his index finger, curious where this was going.

She proceeded to remove the ribbon from her hair so she could tie it on his finger. "This is so you remember. The field trip is in June. You're going to come with the Bumble Bee class. *Not* the Blue Bird class. And don't forget your lunch box and thermos. I'll save a seat for you on the bus so we can sit together and see if we want to trade snacks."

Sweet lord, the child was going to kill him with all this cuteness.

"Promise you won't forget?" She hit him with her big, unblinking eyes. *And* he was done for. "I wouldn't miss it for the world, munchkin."

"Yaaay!" She smacked a kiss on his cheek and then hopped on back to her parents, who were waving at him and mouthing thank-yous.

Okay, so maybe he'd be going to *one* of the town events he'd gotten invited to.

After the pitch-perfect symphonic chorus of awws around him faded, they finally let him get back to the near-religious experience he'd been having eating himself into a blissful coma.

Seriously, between Emma's Reuben and tonight's meal, this was the best he'd eaten in years. With his parents not wanting to be his parents after he'd entered juvie, he hadn't really learned to cook. And because he'd been living paycheck to paycheck ever since, mealtime usually consisted of whatever edible thing he could buy on a budget to keep from starving.

Which was why he was all but licking his plate clean when Barb returned to his table with dessert.

"What's this?"

"Kansas Dirt Cake. It's good—trust me," she answered with an encouraging smile.

Well, of course he knew what Kansas Dirt Cake was; the Oreo-based dessert was a favorite staple around these parts. "Sorry, what I meant was I didn't order this." But damn did it look tasty. He did some quick calculations to see if he could afford to splurge this week.

"Oh, no worries. This is on the house. Sally's way of making sure you come back to the diner again. Dig in. I'll be back with more coffee."

He got a little misty-eyed looking at the decadent masterpiece. He couldn't remember the last time someone had given him a cake just because . . .

Actually, yes, he could. Mentally ducking to avoid the resulting sucker punch of his teen memories, he swiftly shifted his mind away from the depressing topic before it could ruin the first forkful of his first homemade dessert since he was sixteen.

Thank goodness he did because *lord have mercy*. An embarrassingly loud groan escaped him when the perfect combination of cream, cookies, and crust hit his taste buds.

Barb gave him a knowing grin. "Good, isn't it?"

"*Good?* This is the best dirt cake I've ever had. My compliments to Sally."

"Actually, you can redirect those compliments to Emma. Sally gets all her desserts from Emma's bakery. That's what makes this cake so yummy. It has Emma's homemade chocolate cookies—none of that store-bought stuff—along with her special s'mores pudding."

"S'mores pudding?" Really, he was just making small talk so he could slow down and savor the dessert. Left to his own devices, he'd be digesting the entire thing by now.

"Yep. She makes the best puddings. Fancy designer flavors, too. Stuff like baklava, and a couple with beer and whiskey. All her cakes have 'em."

One of the dairy farm owners he'd met earlier came over to join the conversation—Janice? He couldn't remember. He'd met like fifty people in the past hour. "Her cakes are half the reason I come here as much as I do. I'm not kidding, I almost cried when I heard her bakery was going to be shut down for a few weeks."

Barb smiled. "Emma is such a sweetheart. As soon as she found out her bakery was going to be closed for business for a bit, she called up Sally to set an early-morning schedule to bake the daily diner desserts over here so we'd still have cakes and pies until she reopened."

Yep, that was the Emma he remembered. To this day the kindest person he'd ever met.

"Don't you go breaking her heart now," threatened Barb with a finger wag.

Before he could stop that bit of town gossip from starting—a sure-fire way to become the victim of an attempted ass kicking by Emma—Barb lit up. "There's your girl now."

Even with that advance warning, Jake still wasn't ready for the impact of seeing "his girl" enter the front door of the diner. For chrissakes, you'd think he hadn't just seen the woman a few hours ago by the way he couldn't take his eyes off her.

Barb arched an observant eyebrow. "Well, well. I think maybe I'm warning the wrong person. Don't you go letting *her* break *your* heart now."

Guess her soothsayer powers weren't always quite so accurate.

"Lost my heart a long time ago," he admitted quietly, for Barb's ears only. "So you don't need to worry about me." *Nothing to break here.*

"Oh, I'm not worried. I think you'll be just fine." She patted him gently on the shoulder in a sage seer way. "That said, word to the wise so you're not caught unaware. Most of us only call things in our life lost when it's something we hope to find again one day."

Jake had no way to respond to that. Not that Barb was waiting around for him to try. She was already charming the socks off the folks on the next table over, leaving him alone with his now tornado-like thoughts just as Emma and the woman she'd entered the diner with made their way over to his table.

His well-rooted manners on autopilot, he stood to greet both women . . . only to find himself voiceless when he realized who exactly he was looking at.

Megan Stevens.

Every one of the news articles he'd read about Emma's sister's injuries assailed him then like bullets to his brain. *A fourth of her body.* All but one of the papers reported how the fire had burned a fourth of her body. The odd one out described it a bit differently, using a quote from a neighbor who'd witnessed from afar what Jake had seen up close. To give journalistic credit where it was due, the lone article's use of the word *torched* instead of *burned* was a far more accurate description of what little Megan Stevens had endured that night. Of that Jake had no doubt.

Now, seeing the healed but ever-present evidence of what those scorching flames had done to her skin all along her jaw, neck, chest, and the length of her arm almost unmanned him.

He stood glued to the spot, unable to face her—the innocent victim who, like Emma, believed *he* had caused the fire responsible for all those heartbreaking wounds.

Chapter Nine

"Hi, Jake. I've heard so much about you."

Jake stood there numbly, wondering if Megan's foreign-sounding words, like her bafflingly genuine smile, were simply getting lost in translation as a result of his grief-fogged senses. Had to be. Because there was just no way in the world Megan Stevens was actually standing there smiling at *him* and offering a kind greeting.

Jake shifted his gaze over to Emma, expecting her candid honesty to burst through his foggy bubble. But what he found instead was a look of reassurance, bordering on comfort, as she said encouragingly, "Megan saw you outside the bakery yesterday and has been wanting to meet you ever since so she could talk to you about the library job."

All righty then. It was official. His confusion was now complete. Clearly he'd lost his ever-lovin' mind. Or somehow ended up in a parallel universe with the Stevens sisters.

He stood there in silence, not wanting to hinder his brain's ability to glean some important observations from this strange new world to navigate him around somehow.

Huh, would you look at that. Megan's hair is darker than Emma's. More a light mahogany to Emma's golden pecan. Last year he'd installed wood floors in those exact colors.

That's it, brain—work with what you know. Wood exists in other universes, right?

Just when he was starting to think this was all a weird daydream he simply needed to snap out of, the Megan before him morphed right back into that terrified little nine-year-old girl he'd *felt* scream as her body got charred to a crisp as he'd carried her out of the fire.

Instantly his muscles locked up as he felt the furnace around them closing in . . .

"*Jake.*" Emma's concerned voice finally managed to pull him out of his spiraling memories. "Jake, you okay?" The sisters exchanged a look.

Seeing the supreme worry in Emma's expression was the only thing that helped bring him back to reality. "Sorry, guess I blanked out there for a bit," he replied finally, his voice sounding as if he'd swallowed some gravel. "Early morning."

He kept his eyes on Emma like a lifeline. The disappearance of Megan's smile did make him feel less discombobulated, but nothing could really make it any easier to face her.

The silence stretched on. So he moved to sit back down. A bit rude, true, but if it helped put a swift end to this awkward reunion, he'd try anything.

Of course, the universe wasn't that kind.

Megan immediately deposited herself in the seat across from him. "As I'm sure Emma already told you, I'm the head librarian here in Juniper Hills, so I'm strongly invested in the upcoming library remodel. Paul told me there was a chance you might not be working on the project, after all. I just wanted to chat with you a bit and hopefully get you to reconsider."

He glanced back over at Emma in what he hoped was well-concealed but *very* clear alarm. She answered with a sharp chin jerk, motioning for him to turn his focus back to Megan.

He did . . . and swore he was watching one of those slow-motion zooms on Megan's wide, softly pleading eyes. He could almost hear the accompanying emotional violin music.

This did *not* look good for him.

Thoroughly unclear on what Emma expected him to say to her sister—considering their agreement and all—Jake just went with vague and evasive. "Like I told Paul last night, I just don't think I'm the right carpenter for this job." *There. It's me and not you. A classic.*

It took a few seconds of everything in the diner sounding jackhammer loud for some reason before Megan then proceeded to shock the hell out of him by drilling him with a stubborn stare and a voice steely with feet-dug-in-the-dirt determination. "I disagree, Jake. I've seen your work. You'd be a great fit for the project."

"You've seen my work?" Suddenly he wondered if Carter had been in direct contact with her. His brother wouldn't possibly do that—would he? That was too much, even for him. "You've been working with the folks at SME Enterprises on the remodel?"

"No, Paul is handling all that; he's the one who showed me your portfolio. I haven't actually met anyone from SME. But I didn't expect to with a company that size. Thankfully"—she gave a smiling shrug—"it's like they read my mind for the design of this remodel."

Yeah, funny how that worked out.

"Anyway"—she was back to her fierce-fairy face—"like I said, Paul showed me samples of your work, and I think you're phenomenal. The kids' rooms at the farm and the indoor playroom for the foster home a few years back were my favorites." The imploring eyes returned. "Please, won't you reconsider? You're the perfect carpenter for this remodel; I'm sure of it."

She was dead-on that this was the ideal job for him. But an agreement was an agreement, and Jake always kept his word. The one time he didn't had nearly destroyed him.

He wasn't going to do that to Emma again.

Plus, there was that whole thing with him not being able to look at Megan without thinking of the pain she'd gone through, the years stolen from her childhood. The scars she still lived with. Emma was right; his working on the library was a disaster waiting to happen.

Speaking of which, why wasn't Emma defusing the situation? Megan was like a speeding train running him over, and Emma wasn't saying a thing. Was she punishing him?

Just then Megan finally paused long enough to take a breath and rev up for what looked to be another long spiel—this time with visuals, judging by the way she was pulling out her phone. He took that opportunity to steal another glance over at Emma.

Only to find her trying to communicate with him in some telepathic language. For ten frustrating seconds, all he got from her were loaded head tilts, pointedly wide eyes, and brows arching in time with the three quiet, ardently high-pitched squeaks that escaped her. Last came the intense stare he interpreted as her trying to beam her thoughts into his head.

He felt as if he were in Star Wars talking to R2-D2.

"Emma, could we talk in private?" If she said no, there was a very real chance there would be cartoon whoosh marks in the air trailing his escape soon. "It'll just be a minute."

Megan looked from him to her sister before standing. "I'll be over in the front with the Constantini kids." She dropped a puppy–pit bull look on him. "Don't run off."

The second she was out of earshot, Jake turned to Emma and hissed, "What the heck is going on here? I've never been so lost in my entire life."

Emma fell into the seat next to him, looking positively uncorked. "Totallymyfault. I'd planned on discussing this with you today when you first came in, but I got distracted digging up that old bag of decaf I never use, and then I had to go pick up the portable generator, and of course the whole sex-noises-while-you-eat thing made it impossible to think about anything else for a really long—" She flushed and clapped a hand over her mouth.

He couldn't decide if he wanted to gently pry her hand away from her lips so she'd keep going with this rushing-river-of-consciousness glimpse into her mysterious mind, or if he wanted to in fact stem the word flow by doing something crazy like dragging her onto his lap and kissing the hell out of her. *Decisions, decisions.*

"Anyway." She directed all her focus on flicking a tiny cookie crumb off his table. "I meant to tell you that Megan and I had a talk about you after you bid on the repairs yesterday."

Should've picked option B when you had the chance.

Emma shook her head as if a little stumped herself. "Let's just say she reacted the exact opposite from the way I did about you being here. She didn't care one iota that you were the same Jake from Riverside. And later, when she realized you were also the carpenter whose work Paul had shown her, your past projects were all she could talk about for the rest of the night."

"But you didn't *know* she'd react that way." Reeling from the info that Megan knew who he was and still wanted him to work on her library, his polite filter fell a bit as he asked the most obvious—to him—question. "She could've very well freaked out like you did; wouldn't that have been counterintuitive to your plan for us to have a clean slate and pretend we just met?"

"I know it sounds self-sabotaging, more so since Megan didn't even recognize you after all these years, especially with the beard. But I swear that wasn't my intent. Yes, I want us to have a fresh start, but that's between us. You and Megan—that's between you two." She made a motion as if she was going to touch his arm but then pulled back at the last second. "I saw your face when you saw her scars just now." Empathy swamped her expression. "That couldn't have been easy. Truthfully, yesterday, when I said you shouldn't work on the library, I'd really only been thinking about Megan. Awful as it sounds, I hadn't even considered how hard just being around us would be for *you*, as well. You went through that fire every bit as much as we did—"

No. Hell, no. This was getting dangerously close to another apology. For the worst possible reason yet. He wasn't having it. "It's fine, Emma. I was just caught off guard."

"It's more than that, and we both know it. I'd understand if you wanted to rethink—"

"I'm not quitting on your repairs." Even he was shocked at how forcefully that came out.

"Are you sure?" She looked genuinely concerned.

Another emotion he didn't deserve from her. Not about this. "I'm sure."

Megan rejoined them. "What are you sure about?" she asked as she smiled back at the family of what looked like a dozen kids she'd been chatting with.

"Hey, so how are those Constantinis?" Emma said evasively with an overenthusiastic wave at the kids, now tossing balls of yarn near the register while their mom paid the check.

Was it just him, or were there a lot of random yarn balls in this town?

Megan gave her sister a dry, your-shtick-needs-work look. "They're doing good. Still bummed out every afternoon, though." Turning to Jake, she explained. "The Constantini family used to come to the library for books every day since they could walk over from their house. But with the temporary satellite library in the pop-up office space on the other side of town now, they haven't been able to come by because their dad doesn't get home with the car until supper."

She bounce-bounce-pivoted excitedly back to Emma. "And guess what? I brought up your 'library on wheels' idea to see if it's something they'd want, and they went *nuts*."

His sudden awareness of at least fifteen—no, *twenty*—baskets of yarn around the diner momentarily forgotten, and the entire overload of emotional luggage from the past ten minutes temporarily put in a locker in his brain, Jake asked curiously, "Library on wheels? How would that work?" *And can I play, too?* Already his imagination teemed with mental sketches for building a cool wooden cart of books, sort of like in old horse-drawn merchant times.

"Don't laugh. But I was picturing something like an ice-cream truck," confessed Emma. "Only with books instead. Megan could pick a selection and drive to different areas of town a few afternoons a week since a lot of kids here help their folks out on farms or their family shops after school and can't get to the library before it closes. This way the books can come to them."

Megan nodded. "Isn't she a genius? She does something similar with the free Christmas cookies she makes for everyone in town, but in a fun take-some-and-pass-the-rest-along way."

Bright badges of pink immediately painted Emma's cheeks. "Not *everyone.*"

Yeah, he'd bet good money it probably was everyone. The woman was just so dang sweet. "Need any help moving things past the idea stage?" he offered.

Lordy, he'd stepped in it now. When two sets of DNA-matched eyes looked back at him in delighted surprise, he had to wonder if it was something in the water here that was overriding his factory settings of never making promises before knowing all the facts. Maybe it was all the juniper trees. "If you want, I was thinking I could make maybe a traveling book buggy wagon with a trailer hookup so you wouldn't have to haul boxes of books out of your car at every house, especially out in farmland. It'd be sort of like Emma's ice-cream-truck vision."

An eye-crinkling, hands-on-cheeks, five-out-of-five-dentists-approved smile spread across Megan's face. "I *love* that idea! Oh my goodness. See? This is why you *have* to work on the library remodel." She shot her two index fingers up in the air quickly. "Before you say no again, I want you to come to a barbecue I'm having for my library coworkers tomorrow. This way you can meet all of us first before you lock in your final answer."

His lips twitched over seeing Megan with the same 90 percent innocent, 10 percent devious smile that Emma had. "Meaning you'll be kind enough to feed me while you all gang up on me?"

"Yep." Her smiled turned sixty-forty. "I won't take no for an answer. It'll be out in my backyard tomorrow evening. Ten of us total, including you and Emma."

Okay, time to get real. Emma may have said she wanted him and her sister to figure out their own 2.0 reunion plans, but as far as he knew, their agreement was still intact. Which meant that even though it was plain un-midwesternly to say no to a barbecue, it was probably safer if he—

"I think a cookout is a great idea, Megan." Emma smiled. "What can we bring?"

Say what now?

Leave it to Emma to send him back out to the desert again with a toy compass that was really just one of those board game spinners you flick to stay in the game.

"But isn't it early for a cookout?" Now he was just grasping at straws to get his bearings.

Megan gave him a "nice try" head tilt. "Don't know about you folks in the city, but here we haven't had any slush on the ground since mid-March. With the grill and fire pit going, it'll be the perfect temperature for a nice barbecue in your honor. Everyone's excited to meet you."

Wow, she was a persistent one.

Emma the ever so helpful chimed in again, shooting Jake an I-know-your-weakness brow quirk. "If you don't come, you'll miss out on Megan's cooking. FYI, she cooks the way I bake. In fact, the corned beef from that Reuben sandwich you ate is actually her recipe."

Well, that was a well-aimed blow. Now conflicted as well as hungry again, he stared at her in temple-throbbing silence while another big family stopped by to chat with Megan.

"You should just give in and say you'll come," whispered Emma. "Because if I know my sister, and I do, there's no way she's backing down." The smile that softened her eyes as she watched Megan get up and go play yarn toss with the kids was the picture of pride.

"So you *want* me to take the library job?" Just trying to get clear as mud on this.

"Good gracious, no. I still think it's a terrible idea. But *Megan* wants you to take the job. And I'll always fight to get Megan whatever she wants."

"Including me."

"Yes."

"Then I'll call Paul and accept the library job." Simple as that.

"No!"

He sighed. Would he never understand this woman on the first try?

"Megan inviting you, or anyone for that matter, to her home for a barbecue is a *huge* freaking deal. You can't tell because she's in semi-lioness mode right now over the library project, but Megan is usually painfully shy thanks to the scars and not being social for years. So you *have* to come. Or she won't have a reason to go through with the barbecue."

Jeez, then of course he was going to go. No question about it. But he was curious . . . "If I say no, would it be safe to assume you'd dog me and make me crazy until I change my mind?"

Her lashes fanned her cheeks as she nodded somberly. "Like a rabid Chihuahua."

Why did he like the terrifying idea of that so much?

"Oh, just say yes. We can go together." Her eyes danced even as her freckles pinked up over the brassy edict. Man alive, no one did cute, sexy, and *bossy* like Emma did.

She leaned in and added in a regretful tone, "Listen, if you're hesitating because of our agreement, I take it back. I'm sorry."

His amusement disappeared. He really *hated* hearing her say those words to him.

"I just mean I shouldn't have made the stipulation," she clarified. "Of you turning down the library job. I was out of line." She brushed another microscopic crumb off the table. "*Sometimes* I can get a teeny bit overbearing, particularly when it comes to protecting Megan."

You don't say? "Hey, if the type A cape fits . . ."

She gave him a sighing head shake. "The struggle is real I tell you."

Chuckling, he reassured her, "You weren't out of line. You were being a good sister."

"A *protective* sister," she corrected swiftly.

What a strange thing to argue. It was almost as if she took exception to the compliment. Which was just crazy. But in the spirit of Jake and Emma 2.0, he didn't pry. For now.

Instead he asked the only question he had left on the matter. "You sure you're going to be okay with me being in your town for an additional few months after I finish your repairs?"

"I am. Actually . . . I think I'd be more than okay with that."

Well, hell. He tried not to read more into that.

"But remember," she whispered as if they were exchanging trade secrets. "You still have to come to the cookout, and let Megan 'convince' you then. Oy, I can't wait to see her face."

Good lord, they just didn't make 'em this sweet anymore. "Sounds like a plan."

She beamed.

"So is that it? That the last of your orders for me for the time being?" he teased.

Her hands perched themselves on her hips in flagrant indignation.

Ah, damn. He liked watching her get ruffled. "I bet there's at least one more in there. You've already got something in mind for me to bring to this shindig—don't you?"

She pursed her lips, looking both torn and miffed, the latter probably on account of his grinning at her like she was a fuzzy kitten batting a string.

"Now that you mention it, how about you bring beer?" she suggested casually. "Megan doesn't drink the stuff, but everyone else probably will, right? Since it's a barbecue?"

Her framing all that in question form was a noble effort.

That he just *had* to mess with. "How about wine instead?" He was totally bluffing, of course. He never drank the stuff. And he had a strong hunch that Emma didn't, either.

She scrunched her nose as if he'd just asked her to sniff a four-letter word.

See? His recon had been thorough. From what he'd gathered by being in her home and bakery all day, the only wine Emma had was of the cooking variety, and she didn't even own a single wineglass. But she did have a connoisseur's collection of brews in her pantry, along with about four different kinds of beer glasses and a few ice-cold frosty mugs chilling in her commercial fridge.

It was all a thing of beauty, really.

"Wine is good for you," he argued innocently. That was a health fact, wasn't it? "Sort of like . . . *decaf coffee.*" His grin broadened when her eyes narrowed to slits. "I can bring a nice robust red and a crisp white to pair with the food." Now he was just pulling crap he'd heard on TV. Wasn't there also a pink wine? He bet she'd *really* get annoyed with a pink wine. And exactly how sparkly were those sparkly wines?

Emma didn't last long at all. "Oh, will you just bring beer," she growled. "Craft or microbrews are what most folks here drink. Bottled. Local ales or dark lagers if you can."

He wasn't sure what he was finding a bigger turn-on, all the dirty talk with the beer or the fact that she was using that bossy, riled-up tone of hers. Probably both.

Truth be told, Jake had always thought of himself as a fairly uncomplicated guy. But evidently he had very complicated tastes and triggers. Case in point, against all that was sensible and sound, it appeared he was becoming a bit of an addict when it came to getting a rise out of Emma, and making those sexy freckles of hers firecracker hot. He just couldn't seem to help himself. It was like being near those bright-red buttons you weren't supposed to push lest the world combust or something. That "or something" was undoubtedly going to make the next few months the most ill-advised and straight-up volatile ones of his life.

A part of him felt as if this was something he'd been seeking for a long time.

Chapter Ten

Megan's barbecue was a huge hit.

And Emma was over the moon. She hadn't been exaggerating last night when she'd said to Jake that this cookout was a big deal for her sister. A chance for Megan to finally start venturing a bit further out of her shell like she'd been wanting to for so long. Granted, Emma still couldn't quite wrap her brain around *Jake* being the nudge Megan had needed for this monumental step in her life, but she wasn't going to look a gift horse in the mouth.

Emma peered at the grinning smile of the garden gnome currently keeping her excellent cookout company in Megan's backyard. "I'm so proud of her, Gnomeo," she gushed. "I mean look at her. A born hostess! And did you see her face earlier when she got Jake to agree to the library job? *Gah.*" She clutched at her heart. "My baby sis may not have mastered her full lioness roar yet, but she's getting there."

She clinked bottlenecks with Gnomeo, who had her first empty. Though she was a girl who loved her beer, she was still a lightweight who usually drank only one a night. Which was why those brew sampler variety packs were so perfect for her. *And* why on nights like this when she doubled down on her limit, she ended up being a cheap date . . . for a garden gnome.

"Gnomeo," she whisper-confessed. "I think I'm a bit tipsy." Tipsy enough that her having a heart-to-heart with a ceramic figurine she'd liberated from Megan's tulip bed wasn't all that weird. But not nearly tipsy enough that she wasn't questioning how an inanimate object was *chuckling back* in response. *There it was again.*

Wide-eyed, she decided to do a much-needed test to see if the gnome had indeed come alive. Slowly, warily, she leaned forward to do some very scientific finger poking.

"I brought you a bottle of water."

"Holy crap!" Emma jumped three feet in the air and whirled around. "Dagnabbit, I thought you were the gnome."

"Wow, you sure know how to low-kick a man in his misters."

God that voice.

Hearing Jake's deep growl tinged with amusement suddenly made her feel shockingly sober. The power of insta-lust to burn off the effects of alcohol. *Huh, I wonder if we could bottle his voice and create an app? We could make a fortune!*

It was possible she wasn't quite as sober as she'd thought.

Jake casually slid the beer bottle she'd been nursing out of her reach and took a seat next to her so she'd have to snake her arm all the way around him if she wanted to retrieve it.

Dooo it! Go get it! Ooh, then put it in his lap so you can go get it again!

Her inebriated inner vixen was a total hussy.

"Jake, I think I'm a little drunk."

He took a sip of his water and just grinned back at her.

"I'm finishing my *second* bottle of beer already."

His lips twitched again. "Never took you for such a big drinker."

Even though it was dark, Emma could see his eyes dancing with amusement. *Note to self: Build a sarcasm detector into the Insta-Lust Sobriety App.*

"I don't usually drink so fast," she confessed, her eyes dropping to that ruggedly sexy cleft chin of his, partially buried in that scruffy lumberjack beard she was dying to pet. "I think I tanked that first bottle because you'd just arrived. You make me nervous."

Oh, great. Seemed her inebriated inner vixen was a very *honest* hussy.

Jake took another drink of water. "If I wasn't getting behind the wheel tonight, trust me, I'd be in the same boat. But since I've got that three-hour drive ahead of me, I had to settle for a heaping bowl of bourbon chili to take the edge off before I came over here."

She blinked in surprise. "So I make you nervous, too?"

"You scare the crap out of me, sweets," he corrected.

Her shoulders fell. "Oh. Have I been awful?" Having Jake walk back into her life had been hard, yes, but that was no excuse for any unkind behavior on her part. She'd tried really hard to treat him like she did all the other guys in town.

"Of course not. You've been great." His gruff voice softened, and the corner of his mouth drew up on one side. "Considering how much I provoke you, you've been a saint."

She gaped at him, too vindicated to scowl. "So you *have* been doing it on purpose! I knew it! Megan thought I might just have an abnormally short fuse around you."

Jake had the grace to at least look sheepish. "What can I say? You make it really fun to chop away at that fuse of yours."

Arms crossed, she tried not to get charmed by those twinkling green eyes that promised even more fuse chopping to come. "You're kind of insufferable—you know that, right?"

He winked. "Only around you."

She opted not to reply, choosing instead to focus on getting those slap-happy butterflies in her stomach to stop reacting to that wink.

The guy was still the ballsy smart-ass who'd always been able to make her both laugh and swoon harder than anyone else could. Earlier, when he'd arrived with three fabulous cases of seasonal microbrew samplers she'd never tried before, she'd had to bite her cheek to keep from chuckling when she spied the bottle of *glittery* pink sparkling wine he'd brought, as well. The punk. But he'd caught her 100 percent unaware when he'd also furnished a variety pack of specialty *root beers* for Megan's nonalcoholic drinking pleasure.

It was stuff like that that made him the swoon whisperer.

Heck, he was whispering something right now to her inner hussy, just by running his eyes over her face as if drinking her all in. Slowly. Appreciatively.

"You should eat something, sweetheart," he said huskily. "Soak up some of that beer."

Keeping tabs on whether she was getting enough to eat at the party? That swoon whisperer handbook was *good*. A fact he further proved by promptly standing as soon as she did, forcing her to bat down a few more F0 gale tornado butterflies in her tummy.

Charming gentleman manners. Evidently one of her knee weakeners. *Good to know.*

Soon as they made their way to the backyard deck, Jake immediately became the center of attention again, as he had been for the past hour—after he'd formally accepted the library job. A decision he credited equally to Megan's persuasive skills and red potato salad.

Both compliments had earned smiles from Megan so radiant, Emma had gotten a contact high. The man was a prince.

"So, Jake," called out Megan, "how are you liking our little town? Folks been treating you well so far?"

Despite his continued inability to look Megan fully in the eye, he said, "Everyone's been great, and the town is awesome. Shoot, I'd move here in a heartbeat."

Emma did a double take at the more-intoxicating-than-beer notion of Jake being close enough for her to see every day.

Jake arched a brow over her reaction. "Why so surprised? I love it here. You've got history and character in spades, both of which I'd take over a cookie-cutter new development with shiny bells and whistles." His eyes dared her to disagree with him.

Seriously? Of all the men to cross her path, the universe chose *Jake Rowan* to share her exact thoughts about this town. "I agree completely," she admitted.

"I'll drink to that." Dennis, Megan's boss, raised his beer bottle in salute.

Everyone followed suit, which earned another effervescent grin from Megan, who was gleefully joining in the toast with a fluted glass of her special root beer.

"I do have one kind of strange question, though." Jake turned his puzzled expression to Emma. "What's with all the balls of yarn everywhere? I swear every single shop and eating joint in this place has baskets of yarn tucked into every nook and cranny."

At that Emma finally felt her nerves dissipate. Thinking about her town was always excellent in that regard. She grinned. "I'm surprised no one's told you that Juniper Hills is pretty much the go-to hub for specialized hand-spun yarn you can't find anywhere else in the United States. If you're looking for it, chances are we have it. If you can't find a particular color or texture in one of our shops, all we have to do is call around the neighborhood and someone will check their spinning piles at home and walk it on over if they're done working on it."

"Over half the folks here do some yarn spinning or dyeing," added Dennis's wife, Sandra. "We have full-time, part-time, and seasonal yarners, and 'yarn artists' who make one-of-a-kind yarn I'm still shocked sells for as much as it does. We've even got some teens here who've been selling their own yarn online since they were kids, and now have enough saved for college."

Jake stared at her in disbelief.

Emma smiled proudly. "Those kids are incredible. Some have gotten really innovative in how they process the fibers and combine textiles. We're talking yarn unlike anything you've ever seen—next-level-type stuff, made with all the traditional handmade detail and care they learned growing up. Using old equipment and tools in new ways, I guess you could say."

The corners of his eyes crinkled. "See what I mean? A town with kids that apply old-school love to new-school specialty yarn. Along with the out-of-this-world pudding I keep hearing so much about, that's a sales pitch and a half to raise a family and grow old here."

A soft gasp escaped Emma before she could call it back. She wasn't sure if it was his casual reference to her pudding or the ovary-wrecking comment he'd made about raising a family here that was affecting her breathing. Both, probably.

Or it could be because of the way he'd just looked at her.

It wasn't his usual quietly intense stare that always made her knees wobbly whenever she'd catch him doing it. No, this one was more reflective. All encompassing. And . . . free. As if he were letting his eyes wander over the contours of a forest to look his fill of the whole picture, yet still managing to observe the individual nuances of every leaf at the same time.

To be fair, she'd started it. By staring at him first. She hadn't been able to stop herself when, prompted by his own reference to the topic, he'd gotten up to go ladle himself a helping of her seven-layer pudding trifle. While everyone else chatted more about an insanely soft yarn the oldest Constantini kids had made that was the unexpected love child of an impulsive angora and hemp experiment, Jake settled back down and took his first bite . . .

"Oh my God." A sound that was grittier than a gasp and more confounded than anything else tumbled past the spoon between his lips. "What *is* this?"

Her stomach dropped.

Until she heard it. A low, purring groan like he'd made when he'd tasted the Reuben.

"This has got to be one of the best things I have ever put in my mouth." He released a reverent male sigh and dug in for seconds, eyelids at half-mast.

Her heart did a somersault.

Megan peered over to see what he was eating. "That's Emma's nut medley trifle. Good, huh? She makes it with seven kinds of nut puddings with matching cookie crumbles."

Instead of answering he made more sexy, stormy noises that made her skin hum.

No one else seemed to notice. Meanwhile she was squirming in her seat, feeling as if her reservation were being called over a booming restaurant-wide intercom: *"Porn, party of one?"*

"Jake, I meant to ask. You from around here?" queried Dennis, effectively dousing all porny thoughts and replacing them with mildly rattled ones. "You sure sound like you are."

Emma shot her gaze over at Megan, who was now as stiff as a statue.

"My family moved around a lot when I was younger," Jake sidestepped smoothly. "So I've lived all over the Midwest. Right now I live a few hours away over in Kansas City."

Emma exhaled in relief. She wasn't sure what exactly worried her so much about folks here discovering Jake's link to their past. It felt partly like apprehension—over losing something she wasn't ready to part with—but mostly like plain ol' protectiveness . . . and not *just* over Megan.

"But you're a small-town boy at heart—am I right?" prodded Claudia, the soccer mom who worked the library checkout midmornings around her kids' school pickup schedule.

Jake's beard rippled in an almost smile. "You got me. I liked small-town living the best. Definitely made for some great memories growing up."

"Any favorite ones?" The ever-inquisitive Blake, a college intern majoring in library science with a minor in anthropology, studied Jake the way he did all humans. "Whenever I get homesick for New Mexico, it's always interesting which memories I reminisce about most."

Emma found herself holding her breath again. This time to make sure she didn't miss Jake's response. She wanted to believe he still had some good memories, to believe that juvie and the fire and Peyton's death hadn't extinguished them all for him.

"I think," he said quietly to his captive audience, "my favorite small-town memories are mostly about the girl next door." He slid his hooded eyes over to her and snagged her gaze for a full beat. His eyes went from the calm sage green they normally were, to the dark mossy green they sometimes got when he was deep in thought. Instantly, she felt herself get sucked into his orbit like she used to when they were teens. "Looking over my family's fence and seeing her out in her backyard, giving the sun a reason to shine, was always the best part of my day."

"Oh my lord, that's about the sweetest thing I've ever heard," exclaimed dear old Betty, the weekend librarian who was the spitting image of the granny from the Tweety Bird cartoons.

As soon as Jake turned his attention back to the group, albeit reluctantly, Emma felt the tether snap, releasing her to hotfoot it to the kitchen in search of the undetermined-as-of-yet excuse for her escape. *Paper towels? Yes!* The three rolls outside weren't nearly enough.

Megan materialized out of nowhere to join her in the pantry as she hunted for the elusive paper towels with the colorful fruit patterns. "You *like* him."

It wasn't a question or a teasing taunt. It was an observation.

Or an understatement, rather.

This was bad. Okay, not bad per se. But dangerous for sure. So dangerous.

Damn the universe for being twisted enough, mean enough to have her start thinking about Jake in this way again. She couldn't possibly be having feelings for the man responsible for everything she and her family went through . . . could she?

Chapter Eleven

Jake knew he should stop looking at her, stop craving something he could never have.

But it was impossible.

He hadn't been entirely truthful earlier; he was definitely a little drunk . . . simply from being near Emma for the past few hours. All night he'd been drinking in her laughs, her genuine sweetness, her antagonized snark (for which he took full credit). The woman got to his head faster than whiskey, and warmed him from the inside out about the same way, too.

Talk about lowering his inhibitions.

At one point he'd even reached over to untangle a few strands of her ponytail that had gotten caught on the tree and brushed his knuckles across her jawline in the process. Though there hadn't been enough light in the yard for him to see for sure, the sudden blast of heat coming off her cheeks had instantly flooded his brain with teenage memories of that sexy little blush of hers.

He may as well have tossed back a shot of tequila.

It'd been all he could do not to drop his lips down onto hers right then and there, or at least pull her closer to a lantern so he could see the tanned, barely there freckles scattered across her cheekbones make an appearance. They were faint, but he knew a lot of girls back in high school who would've taken extra measures with makeup to hide them completely. Ditto for most women he knew now. Not Emma. She never used to wear makeup back then, and she still didn't from what he could tell.

He dug that. A lot.

Seeing her cheeks get a tiny bit more flushed with each sip of beer she took reminded him of the afternoon he'd once spent teaching her how to play poker. He'd lost all his peanut M&M'S to her that afternoon, partly because he'd been distracted beyond saving, but mostly because he hadn't been able to bring himself to fold whenever those freckles—the sweetest tell ever—would reveal fairly blatantly that she was sitting on a winning hand.

Her candidness had always been the damnedest thing. Now, though, those freckles weren't so much cute as they were sexy. Fires of hell, everything about the woman was sexy. The way she walked, talked, laughed, and thought. Even the way she'd attempted earlier to cartwheel around Megan's backyard—not quite successfully—just to see if she still could.

But the biggest turn-on of all? The way she snuck in those big, blue, open-window-to-her-soul glances at him the few times she'd let her guard down. Because that right there was Emma just being herself. Uninhibited. Real. And more intoxicating than moonshine.

"If you stare at her any harder, you'll set off my smoke detectors," teased Megan.

He winced, both because he'd been caught and because of her choice of words.

As if reading his mind, she gave him an empathetic head tilt. "You'll get used to it; I make a lot of fire jokes."

He'd noticed. Since yesterday, she'd made at least a dozen. And from what he could tell, he was the only one in town utterly ill equipped to handle it well.

"It was a defense mechanism at first. You know, fight fire with fire," she admitted, sounding pleased she was able to squeeze another in. "But then I just got *really* good at them."

Despite feeling as if he were going to get a window seat to hell for doing it, he laughed. "You are nothing like I expected."

"While *you* are everything I remember Emma going on about when we were younger."

Her hushed tone was as effective as gravity in reminding him of his norm while he was here in Juniper Hills. Here, for the time being, he wasn't the man with the "bad" past.

He was the one who'd agreed to have no past at all.

To be perfectly honest, the latter was harder to stomach at the moment.

"You can talk about the fire with me, you know," she said, again reading him like a book. "That whole pretending to meet for the first time, that's just Emma's thing. What she needs, how she needs to handle this. But you and me, we can still be Jake and Megan from Riverside." She shrugged. "So long as it doesn't poke a hole in her plans, of course."

Just as protective as her sister. Not surprising. "Meaning as long as I don't blow my cover with folks in town, I don't have to pretend that I'm not the person who saw your little face when you saw your own burns for the first time that night? That I'm not the one who sat beside you until the ambulance came, wishing I could rip my own skin off and make yours better?"

Tears filled her eyes almost as quickly as she blinked them away. "Yes. In fact, I'd prefer you didn't. Because that's exactly how I remember you. My hero."

His breath hissed out in white-hot denial. "I'm not."

"*Yes.* You are."

A zero-to-sixty temper like her sister. About this at least.

"You saved my life that night, Jake. To me, it never mattered how the fire started. Heck, fires start for a million reasons. What mattered is that you made sure I made it out of there. Period." A woeful angst hit her voice finally. But not over her wounds. "I'm just sorry your life got so wrecked in the aftermath."

God, he hated it as much when she said that *s*-word as he did when Emma said it.

"I'm not my sister," she preinterrupted his broaching of the topic.

Her bold, listen-here-mister tone trapped his attention. He raised a brow to give her the go-ahead to elaborate.

"I'm not Emma," she emphasized. "So if I want to tell you I'm sorry, I will. For the most part, my sister is and will always be fiercer than I can ever hope to be. She's a real-deal badass. But when it comes to the fire, and to you, let's just say she's a work in progress."

His frown dissipated. "That's the way she described herself when we first re-met."

"Didn't say she was an *unenlightened* work in progress."

Smothering a reluctant smile in his beard, he shook his head and sighed. "So you're saying you're going to keep saying the *s*-word around me." He wasn't so much asking as he was accepting the reality of the situation.

"I'm saying"—she gazed over at her sister, sadness clouding her eyes—"that I may have come out of that fire with the visible scars. But Emma is the one with deeper ones."

Damn. He'd suspected as much. Grief engulfed him. "What can I do to help her?"

"Just be you. And . . ." She exhaled heavily. "Just be ready. It'll take a while, but Emma will eventually make herself deal with Jake from Riverside and Jake 2.0 being the same guy."

She didn't have to paint him a picture beyond that. They both knew that when the time came, it would be hard for all of them to weather—

The peal of his cell phone ringing shattered their shared silence.

Carter.

Torn, Jake volleyed his gaze back and forth between his phone and Megan. Thankfully she made the decision for him. "The fact that you're still sticking with a cell that sounds like it's survived a drop in the disposal tells me you don't need my advice on how to help Emma." She got up and headed back to the house. "But I'll be here to listen if you ever need to talk."

And then she was gone.

Jake walked over to the side gate leading to the street he'd parked on, just barely managing to answer the call before it went to voice mail.

"You still pissed?" asked Carter, for once not using his Stepford brother phone etiquette.

Was he still? "Yes and no. Good call waiting me out those few days." When Carter didn't respond, Jake took the training wheels off. "Dude, what the hell were you thinking?"

A muffled, weighted sigh fogged the phone line. "Wasn't. Thinking, that is."

That much was obvious. Jake hopped in his truck and waited.

The silence lasted maybe a few seconds before Carter broke. "How is she?"

Somehow Jake knew he wasn't talking about Emma. "Megan's doing good. Sweet girl. An interesting combination of shy and ballsy. She looks happy, far as I can tell."

Another pause. "And her burn wounds?"

Jake answered that one as gently as he could. "About as bad as we'd thought."

"She's still badly scarred?"

"Yes. But . . . just on the outside seems like."

A ragged breath was Carter's only indication he was still listening.

"So, how long have you been keeping tabs on her?" A few days ago, the first thing Jake had wanted to ask Carter was how he'd managed to even find the Stevens girls. But the longer he'd thought about it, the more he was certain this entire thing had deeper roots.

"Since the fire," Carter replied quietly.

That explained a lot.

There were times Jake used to question why Carter hadn't taken a more front-seat role in his own corporation. From its inception Carter had always been the brains and muscle behind SME Enterprises but not the *face* of the company. Never that. Even though he was the majority shareholder. Instead he'd appointed his college buddy and cofounder of SME, Geoffrey, as the more visible co-CEO, choosing to stay practically anonymous over the years. As a result very few knew who Carter was, let alone that he ran SME while Geoffrey took all the credit.

On Jake's part, he'd always respected Carter's choice to be a success in private instead of flashing it around in the public eye. At first he'd suspected it had to do a little something with pissing their dad off, though Carter neither confirmed nor denied one way or another. But now he wondered if Megan was also one of the reasons he'd maintained his anonymity. Carter couldn't exactly do things like pay to renovate her crumbling library if his name was out of the shadows.

"Is this the first time you've helped her out without her knowing?"

Carter ignored the question and asked one of his own. "Tell me the truth. Do either Megan or Emma even know you have another brother besides Daryn?"

Ouch. He hadn't expected Carter to want *that* much truth. "No. They don't." The technical reason why was simple. The fire had happened about a month after Jake and his family had moved to Riverside, and Carter hadn't made the move with them since he was already in California starting his freshman year of college early in a summer program for superhigh achievers (that wasn't the actual name for it, but it was close enough).

Since Carter wanted the brutal truth, Jake gave it to him. "That summer was the first time you weren't the center of attention in our house, our town. It was the first time I was out from under your shadow, with a great girl seeing *me* and not just all-star-everything Carter's younger, less awesome brother. So . . . I never brought you up in conversation with Emma." Because his time with Emma was the first and only thing that had ever been his and his alone.

Of course, he'd never begrudged the Carter hand-me-downs of clothes and toys—and as he got older, the hand-me-down shoes to fill, as well. But unsurprisingly, none of it had ever fit as if it were made just for him. Not like Emma had.

"Then after the fire, Dad made sure the Carmichael name—and you—had complete insulation from everything that went down that night with the fire and Peyton's death. By the time Dad got done calling in favors and strong-arming court orders and getting paperwork signed in blood, the three Rowan kids had a *pet gerbil* more closely related to us than you were."

In a way there was a certain poetic justice to it all. That summer the girl of his dreams had lost a brother because of a tragic fire. It was only fair that, in effect, Jake had, too.

Analyzing it all here outside Megan's home was just too much. Jake couldn't keep the sharpness—or bluntness—out of his next words. "To think, all these years of your dogged bimonthly calls and look at us now—you're *relieved* they don't know you're my brother."

"That's unfair, Jake, and you know it," Carter all but snarled in frustration. "Dad may have been the one to get you to falsify that confession and change your last name, but *you're* the one who decided I was no longer your brother. You never gave me a chance to fight for you!"

That knockout punch opened up an acid-laced hole in his chest Jake thought he'd cauterized long ago. Of course Jake remembered how stricken Carter had sounded when their dad had discussed his plan with them, how Carter had thought it inconceivable to sacrifice even a single minute of Jake's life for his. And Carter was right; Jake hadn't let him oppose it harder. "It's not that I didn't want you to fight for me; it's that I knew you wouldn't have won that battle." Not with their dad rebutting Carter's protests by describing—in detail, right in front of them—how Jake's life and future were basically insignificant in the grand scheme of things, an expendable liability that would run its course and become a sad but acceptable casualty.

Quote, unquote.

It didn't matter that the time he'd spent in juvie was a far lighter sentence than what Carter would've served in prison as an eighteen-year-old tried as an adult. It didn't matter that he loved Carter enough to take the fall for him all over again if history were to repeat itself.

What *did* matter was that when their father *chose* to sacrifice Jake's future for Carter's, *chose* to value Carter's life over Jake's, their relationship as brothers didn't just get strained. It broke. Severed. *Shattered.*

So, yes, Carter was also right about the role Jake had played in severing their relationship. It had been Jake who'd wanted that bullet of betrayal their father had fired to be a through-and-through gunshot wound, instead of one that kept the bullet lodged inside him forever.

Yet here they were.

"For chrissakes," rumbled Carter, now sounding pissed, "you never even let me visit you in juvie. Not on holidays, not even on your birthday."

Jake flinched. That was a direct hit where it hurt. Unlike his parents, his siblings had all wanted to come see him on his birthday. But he just . . . hadn't wanted them to see him like that.

Hell, even now the mere mention of juvie between him and his siblings felt like an anchor that kept them from moving on with their lives. And at least where Jake was concerned, it was an anchor that kept him barely skimming the surface of life, bobbing for air, constantly having to make that active choice to keep kicking and fighting just to avoid going under.

"You know what?" Jake murmured tiredly as he tried blocking unwanted memories that now looked a whole lot different than they had back then. "I think Emma has the right idea. She wants to keep our history buried. Pretend like we just met. And it's been working great for us."

"Bullshit."

Dammit, he hated how good Carter had always been at that card game. "I'm not bullshitting you. Everything is better now that she and I cleared the slate and started fresh."

"You didn't clear the slate. You two just dumped the old, tarnished, *repairable* one on the side of the road and randomly picked up a new one."

Funny how hearing your own thoughts come out of someone else's mouth make them sound so much harsher. "Well, the main thing is that it worked. We're all good."

"Yeah? So does that mean you don't still have a massive crush on her anymore?"

See, *this* is why you should never tell family anything.

Rather than answer the obvious, he took a move out of Carter's evasive maneuvers playbook and boomeranged the inquisition back. "This isn't the first time you've helped Megan out financially, is it?"

Shockingly, after drawing in a deep, worn breath, Carter fessed up. "No. But it's the first thing I've been able to do for her in a pretty long while." His tone turned bristly. "The girl just doesn't need much anymore. She's too damned independent. And *content.*"

A crack in Carter's polished outer layer. Unprecedented.

Studying the storybook cottage before him, Jake couldn't resist poking at the unhibernated bear a bit more. "Let me guess. You've been brainstorming ways to pay off her house." Actually, that didn't sound too far-fetched—this *was* Carter they were talking about here.

"Yes," Carter groused back, and Jake had to stifle a shout of laughter.

"I've contemplated just hiring actors and sending one of those giant sweepstakes checks to her home, but knowing her, she wouldn't just turn down the money—she'd insist on finding another Megan Stevens who needed the money to give it to."

This was a whole new side of Carter, and Jake couldn't be more entertained.

"At least back when she had medical bills," continued Carter like a runaway train, "all I had to do was make anonymous donations to the—" Carter cut himself off around the same time Jake felt his eyebrows nearly hit the ceiling of his truck.

"You paid for her hospital bills?" Jake asked quietly.

Carter hesitated, but eventually he admitted, "I saved up every spare penny I had to make small dents in her mounting debts. They weren't really substantial donations until SME started doing well." His voice deepened with emotion. "The day I saw the balance at zero . . ."

Dammit, the man really did deserve the paragon pedestal he stood on. This time there was no lingering bitterness in Jake's voice when he reassured Carter. "Megan won't figure out your connection to me. I'll make sure she never knows you had anything to do with the fire."

"If you're trying to make me feel better, you're failing pretty miserably."

No. Of course his perfect brother wouldn't feel good about that. "It is what it is. For both of us. I don't mind, Carter, honest. I accepted my fate the day I signed that confession. I'll continue to stand by my decision, and you'll get to live to fight another day as Megan's white knight in the shadows. That's our status quo."

A self-deprecating grunt was Carter's only reply.

They sat there in silence for a while before Carter said gruffly, "Sorry I didn't tell you more about the job before sending you down there. I just . . . couldn't risk you not showing up."

"Water under the bridge." He paused for a beat to measure his next words carefully. "So are you going to keep this up forever?"

"Are *you*?" Carter retorted, sounding just as concerned. "This plan Emma has for you two to pretend you don't have a past. How long are you going to go along with it?"

"As long as she needs. Don't worry. I don't have any grand illusions of finally getting the girl or anything. Emma made it abundantly clear that she and I are in a temporary Jake and Emma 2.0 unreality truce for a finite amount of time." Depressing. But at least he knew where things stood. "Gave you my answer. Your turn."

A tattered sigh vibrated over the phone line. "I honestly don't know how long I'm going to keep this up. All I know is that her injuries are my fault. I'm responsible for her. And for the way *your* life went down, too. So maybe I'll never be able to stop trying to make things right."

Jake knew that telling Carter this wasn't his wrong to right would just fall on deaf ears. So he didn't try. Instead they sat there in their first nonawkward stretch of silence ever.

It was nice.

"Jake?"

"Yeah?"

"Can I ask you a favor?"

"Shoot."

"I know my asking anything of you is the last thing I deserve, but . . . could you keep an eye on her for me? While you're there. Let me know if she needs anything at all? Or just as important, if she *wants* anything at all?"

On the one hand, Jake didn't want Carter to feel burdened by the type of deep-seated guilt that could prompt a request like this. But, on the other, he hoped that *was* what Carter was dealing with. Because if not, that meant there was more involved here. More at stake.

"Sure thing, man. No problem. Consider me your eyes and ears." Hearing Carter's muffled sigh of relief, he added, "All shit aside, you're a good guy, Carter. You *can* start forgiving yourself, you know."

Carter didn't even hesitate before tossing back, "Said the pot to the kettle."

Chapter Twelve

Emma saw the sadness clouding Jake's expression when he returned to the barbecue after finishing his phone call.

His eyes met hers, and the well-masked but not-quite-hidden look of quiet torture on his face stole her breath. *He's been thinking about that night.* How many times had she felt the way he looked? Like the nightmares didn't realize they were off the clock once the sun was up.

She started to make her way over to him. They may never get past what happened that night, but, if anything, no one deserved to be alone when the memories of it returned.

Because they always returned.

What they'd all gone through in that fire . . . no one could possibly understand. Sure, therapists and other well-meaning folks could say until they were blue in the face that they understood and that there were "proven methods" that would help make it better. But in her experience, none of that had been half as effective as having someone who'd lived through it, too, simply sit beside you and stare life down alongside you. Someone you trusted to pull you out if you found yourself falling into the shadows that followed you.

Emma wasn't sure what she was going to say to him, or if they'd even talk at all. All she knew was that she wanted to be there beside him if he needed her to be.

Only it looked as though Megan had the same idea.

Emma hung back and watched as her sister went over to cheer Jake up. She was a tiny bit jealous, yes, but mostly just grateful when Megan was able to get Jake smiling again.

God, he had a great smile.

With that Superman chin and those green eyes that could down-right dance in the light when he was laughing, or practically smolder when Emma would catch him looking at her—

Huh, sort of like he was right now. *Waaait a minute.* Why was Megan looking at her, too? In that unsettling, brow-raised, I've-got-an-idea look.

Uh-oh.

"I'll go get it," Megan announced to Jake loudly before ducking off to the kitchen.

Emma made her way over and leaned against the deck railing next to Jake. "Get what?"

"This!" called out Megan proudly as she practically bounced on a pogo stick all the way back from the kitchen. "See, Jake. I told you, great, right?"

Oh good lord.

Megan was waving around the gift Emma had knitted for her—or attempted to, at least—two Christmases ago. An indescribable work of art with more knots than knitting stiches and no discernable shape whatsoever.

They liked to affectionately call it the yarn blob.

Emma watched Jake's eyes twinkle with humor even though he said not a word while Megan went on and on about how much she loved the weird little thing.

Megan carefully turned the blue shower-puff reject in her hands, grinning at it the way parents grinned at kids when they drew them artwork that no one else in the world could figure out. "Emma made this for me. Haven't decided on a perfect use for it yet, but I will."

Emma couldn't stop herself from smiling over Megan's utterly guile-less positive energy. Her sister was hands down the purest soul she knew, with about enough hope and faith to power Santa's sleigh every Christmas. And then some.

When Emma had first given the blob to her, Megan had tried so valiantly to fit her teapot into the misshapen thing, all the while sighing over it as if it were the most beautiful thing she'd ever received. Where Megan was concerned, it really was the thought that counted—she'd take a nonusable home ec disaster made from the heart over an expensive store-bought gift any day.

Megan's eyes softened at the corners as she patted the yarn blob. "Emma is actually the one that got me started with knitting years ago, back when I was in the hospital recovering from my burn injuries. She set up an online store for me and helped me sell scarves, hats, and all sorts of kids' clothing all through high school."

Emma shrugged. "I had to. I was getting calls left and right about folks wanting to buy everything you made."

Smiling, Megan looked over at Jake as if getting ready to let him in on a secret. "That may have been the case later on, but in the beginning, Emma used to spend hours peddling my knitted pieces all over the hospital, making sales pitches to nurses and folks in the waiting rooms. She even got the maternity ward to agree to buy fifty red-and-green newborn caps during the holiday season for all the babies born the last two weeks in December. Just so I'd have enough money to buy a Christmas gift for my dad that year."

Emma didn't need to look up to know Jake was staring intently at her. Focusing her attention on the beer bottle label she was now care-fully peeling off as if she were performing brain surgery, she smoothly redirected the conversation away from that first year she'd hounded everyone and anyone in the hospital who made the mistake of not duck-ing when they saw her coming. Not just because she hated being in the spotlight, especially over this, but more so because it inevitably made her remember how helpless she'd felt at the time, watching her little sister live out her childhood alone in a hospital. "So what prompted you to go looking for that ugly thing I knitted for you anyway?"

Megan gasped in genuine offense. "It's *not* ugly!"

Yes, it really was. But Megan tended to look at the world through a totally different lens than the rest of them, so Emma just smiled and amended her statement, "Okay, not ugly. But certainly not useful." She lifted a self-deprecating shoulder at Jake. "It's supposed to be a teapot warmer." But what it had ended up looking like was a sad doily with a beer belly.

"I swear I followed all the directions in the knitting book." In the beginning, at least. When she quickly found herself unknotting the possessed yarn blob every two minutes or so, the bad-bad book went bye-bye. "Worked on the thing every night."

"And *that's* why she's the best sister ever," Megan declared with an I-told-you-so smile at Jake.

Emma looked at her sister incredulously. "*This* is your evidence of that?"

"Yup," replied Megan resolutely. "Because no matter what you have going on, or how tough things get, you *always* think about me and what you can do to make my life better, happier. You were fresh out of college when you decided to move us out of Riverside after Dad died because you thought I could become the yarn queen of the Midwest out here, remember?"

Emma blinked in surprise at the reminder of how they'd found themselves in Juniper Hills to begin with. At first her only goal had been to be on the other side of the Missouri River. New state, new start. "I saw how much you liked it here that day we'd stopped by to buy some of that fancy yarn you were looking for."

"Exactly. You were twenty-three years old with a sixteen-year-old sister you had to suddenly support with the measly life insurance Dad had. And instead of taking on that daunting task in the town you grew up in and had friends you'd known your whole life, you decided to pick up and transplant us here . . . for me. You kept a roof over my head and managed to build a successful bakery from the ground up all by yourself."

"We were a *team*," maintained Emma firmly. "I didn't do any of it on my own. You were working by then, too, remember?"

Megan shook her head. "Hardly. You practically tackled me if you saw me doing anything but studying and knitting back then." Turning to Jake, she explained. "After my recovery, I tried going back to school, but we eventually decided to homeschool, and I graduated at sixteen. So I'd been taking college courses online at the time—"

"On a *full ride*," interjected Emma proudly, happy to be moving the discussion away from the sad aftermath of the fire to the way her incredible baby sister had managed to take life by the horns and show the universe she wasn't going to let it kick her around.

"It was a scholarship for students who'd overcome adversity," Megan clarified modestly.

"Which you clearly deserved seeing as how you were on the dean's list all through college." Emma beamed at Jake. "She kicked ass in every single class she took."

"Not in Life Survival 101 like you did," countered Megan in a lavishly proud tone of her own. "You aced that better than anyone your age could've."

"Again, I couldn't have done it without your help, Meg. I mean that." In all honesty, seeing Megan accidentally discover her calling working part-time at the library had fueled Emma like nothing else could've. Failure simply hadn't been an option.

Megan sighed and turned back to Jake. "She does this all the time. She never lets me thank her for all she did for me."

"It wasn't a big deal," Emma mumbled in response to Megan's excessive praise, while paying inordinately fascinated attention to the microscopic surgery she was nearly done performing on her beer bottle.

Success!

Emma finally got the entire label off without tearing it at all. Clearly, the frustrating years she'd spent trying to reuse old stickers as a kid had not been in vain.

She reached for the empty water bottle next to Jake to try her new-found skill on a different patient—it was either that or meet his probing gaze, which she hadn't felt budge throughout this entire conversation.

"Yes, it was so a big deal," maintained Megan with a meaningful look at Jake. "Told you she'd disagree with us."

Us? So that's what they'd been talking about earlier with all the smiling?

Thankfully, Megan's boss and coworkers provided a much-appreciated diversion when they came by with their good-byes and thanks to Megan for hosting.

A few minutes later, when Emma and Jake were the only two still left outside in the backyard, he leaned over to gently pull the now-naked bottle from her hands. "I always knew you'd grow up to be something special, Emma Stevens." It was a soft murmur that might have gone unheard if not for that low growling voice of his that Emma's ears were now hardwired to pick up, sort of like dogs with that special whistle.

They heard Megan shut the back door to the kitchen with a resounding click in her not-so-subtle attempt to give them some more privacy. First the demonic dating app and now this. Her little sister was turning into quite the meddling matchmaker.

Jake backed up to put a few feet of space between them. "We probably shouldn't stay here in the dark like this, before your sister gets the wrong idea about us."

Was it? Right now being near Jake felt anything *but* wrong.

When Emma made no move to back away from him, or agree with his statement, for that matter, he settled back against the nearest tree and surveyed her, looking as surprised as he did intrigued. In the comfortable silence that followed, she allowed herself the luxury of getting her fill of the man. Lord almighty, he was handsome as sin. And so beautifully brawny. Heaven help her. His heavily muscled forearms were centerfold-arm-porn worthy.

Staring at the anatomical work of art now, this close to her, Emma finally noticed that he wasn't wearing the rugged wristwatch he'd had on at the bakery earlier today. It took her a second to figure out why the sight of his naked wrist was having such a marked effect on her.

Back whenever he used to talk to her over the fence separating their two yards, he used to always drape his arms over it. Casual-like. In the beginning, looking up at the top of the fence, all Emma could see of his six-foot-tall frame were his arms. Until she'd dragged a big rock over to stand on so she could at least be eye level with him.

One day she'd slipped off the rock and smacked her face into the fence. In addition to an egg-shaped lump on her forehead, she'd gotten a tiny little scratch on her cheek from his watch. It was hardly even a scrape, but it had upset Jake something fierce.

After that he'd never worn a watch during their chats again.

Seeing him now with a deep watch tan that indicated the man hardly took his watch off, Emma was finding the whole breathing thing a bit difficult. The logistics of blinking were also lost on her as she wandered deeper into the darkening forest-green depths of his gaze.

She was quickly finding that his eyes were like that mood ring she'd had when she was a kid that didn't actually measure mood so much as it did *heat*. Earlier, when they'd been alone and she'd told him he made her nervous, his eyes had gone from sage to hunter green.

Right now? His eyes were nearly black.

Okay, maybe he had the right idea of putting some space between them.

Emma backed up a few steps until she bumped into the grill.

"Careful!" He shot forward to pull her arm away from the still-cooling cooking grates. Running his calloused fingers over her skin gently, he inspected every inch of her arm, voice laden with concern. "Did you burn yourself, baby? Come over to the light so I can see."

Her heart rate went double time. "I'm okay, Jake. It was hot, but not enough to burn me. Stupid of me not to watch where I was going."

After giving her arm another thorough once-over, he exhaled with relief. "Stay here. I'll move the grill back onto the deck." The man then picked her up by the waist and deposited her on the seat farthest from the grill, putting a cold bottle of water against the one area of her arm that was now just a tiny bit pinker from coming into brief contact with the grill.

Seriously. Swoon. Whisperer.

As Jake efficiently wiped down the grill with a cool rag, he asked curiously, "Why on earth did Megan buy such a big grill? I kid you not—I saw her rolling it closer to the table on the grass earlier, and she nearly got run over by the thing."

Yeah, Emma had seen the same thing. Chuckling softly, she explained. "I tried to get her to pick a smaller one, but she'd just been named head librarian and she wanted to buy something 'extravagant' with her pay raise."

"Your sister always been this live-on-the-edge?" he asked, deadpan.

Shoulders shaking with more light laugher, Emma got up to start moving the chairs back up onto the deck. "An outdoor kitchen *is* living on the edge for her. She'd bought the grill, three picnic tables, enough seating for a dozen, and that big fire pit around two years ago with the goal of throwing her first party—"

Oh my.

Emma stopped talking and just watched—rubbernecked really—as Jake used his burly mountain-man arms to grab the edges of the big grill and pick it up like it weighed no more than a waiter's tray. After he tucked the grill in the back corner on the deck, he did the same with the wide picnic table that had taken three of them to haul down earlier.

"So was that first party a hit?" he asked, oblivious to the focus of her attention. "Was the big-ass grill worth it?"

Dragging her eyes away from the display of muscles flexing across his broad back, Emma climbed up the steps, bringing the last of the chairs with her. "I don't know—you tell me. Did you enjoy yourself tonight?"

Jake looked back at her, startled. "*This* was her first party?"

Megan opened the door then and joined them on the deck, answering Jake's question with a shy attempt at humor. "Yes. I've just been prepping for it for two long years is all." Chewing on her bottom lip, she asked quietly, "Was it okay?"

"Best barbecue I've been to in ages," replied Jake without any hesitation at all. "And I'm a Midwest boy, so you know I take my barbecues seriously. Ask Emma." He winked. "Those sex noises I was making when I tasted your ribs and baked beans, I wasn't faking them one bit."

"He wasn't," Emma confirmed wholeheartedly. "Those were all completely authentic."

At Megan's pointed double-brow raise, Emma replayed the exchange and felt her face go up in flames. "Not that I know what Jake sounds like during sex!" she all but shouted to clarify.

Even Jake looked ruffled. Unlike her traitorous cheeks, though, his natural pelt of sexy beard hid any visible embarrassment. "Um, yeah, what she just hollered. There has been absolutely no sex having between us. Yesterday Emma just heard what I sound like when I eat something I can't get enough of is all."

Lordy, even that sounded dirty.

Clearly Jake thought so, too, because he smoothly averted his eyes and busied himself with surveying the yard for an escape portal of some sort.

Apparently he found one in the hanging lanterns Megan had put up in the trees. Pointing at the ladder, he started shuffling sideways in that direction. "I'm just going to . . ." He didn't even bother finishing his sentence before he darted off into the yard, effectively deserting Emma to deal with Megan's amused looks on her own.

She scowled at Megan. "Don't you dare start."

"Wouldn't even know where to begin," Megan reassured her, eyes twinkling.

"Stop making this perverted."

"I will if you will."

Jake cleared his throat loudly from the now-dark yard. That hadn't taken long. "Okay, lights are taken care of. You know, since my truck's parked out on this side of the street, I'll go ahead and see myself out, let you girls have your bonding time to talk about . . . stuff."

Emma gave him the evil eye after hearing the ill-disguised laughter in his voice and the suspicious shaking of his shoulders.

He gave Megan a wave and a warm smile, "Again, great barbecue. Thanks for inviting me; it's been a while since I've been out with friends."

Then with one final good-luck look Emma's way, he took off.

The traitor.

He was so getting more decaf tomorrow.

"Hey, he left one of the lanterns on," remarked Megan after Jake's truck disappeared down the street. She went over to go turn it off while Emma finished tidying up the deck.

At the first sound of Megan's mirthfully delighted laughter, Emma quickly went over to see what had her sister eagerly taking out her phone to take a photo.

"Look, Emma—look what Jake did." She made a ta-da motion with her hands, directing Emma's attention to jolly little Gnomeo sitting directly under the hanging lamp he'd left on.

At least she thought it was Gnomeo. The gnome had undergone a bit of a makeover.

Megan giggled and snapped another photo.

It appeared that somehow during the night, Jake had been able to accomplish what they hadn't been able to over the years—he'd discovered the perfect use for the yarn blob. The fuzzy blue teapot warmer reject was now sitting atop the garden gnome's head, tilted over one bushy ceramic eyebrow and poofed up just so. "He looks like he's wearing a bright-blue beret," chuckled Megan. "I love it! And oh my gosh, look—Jake even twirled the black beer label you removed earlier and stuck it under Gnomeo's nose to make a curly French mustache."

Emma spotted the final new accessory about the same time Megan did.

"Hey, is that . . . it is!" Megan gave a puzzled frown, still chuckling. "How random. Not sure how I feel about Jake giving up one of his condoms for Gnomeo, but it sure is funny."

Seeing that the condom packet Jake had placed on the gnome's outstretched palm was the extraslim fit she'd jokingly left for him the other day had Emma bursting out laughing.

She broke down and got her phone out to take some amused photos, as well.

The man was proving himself to be a worthy opponent in this strange little game they were embarking on.

Chapter Thirteen

"I'm just saying he's good for you."

Emma began mentally arming herself as Megan went full tactical and launched into her favorite discussion topic this week: the 1,001 reasons Jake was perfect for Emma. To be perfectly honest, Emma wasn't a fan of today's arguments. "No, what you said was that you thought I was a spinster before Jake started doing the repairs here."

"*Living like,*" Megan corrected. "I said you were living like a spinster. You were always in bed by ten. You only agreed to dates if I'd guilt or trick you into them. You rarely went out, even on nondates. And when you did, half the time you were in your apron around town—"

"Because I always had to come right back here to work," replied Emma, a touch offended. Her aprons were cute, dammit.

"My point exactly. You were always working."

"Meaning I'm a hard worker. That does not a spinster make."

"Okay, fine, I retract that part. But I have a ton of other evidence to support the underlying concern in my case." Megan crossed her arms and got a torpedo target lock. "Do you know that the Old Biddy Brigade practically threw a ticker tape parade last week after one of 'em saw you in the checkout at the grocery store buying condoms? Apparently, this was the first confirmed condom sighting in your possession in a few years. Multiple sources confirmed it."

Oh. My. God. They were not having this discussion. Emma pivoted and headed back up to her apartment. *Retreat, retreat!* Was nothing private in this town?

"They were downright bummed when Jake informed them that the condoms had in fact been part of a joke and nothing more."

Nope, evidently nothing was private. And clearly she needed to have a talk with her carpenter about giving ammo to the enemy. "Why was Jake even talking to the old biddies in town about me?" And in relation to *condoms*.

"I heard they cornered him last Friday, wanting to know if you two were going somewhere special that night. My guess is the conversation transitioned naturally from there."

This was worse than when she'd dated the two-timing taxidermist they'd essentially chased out of town. Rumor had it that he'd had to go to the ER on his way out owing to a run-in with a motorized scooter that ended up breaking his big toe.

Those Medicare Part B senior mobility scooters were no joke.

"Jake and I have just had a few meals together around town. With the bakery closed down, I've obviously had more time on my hands, so I've been trying out a bunch of restaurants I haven't ever had the chance to dine in with my crazy schedule. And sometimes Jake and I find ourselves needing to eat at the same time. So we sit at the same table. Since I get a town discount at all the restaurants, this way he gets to save a few bucks on his meals. That's all."

"So this is strictly economics between you two? Not chemistry?"

Yes, but the subject you'd really rather be studying with the man is sex ed, admit it.

Lately it had become very evident to Emma that she didn't have Jiminy Cricket whispering in her ear, but rather his wild and juuust this side of indecent twin *Jezebel* Cricket.

"Hate to disappoint all of you, but Jake and I are just friends."

Bizarrely. Unexpectedly. *Unequivocally.* Friends.

That is, if the newfangled definition of a friend could also encompass a person she'd barely been able to stop thinking about for the past week.

"Besides," Emma continued, hoping her thoughts weren't reflected in her words, "even if there were some lingering *chemistry* with Jake, there's no future there."

Megan looked stunned, to say the least. "Wait, you think Jake's not the settling-down-with-a-wife-and-kids type? Because if so, I'd say you're crazy."

Picturing Jake in that scenario made a surprisingly sharp stab of pain hit her square in the chest. "That's not what I meant. Of course he'd make an amazing husband and father."

"Then what's the problem?"

"*I'm* the one that isn't happily-ever-after potential where Jake is concerned. He's a great guy. He deserves an equally great woman to marry and have a whole mess of great kids with."

Megan's expression morphed from confusion to astonishment. "Em, what are you talking about? You want the whole white-picket-fence future—I know you do."

Actually, the fence she wanted wasn't a white picket one. It was tall and unpainted. A rustic wooden fence that had a pair of burly lumberjack forearms draped over the top every afternoon just before sunset, straight out of the fairy-tale endings she'd dreamed of for more years than she'd ever allowed herself to admit before now.

But that's all it was—a fairy tale.

Emma remembered how one of her therapists had explained that the death of a child can often break up even the best of relationships, even the most loving ones. Like the one her father and stepmother had found. They'd been second-round soul mates; all anyone had to do was see them together to know that. That they'd found each other later in life made their fairy-tale marriage that much more destined to be.

Yet even *they* hadn't been able to survive after Peyton's death.

So what possible chance did she and Jake stand?

None. Not with a child's death already between them . . . a child they'd *both* failed to save.

"Em, talk to me."

Emma blinked the memories back and pasted on a bright smile. "Let it go, Meg. Jake and I have an understanding. An arrangement. We're Jake and Emma 2.0 for the duration of his time here. No sad past. Just fun, uncomplicated times in the present."

And no future.

"Morning, ladies." As if she'd conjured him to the bakery, Jake 2.0 walked through the front door in all his steel-toe-boots-and-stone-washed-denim glory.

While he walked around her bakery looking all serious as he scribbled measurements for this and used his hammer on that, Emma saw it—glimpses of the boy next door who'd stolen her teenage heart seemingly a lifetime ago.

The boy she needed to view as an entirely different person from the man before her now just to function and get through each day.

The boy she'd vowed to never give another thought to after waking up in the hospital with one badly burned sibling, and one dead one.

The boy she still found herself thinking about even now whenever the sun would set just so, and the grass fields would turn a golden green for a few fleeting minutes.

"So that's that?" asked Megan skeptically. "You and Jake are just going to keep pretending the past doesn't exist so you can enjoy each other's uncomplicated company in the present until the bakery repairs and the library renovation are over?"

Christ, that sounded twenty different kinds of unhealthy. "Yep, that about sums it up."

Megan shook her head slowly in a you're-lucky-I-love-you sort of way. "Okay then. A bunch of us from the library are going to go see Blake's girlfriend's art show—you met her at the barbecue. They invited your 'new friend' Jake also, so bring him along. Blake's older brother will be coming, too, so everyone will be paired off. I don't want you to be the odd one out."

Emma felt mild panic start to set in. "You mean this is going to be a group date?"

Megan shrugged. "If you want to label it. It'll be casual. And fun. Right up your alley with this whole 2.0 arrangement, right?"

The woman was evil and was cut off from any morning cupcakes for the next month.

"So you'll invite Jake then?" pressed the demoness formerly known as her sister.

Emma drew it out, hoping Megan would back down.

She didn't. "Sure. Sounds like a fun night."

"Excellent. You have three days to ask him out." Megan waved and skipped down the staircase toward the front door, waiting until the very bottom step to sing out, *"Good luck."*

Make that *two* months for the cupcake strike.

It was officially day three.

You can do this. It's no big deal. So she'd never technically verbally asked a guy out before—one good thing about the demented dating app her sister had signed her up for. How hard could it be? This wasn't even a date, really. It was just a couple of friends hanging out.

And that's why the very idea of asking Jake to go to said event was giving Emma something close to Midol-worthy cramps.

Even the silent pep talk she was giving herself about doing this was making her cheeks warm and her ears hot to the touch. Which meant her freckles were out in full force. She didn't have very many, just a light dusting across the bridge of her nose and the ridges of her cheekbones from a few too many summer sunburns out at the lake. In fact, she'd actually never really been all that conscious of them until now.

Until she'd first realized that Jake was utterly fascinated by them.

She'd caught him staring at them a few times over the past week, and damn if she hadn't blushed like a schoolgirl each time. Which, of course, just seemed to intrigue him even more.

Not that he did anything about it.

Nope. That man was the *perfect* Jake 2.0. Kept to the restrictions of her plan to a T. The ideal casual stranger turned friend. In fact, he did such a great job, she hardly ever thought about their history anymore—"their history" meaning the fire. Not the massive crush she'd had on him from the second he'd moved into the house next door that summer.

That was why this thing she was about to do was *no big deal*.

It was not as if she planned to shave her legs above the knees and go out to buy condoms or anything. *Oy. Condoms.* The disturbing reminder of the old biddies and their multiple sources knowing that it'd been more than *three years* since she'd last bought a box of the stuff wasn't helping one bit. *Jesus, don't think about that now, woman.*

Because, well, freckles.

Just quit stalling and do it already, Stevens! "Jake," she blurted out, straight from the far, far end of left field. "Do you want to hang out tonight? Together?"

Okay, *maybe* she could've waited until he was through nailing the baseboard to the wall with his nail gun.

Oh yeah, she was sooo good at this. And what was with the unnecessary clarification of them doing the hanging out together? Sweet baby J, how on earth did other women do this?

After renailing the spot he'd ended up missing by a mile as a result of her little outburst, Jake put down the nail gun and turned around, a slow grin spreading across his face.

If there were an award for sexiest grinner alive, this man definitely deserved it.

He tilted his head next, pinning her with an intense gaze, and she knew she'd just swum out of her league. What had she been thinking? She'd barely even waded around the kiddie pool with floaties when it came to the whole dating scene.

"Did I hear that correctly, or are my ears playing really mean tricks on me? It sounded like you just asked me out on a date."

As he continued to watch her watch him with her cheeks neon bright and her lips apparently glued together, that award-winning grin of his morphed into a sexy crooked smile that made his chiseled jawline even more laser cut and brought focus to that hidden cleft chin, which she was pretty sure held supernatural powers over women's panties.

They didn't call it a superhero chin for nothing.

"It's not a date," she replied immediately—potayto, potahto—as she started dog-paddling her butt back to shallower waters.

Okay, okay, this *was* a big deal. She couldn't ask Jake out on a date!

At that mental announcement, teenage Emma promptly took back the high five she'd given adult Emma after the nail-gun thing and was now stabbing her in the eye with a glitter pencil.

"No? 'Hanging out tonight . . . together' certainly sounds like a date to me. And judging by that sweet blush on your cheeks, it sure looks like it, too."

She knew he was just teasing her. This was how their friendship had evolved over the past two weeks. They busted each other's chops. So she busted right back. "Yes, well, I'm sure lots of things sound and look different when they get lost in that big head of yours."

He let out a deep, untamed laugh. "Ah. Okay, my mistake." Turning back to his nail gun, the maddening man started whistling the theme song from *Jeopardy*, all the while leaving her hanging regarding the whole nondate thing.

"Well?" she prodded, keeping her cool. "You want to go? It'll be casual. An art show in the city and then a bite to eat after, probably." *Much improved. Smooth sailing from here.*

129

He gave her an exaggerated double-shoulder lift. "I don't *know*. See, I have this slave driver of a boss who makes me come in at the butt crack of before seven each morning . . ."

She narrowed her eyes at him. *Jake* was the one who always insisted on coming in so early. And they both knew that. This was all a power game. *Bastard.* "Fine, I'll talk to this slave driver boss of yours, who sounds just delightful if you ask me, and work it out with her so you can come in tomorrow well after seven—" He cleared his throat loudly. "I mean eight," she amended between smiling clenched teeth.

"Well, then that changes everything. I'd love to go out with you tonight. Only . . ." He eyed her suspiciously. "You're not"—he lowered his tone as if he didn't want to alert the elders or something—"going to be 'expecting' anything from me, are you? Just so you know, I'm not that kind of guy. I don't put out just because a pretty girl asks me on a date and buys me lobster."

Emma's jaw dropped in horror. "Wha—no! This—*lobster?*" she sputtered. "I told you it's just an art show. And it's not even just going to be us; Megan will be there, too."

He tsked disappointedly. "Whoa, whoa, whoa. Sorry, babe, that's a deal breaker for me. Not into threesomes—way too racy for my tastes. I've just never been one of those bad-boy types who go for that sort of thing. Whose idea was this anyway? Yours?"

She was two seconds from busting a blood vessel in her head. And strangling the man. "You know that's not what I meant. *Threesomes*—are you off your cracker? And, no, none of this was my idea. I don't even *like* you right now. Megan's the one who asked me to ask you."

"Riiight. *Megan*, of course. It's okay. I'm flattered you asked me out. Really. I just have to think about it. You know, with us working together and all, and you and I having just met a few weeks ago. It's a tough situation."

She very nearly stomped her foot in frustration.

"I'm leaning toward yes, if that helps," he offered with an affectionate head tilt that was at least genuine. "Because, obviously, I think you're great."

Well, that helped *a little* in terms of calming the aggravated fires from hell blistering her brain right now.

"I'll be sure to give you . . . I mean, *Megan* my final answer later this afternoon. I promise." He smiled, casual as can be, before he turned and went right back to work.

Un-freaking-believable. He'd actually used exaggerated air quotes and everything.

Emma immediately started looking around for something to throw at him.

∽

Jake was pretty certain she was going to bash him in the head with his own hammer and knock him out cold. But he just couldn't help himself. The woman was adorable as all hell when she was riled up. Plus, she made it so easy. And so, so addictive.

"If we could interrupt your ménage proposition for a bit." He smothered a chuckle over her murderous glare. "I wanted to talk about the repairs for this wall section over here, just outside the kitchen. I actually don't think we should wallpaper it up again."

That brought her back to business as usual. "What? Why not?"

"Well, when I was repairing the panel of drywall that was damaged in the corner, I saw that there's shiplap wood under it. You see all these old horizontal wood panels? I've actually never seen it myself since it wasn't as common in midwestern constructions back in the day."

As Emma ran her hand across the weathered planks, he made his pitch, "The thing is, shiplap walls are getting popular again, and it definitely adds a unique character, which your bakery is all about. So I was thinking we should just expose it all, sand it down, and stain it. Make it a focal point here."

"But won't that be distracting? With one strip of wall looking totally different from the other walls in the bakery?"

"I think it'll actually fit well. Plus, it'll save you some money. If you're that worried about it looking too different, we can just do it on the bottom half of the wall. I can put a chair molding across the middle with a brighter color on the top half. That way you can have the historic, rustic touch you have going here but still with all the bright colors you like."

It was obvious she loved the idea, but the stubborn little thing wouldn't admit it outright just yet. She had a tell whenever she was holding something back—she literally bit her tongue. He'd caught her doing it a few times over the past week. Just the tiny tip of her tongue would be sandwiched between her perfectly pointed canines. Always on her right. It was the sweetest tell. And sexy to boot.

Every time he saw her do it, he wanted to just yank her in his arms and slide his tongue over those sexy canines. He wasn't greedy. He could share. She could keep the right canines she favored, and he'd lay claim to the ones on her left.

"All right. If you think it'll save us some money, and time, let's go with your idea."

He grinned. "I feel like I need to take a photo to record this moment. You coming around to my way of thinking without arguing about it for an hour."

She huffed and shot him an exasperated look. Before doing that thing he loved whenever she dug one of his ideas. All the woman had to do was flash him that nose scrunch and deploy her freckles out in full force up on her cheekbones, and he'd get hit with a big bolt of stupid from head to toe.

He was sure she had no idea that she could probably get him to build an entire bakery from scratch for free just by supplying more of those scrunching, freckled smiles.

While they were on the category of things that turned him on, the daily double for him definitely had to be that bossy tone she used sometimes to try to regain control of a runaway situation (that he was usually the one messing with the brakes on). Her bossy sass was also damn effective at making him want to hang the moon outside her bedroom window for her.

"It'll look great, sweets—I promise."

Her expression went still for a second, and he frowned, wondering what had just happened.

Her brows stitched together in consternation, even though a contradicting crooked smile was peeking through.

"Something wrong?"

"No," she said in a soft tone to match her smile. "It just occurred to me that no one ever really calls me anything but Emma, or Em."

He blinked through a mental transcript of what he'd just called her. *Sweets.* It hadn't been intentional. The word had slipped out without him even thinking about it. Probably some subconscious thing. The woman was all sweetness and goodness.

"I'm sorry. That was unprofessional. I'll make a point not to do that."

"No, no." She tempered her voice down to casual and breezy. "I like it. You don't have to stop. Like I said, folks don't usually call me by any nicknames. Especially guys."

He gave a silent growl over the idea of any guys calling her anything, period.

"Everyone here is really . . . I don't know, careful? With me and Megan. Which is good. Great really. Plus, nearly everyone treats me like I'm their sister. Again, especially the guys."

Best news he'd heard all day.

The clanging of the front door stopped him from accidentally spilling the beans on how he was definitely *not* in the group of guys in town who intended to treat her like a sister.

Probably for the best he kept that spoiler alert to himself.

Megan poked her head into the kitchen a second later. "Hey, Em! I'm just here to raid your closet for tonight. I know neither of us has anything really fancy to wear, but I was thinking we could try to mix and match some things to get close to a night-in-the-city outfit."

She flashed a broad grin at Jake. "Oh, hi, Jake. I meant to ask, since the art gallery is near your place, are you going to meet us there or come down with us from here?"

Ah, damn.

Jake looked up to study a crack in one of the drywall tiles on the ceiling, all but whistling innocently when Emma held up a hand to interrupt Megan. "Hang on—Jake hasn't even decided if he's going yet. We were just talking about it."

"That's weird. Jake was helping Blake and his girlfriend fix some of the display stands for her art exhibits, and when they invited him to the show, he told them he'd be there—"

The rest of Megan's sentence came to an abrupt halt.

Most likely because Emma was now chasing him around the kitchen.

"You freaking ass! You were already going to come out tonight! You were just messing with me this whole time!"

Emma got close enough to double whack his arm. He juked to the right, and then to the left, and then did an impressive *Matrix* move to avoid the smack she was aiming for his head.

With the passageway out of the kitchen and to the front of the bakery in sight, he made a dash for it. "I think I'll finish the floorboards tomorrow. Big date tonight. See you girls at seven," he called out, ducking to avoid the spare paintbrush Emma sent whizzing past his head. Good thing he didn't leave his hammer behind.

A peek behind him revealed Megan forcibly holding Emma back.

The woman was spitting-nails pissed at him. *But* that was undeniably a tiny smile he could see her doing her damnedest to hide.

Clearly Megan saw it, too, because he overheard her say, "I swear—watching you two with these bizarre mating rituals is like watching Wile E. Coyote and the Road Runner go at it."

Chapter Fourteen

The man was a menace to her sanity.

It was bad enough that he was ridiculously handsome, and criminally sexy, but to top it all off, he was also an unbelievably great guy. A prince among men.

As Emma had discovered at the art show a few nights ago, Jake hadn't just helped Blake's girlfriend with her art exhibit display stands; he'd stayed there till sunup to make sure all the students' display stands were perfect.

And today? He'd started work just after dawn and worked through lunch so he could take off a few hours early to help out old Mrs. Taylor, who needed to get a ramp installed at her house since she'd recently broken her hip and couldn't get up and down her porch steps.

Not long after sunset, Emma finally couldn't take all the quiet. She'd gotten used to having Jake around all the time. It wasn't just the lack of construction sounds, either. The space, and her entire day, felt emptier without Jake's idle whistling or his off-tune singing to old-school country. Not to mention the way he'd tease and flirt with her innocently but mercilessly.

To take her mind off the big lug, she decided to at least fill the space back up with some construction noises. She could kill two birds with one stone by tackling the new hardwood floors in the front of the bakery so they could get ahead of the repairs a little. From what she'd heard from Paul and Megan, the library project was running right on schedule, so Jake would need to get started over there soon.

Since she'd handled the installation of the hardwood floors in her apartment dining room, this was nothing new. Granted, the space she'd worked on was only about a tenth of this size, and the wood she'd used upstairs looked more like big rulers compared with the walk-the-plank pirate pieces Jake had ordered for the bakery, but still she wasn't worried.

Not knowing how Jake felt about other folks using his tools, Emma erred on the side of caution and dusted off the old table saw she'd used on her own floors. After a few trial runs with some old plywood, she was ready to rock and roll.

Measure, cut, glue, position, tap into place. Repeat. Easy peasy.

It was actually kind of soothing.

A few hours later, she was about a quarter of the way done. And her correlated mission of not having Jake on the brain nonstop was also proving a success as a result.

Emma was finishing up laying down the adhesive for the final pieces in the two rows she was working on—her last ones for the night—when her phone rang with Megan's ringtone. If she didn't answer, Megan would just come on over. Standard small-town sister protocol. And when she saw Emma working on the floors, she'd rat her out to Jake for sure. Not just because the two had gotten chummy lately, but because Jake had specifically told Emma to stop doing construction work when he wasn't there in the name of safety.

When it came to that sort of thing, Megan had no sisterly loyalty whatsoever.

Not wanting to deal with a protective, worried Jake this late at night, Emma managed to sprint over to the counter to grab her phone before the final ring, but on her dash back, she tripped on her tools and took a sprawling tumble.

Ouch.

Crap, was it possible to bruise your ass? Sure felt as if it was. Even with the extra padding she had back there to soften the blow, it still smarted.

"Oh no! No, no, no," she cried out when she saw that her smartphone had fallen onto the hardening adhesive. *Crap!* Using the hem of her shirt, she quickly wiped off as much as she could. She wasn't a cell phone warranty expert, but she was pretty sure they might be opposed to covering any repairs when they saw the phone was completely covered in a tarlike glue.

It took a while, but she was finally able to scrape most of the sticky gunk off before it got too hard. And, thankfully, her touch screen appeared unaffected. *Whew. Crisis averted.* Emma immediately hit the "Redial" button to call Megan back, only to see a text from her waiting in the in-box.

Babysitting for Dennis tonight. I'll call you later.

So she'd been worried for nothing. *Double whew.*

Just as she was celebrating sidestepping a land mine, however, Emma discovered one very belated, very important detail that hadn't registered for, oh, the past fifteen minutes or so.

She was still sitting in the flooring adhesive she'd landed in earlier.

And now she couldn't move an inch.

Irony of all ironies, while she had been focused on making sure the industrial-strength glue didn't dry on her phone, that very same glue had been drying underneath her. Which meant that the back of her jeans, from the seat of her pants straight down to her ankles, along with the back of her boots, was firmly adhered to the now fully dry flooring adhesive she'd slathered down earlier.

"This is *not* happening. Tell me I didn't just glue my ass to the ground."

Don't panic.

She calmly placed her phone down and tried unzipping her jeans. If she could just get out of her boots, she could then slide herself backward out of her clothes to get free.

It didn't take long for her to figure out that was a doomed plan. A few hours ago, using her old knee-high winter boots today had seemed like a good idea since she never wore them anymore and had planned to just chuck them after she was through with the flooring. But with the long zipper completely inaccessible under the legs of her jeans, she couldn't get her boots off, meaning she couldn't get her legs out of the jeans.

Okay, maybe now is a good time to panic.

Emma then proceeded to spend the next five minutes exhausting every muscle in her body by trying to forcibly pull herself straight up—gymnastic pommel horse style. But all that did was give her two possibly torn triceps and what felt like two bruised breasts. *Criminy.* She was stuck, plain and simple.

"I'm not going to call Jake. I am *not* going to call Jake."

Emma began examining her options. Calling Megan would be the same thing as calling Jake so she went ahead and filed that as terrifying plan B. All the other shops around had been closed for a while now, so no help there. *Holy moly, is it really almost midnight?*

She supposed she could call the sheriff's office . . .

Yes, that would absolutely be less embarrassing than going to plan B.

Emma plopped backward onto the last set of hardwood planks she'd laid down just before this whole mess and covered her face with both hands.

Then she started cracking up hysterically.

"Emma!"

"Jake?" She popped back up at the sound of his worried, growling shout, and nearly got a charley horse in her abs. Or was that a cramp?

That had probably been the first noncheating sit-up she'd done since high school gym, so for all she knew, it could've been both.

Holding her now-throbbing stomach, she swiveled around as best she could and saw Jake sprinting across the street toward her at a dead run.

He flung open the front door of the bakery with a wall-rattling bang.

Emma cringed when six feet of heaving muscles, topped with a thunderous scowl, greeted her from the door. She waved casually as if she weren't the biggest idiot in the room. "I promise—I was *just* about to call you."

He gave her a look that said he didn't believe her one bit before he stomped over. "Dammit, sweetheart, are you okay?"

"I'm fine, I'm fine."

"Are you hurt?" He crouched down and started scanning her head to toe.

She thought it best not to mention her bruised ass or various strained muscles. Her ego had gone through enough tonight. "No, I'm okay. I'm just stuck."

He grabbed the tool she'd been using to spread the adhesive and tapped the tar-covered ground between her legs. Discovering it completely dry, he scowled at her. "Christ, how long have you been sitting here like this?"

This was one of those best-to-feign-ignorance situations; she just knew it.

She gave him a big shrug.

"Woman, you could test the sanity of a saint. I told you to leave the construction work to me." He released an exasperated grunt and kneeled down beside her to try to yank her up off the ground.

"I tried that already. I think I might've sprained my boobs in the process."

"No being cute," he groused, though a flicker of humor did twitch at his lips. But then all humor fled his features as his eyes darkened suddenly to a deep, intense forest green.

She followed his gaze to see what had brought on the drastic change. *Oh, right.* She'd unzipped her jeans earlier.

And apparently she was wearing her superfrilly pink panties today.

She slapped her hands over herself to cover up just as Jake slammed his eyes shut like an iron drawbridge almost at the exact same time. He remained like that for a few seconds, his unsteady breathing sounding more reckless by the second.

Sure, it wasn't particularly evolved of her, but it was flattering to see him react like this.

When he eventually opened his eyes again, she saw that the ego-boosting flare of lust she'd caught a microsecond glimpse of earlier was now gone completely. In its place was something else entirely. Something raw with emotion. "Baby, your front door was unlocked. Someone could've come in here while you were stuck like this. Someone could've hurt you—"

A dark, stricken look overcame his features.

Fist flexing, jaw clenched, erratic breathing. Within a blink of an eye, he looked ready to slaughter these nonexistent assailants his imagination was conjuring.

Alarmed, she tried to calm him down. "Jake. I'm fine. Nothing happened—"

"Hold on, sweets. Give me a minute. I just . . . need one minute."

Jake was doing his best to slow down the rushing adrenaline that was making him crazed, but he was going to need a little more than a minute.

When he'd first driven up, he'd almost had a heart attack. All he'd been able to see was Emma lying on the ground, hands over her face, with her body shaking as if she was sobbing.

And he'd plain lost it.

It had brought him right back to that night. The only time he'd ever seen her cry. He'd barely been able to keep it together then. Now? Strangely it was even more difficult.

After a few more seconds, now that his brain wasn't overloaded with panic, he managed to calm down enough to peer over his shoulder to make sure his truck was still outside and not halfway down the street. Seeing as how he hadn't even bothered to put it into park before rushing in here and all, he considered that an important win.

"Sweetheart, why were you crying?" he ground out in a rumbling voice he had no way of making less intimidating at the moment. "Are you sure you didn't injure yourself?"

"I was laughing, Jake. Not crying. Because of how ridiculous the situation was. I swear. I'm absolutely fine."

Her soothing voice helped stop the blood rushing in his ears some. But his veins were still ice cold with dread, his muscles all locked in fury and fear. A dozen different horrifying scenarios, each worse than the last, continued to run through his head. What if some predator or psycho had come in and attacked her while she'd been in here defenseless, unable to move—

A gentle squeeze on his forearm stopped another wave of terrifying what-if thoughts from crashing into him.

"Jake, stop. Nothing happened. I just fell and got stuck. And now you're here to help. So everything is fine." Her hand rubbed his gently. "I'm fine."

Finally feeling more human than beast, he looked down and saw Emma gazing at him with concern. Damn woman was too sweet for her own good. Didn't she know that all that sweetness was worse than kerosene for a man running on pure adrenaline? He leaned over and placed a kiss on her forehead. "I'm glad you're not hurt. Okay, hang tight. I'm going to figure out how to get you unstuck. So I can start yelling at you."

She smiled. "Sounds like music to my ears."

He looked down and tried to determine the best way to get her free, all the while keeping his eyes away from the vicinity where he had seen a sexy pair of pink panties peeking out of her unzipped jeans. "Did you already try to drag yourself out of your jeans? That didn't work?"

"I'm wearing knee-high boots, and they're stuck, too. So I think you have to cut open my jeans so I can get to my boot zippers."

Shaking his head, he blocked all the lusty images that one sentence provoked, then hustled over to her utility drawer to grab a pair of scissors. Dropping back down to his knees beside her, he sighed. "All afternoon something in my gut told me you were here doing something like this, even though you promised me you weren't going to."

Her cheeks colored, and he only just barely checked the impulse to brush his lips over her heated freckles.

He settled for using the back of his knuckles, under the pretense of wiping away a bit of sawdust. "I actually would have been here sooner, but I was helping the Taylors install other safety measures inside the house after I got through with the ramp."

This time it was Emma who looked worried. "Were you able to get those done? I know Mrs. Taylor can be stubborn. If you need to go back tomorrow, no worries here. I can—"

"Stop talking," he commanded, feeling positively primal all of a sudden.

At her stunned expression, he gentled his voice and went with the bare and bold truth. "If you bring up working in here again while I'm away, the long and short of it is that I'm going to play dirty to make you take it back. 'Kissing' would be a paltry, wholly inadequate description of what I'd do to your mouth in an attempt to obliterate the mere thought of doing anything like that again from your brain completely.

Then later, much later, I'm going to feel guilty for seducing the lips off a woman whose ass is glued to the ground, so, please, save us both from the inevitable pandemonium and *don't* say what you were just about to say."

Her blush deepened and spread slowly to pink up her skin clear down to her chest.

"I can't believe you just said all that," she murmured in a thick, soft, breathless voice that sounded . . . intrigued.

Yep, she was definitely trying to kill him.

"Which part? Me telling you to stop talking, or me telling you I want to kiss the living daylights out of you?"

"Both."

"Well, believe it, honey. And don't test me unless you want to see how quickly I can get you out of those jeans . . . without the scissors."

A stuttered gasp escaped her lips then, and swear to God, he felt ready to pass out for lack of blood in his brain. "If you're keeping a list, go ahead and add that sound you just made to the things you can't do or say unless you're okay with me throwing you over my shoulder and dragging you off to my cave."

"Jake, now *you* need to stop talking."

He surveyed her rapid breathing and dilated eyes.

Arousal, not anger. *Damn.* He couldn't help himself. "Why?" he asked, leaning in just a little closer. "Are you going to kiss me if I don't?"

She shook her head slightly but didn't move away from him.

"Then why do I need to stop talking, sweetheart?"

"B-because," she whispered, her voice gaining strength little by little, "you're about to cut open my jeans, and if you don't stop talking, my panties will be drenched, and then I'll be too embarrassed to slide out of my jeans."

Her defiant so-there tone by the end simply tested his restraint even more.

"*Holy hell*, woman."

Jake fisted his hands on the ground beside her and dropped his forehead down onto hers. That whispered confession was the hottest damn thing he'd ever heard a woman say. "You're driving me batshit crazy right now."

"You drive me crazy all the time."

He chuckled at her frankly disgruntled response. "Let me ask you something. And be honest. If I told you I needed to go to the Taylors' again tomorrow, could I trust you not to work on the floors again?"

"Yes."

Hmm. He thought about how he'd worded that. Then gave her a look. "Could I trust you not to work on the walls or ceilings or anything else either while I'm gone?"

She snapped her mouth shut and gave him a mulish pout.

He led out a rumbling sigh and put the scissors down.

"What are you doing?"

Sitting back on his heels, he crossed his arms over his chest and waited her out.

"Are you seriously not going to let me free unless I promise not to do work *on my own bakery* while you're out?"

"No," he admitted. "We both know you'd break that promise in five minutes."

She raised her impertinent little nose in the air to acknowledge the accuracy of his prediction.

"But I am refusing to set you free unless you agree to three other, much more manageable conditions," he countered.

With an indignant huff, she crossed her arms over her chest and mirrored his pose. "What three conditions?" she bit out.

"One, you don't do any more big jobs like this without my supervision." He interjected quickly before she could protest, "Or at least tell me what you're up to, especially if you're going to be using a saw or things like an adhesive that could glue your gorgeous butt anywhere it's not supposed to be permanently affixed." *Wow, there's a visual.*

Focus, Jake.

Totally unaware of his off-track thoughts, Emma continued to glower stubbornly at him. But she did eventually concede. "Fine."

"Second condition, you march your little tush upstairs and get some goddamn sleep for a change." At her frustrated frown, he reasoned gently. "Babe, I know you've been burning the midnight oil every day. It needs to stop. You're exhausted. And every time I see you stifle a yawn I get crazy ideas about tying you to bed. Preferably mine. Which then results in me getting a raging hard-on. I know it's hard to believe, but doing carpentry work in that state is not nearly as fun as you might think."

Her eyes widened for a beat, and the pulse at her throat thrummed double time before she replied with a quiet, "Okay."

"Third condition." Now this was just getting fun. "From here on out, you will call me master and make me Reuben sandwiches and bourbon pecan pudding every time I snap my—"

She whacked him on the arm before he could finish his list of demands.

"In your dreams, buddy." Quick like a cat, she grabbed the scissors he'd put down and began swiftly cutting through her jeans.

She had her boots unzipped and was just starting to scoot out of her jeans when he put a hand on her knee to stop her. "You're already there, sweetheart. Have been for a while."

Emma paused, eyebrows lowered in question over his cryptic statement.

"I've been dreaming of you damn near since the moment I first saw you peek over that fence separating our two houses. Don't know that I ever really stopped."

Then he let go of her knee and promptly dropped his hand atop his closed eyes. "Go on. I'll take care of the rest of this floor. You get some sleep, honey."

"You're not even going to try to sneak a peek?" If he wasn't mistaken, she sounded a bit disappointed about that. The little vixen. She had no idea how badly he wanted to not just look, but touch, taste.

Keep.

"I told you, sweets—it's pretty un-fun to do construction work when you're turned on like a lamppost. Plus, I really only have room for one hammer on my tool belt."

Her quiet giggle echoed through the bakery. "I'd say you're full of yourself, but—"

"Hey." He pretended to grab for her. "If I have to preserve your modesty by not ogling you, you should have to do the same."

"*Now* you tell me." She chuckled and scurried away.

He waited until he heard her soft footsteps get all the way up the stairs before he took his hand off his eyes. The sight of the empty jeans and boots on the ground before him had him shaking his head in reluctant laughter.

And, yes, hard as a hammer.

Honestly, how different would life have been for him the past fourteen years if he'd had Emma right there beside him making him crazy the entire time?

"Hey, Jake?"

"Yeah?" he called up.

The words floating down the stairwell were barely audible. But he heard them.

"I used to dream about you, too."

It sounded like a confession, wrapped as a gift. Followed by the soft click of her door closing for the night.

Unforgettable, he decided then, answering his own question on how differently his life would've played out. No doubt having Emma at his side for the past fourteen years would've made each and every day utterly unforgettable.

Chapter Fifteen

The next morning Jake woke up to the smell of hot coffee, hot cookies, and hot woman.

He'd recognize Emma's scent anywhere.

He peeked open his eyes and saw a very bothered scowl on Emma's sweet, dawn-lit face.

Man, what time is it? I didn't even feel her climb in the truck bed.

She settled in beside him and placed the fresh cookies on his chest. Then with his attention now caught, she drilled him with a black look. "You could've frozen to death out here."

He smothered back his incredulous laugh because he knew she was being completely serious. "Sweets, it's April. I was perfectly warm." In fact, he was downright toasty in his sleeping bag right now. The only reason he hadn't climbed out of it yet was because it was handling a morning-wood situation for him.

"With my place being so far, it was easier for me to just crash out here after I finished the floors. I always have my camping gear in my truck since I sometimes get the random urge to go off in the woods, so it worked out great." As exhausted as he'd been, the tucked-away parking spot under the tree across the street from the bakery had been impossible to resist. He'd dragged out his sleeping bag and knocked out the second his head had hit his makeshift pillow.

"Next time, just sleep in the bakery," she ordered as she continued to fuss over him and tuck him deeper into his sleeping bag, as if she expected him to go hypothermic.

God, he couldn't get enough of her.

When he managed to rub the last of the sleep from his eyes, he was finally able to get a good look at the still-worried frown she was wearing, which paired perfectly with the suspicious survey she was taking up and down the street around him. As if she was looking for evidence of some ruffian waiting in the bushes to kidnap him out of his truck.

She was killing him. He went ahead and cataloged this as yet another one of the outrageously cute things she did that turned him on. The list was getting pretty big.

Among other things at the moment, in direct relation.

"Emma, you're going to need to sit about ten inches away from me. I don't exactly have room for a tent in my sleeping bag."

A brief pause. Then: "You're talking in drunken bubbles." She chuckled, clearly not getting his perfectly lucid meaning. "How late did you get to sleep?"

"Not that long ago." Between the coffee and the cookies and the feeling of an early-morning, sleep-warmed Emma tucked against his hip, at this rate, he was going to have to turn over completely to keep himself decent. "Honey, really, you gotta shift a bit for me."

She shrugged and scooted her butt over a bit.

He hissed. "Other direction."

Her eyes rounded as belated understanding set in real quick. *"Oh."*

Soon as they weren't hip to hip anymore, he was able to pull himself into a seated position and adjust enough to keep his flag from saluting her before taking the travel cup of coffee she was holding. "Woman, why are you up at dawn? I thought I told you to sleep more."

He promptly stopped his scolding to release a deep male purr of satisfaction over the strong brew Emma had made for him. After that first day she'd tried to poison him with the horrendous decaf, she hadn't done anything mean with his coffee again. And if he wasn't mistaken, good ol' Sally had shared her recipe for double black with Emma because what he was drinking right now was dark-as-night, caffeinated heaven in a cup.

"Don't turn this around on me, buster. What if some hoodlum had mugged you or something while you were sleeping?"

"Then he would've been sorely disappointed to discover a measly twenty in my wallet." He winked. "Well, that and an extraslim-fit condom of course." Since the condom he'd left in Megan's garden had somehow sprouted legs and ended up in his toolbox for all the world to see last week when he'd gone over to help out at the library site for a few hours—he was still living that one down, by the by—Jake now kept it in his wallet just in case.

At the reminder of the funny-ass stunt she'd pulled, which he was still brainstorming a proportionate payback for, Emma smothered a laugh and finally stopped looking so darn worried over his delicate hide.

He picked up one of the fresh cookies she'd put on his chest earlier. It was still warm from the oven. "Did you get cleared to bake already? I thought you had to wait for the town inspection after we're done with all the repairs."

"I do. I'm still shut down from cooking commercially, but I have a few projects I'm involved in that are not commercial." She pointed at a big box of cookies she'd left by the door. "Every week I donate several batches of cookies to the local youth center for snacks and volunteers. The director is so busy because that place runs from five in the morning to ten at night, six days a week. So this is the usual time she comes by for pickup."

He shook his head. "Just when I think you can't get any sweeter." Grinning over that irrepressible heart of gold of hers, he took a big bite of the cookie.

And grew still as a statue.

"What's wrong?" Emma sat forward, alarmed. "Are you okay?"

Jake took another bite, feeling untethered in time for a brief moment, before he finished chewing. Swallowing, he said almost reverently, "This is the cookie you made for me and my family the day we moved in. You came over and announced they were peanut butter and jelly shortbread cookies . . . and we all thought you were a little nutty until we tasted them."

There was no mistaking the melted home-churned peanut butter and freshly picked jelly filling, which married perfectly with the crisp shortbread. Each bite sent him right back to that summer.

"That's actually the first time I created the recipe for this cookie. I can't believe you remember that."

"Sweetheart, I remember everything about you."

A delighted, gushing "Awww" from somewhere in the middle of the street broke up the moment. And had them scrambling to get out of the truck.

Emma hopped out first and headed right over to the woman in her midforties standing a few feet away from his truck, hands clasped to her chest, sappy smile melting all over them.

"Gloria! I'm so sorry—I didn't even see you."

"No, no. You stay there, I'll come back after I finish getting the cookies into the car," she called out as she turned back around to her station wagon to finish loading up the box of cookies Emma had packed. After slamming the wagon door shut, Gloria made her way over again. "I noticed you two sitting here while I was picking up the cookies, so I'd walked over to say hi. Didn't mean to eavesdrop, and I certainly didn't mean to interrupt anything." Gloria waved his way. "Hi, I'm Gloria. I run the youth center here in Juniper Hills."

"Pleasure to meet you. I'm Jake. Emma's carpenter."

"Oh, *you're* the carpenter! I've heard so much about you!" She looked back at Emma with a smile. "Again, sorry, I couldn't help but overhear—I promise I wasn't doing it on purpose. But I think it's so great that you two grew up together. Were you high school sweethearts? How wonderful that you're also going to be working on Megan's library as—"

Jake barely heard the rest of Gloria's run-on questions. All he could focus on was the distraught look on Emma's face, the way she was wringing her hands, the lost shadows in her eyes while she stared hollowly before her as if one of her nightmares were playing out in real life.

Normally he'd let her handle this sort of thing since this was her town, but she looked as though she was seconds from coming apart at the seams. "Emma and I never went to high school together." Technically true—he'd been sent away to juvie before he'd been able to start. "I met Emma a really long time ago. And actually, we haven't seen each other since."

There. Vague but complete. With just enough info to satisfy and stem questions.

"Oh." Gloria laughed lightly. "Sorry, I guess I let my imagination run a bit there. When I heard what you said, I thought you were reunited sweethearts with this amazing backstory."

Not exactly amazing. I sort of killed her younger brother and scarred her younger sister before we lost touch for fourteen years.

Yeah, too much information.

When a fog of awkwardness fell on them, Gloria looked back and forth from him to the now-silent Emma. "I'm so sorry—was it something I said? My husband is always telling me to look left and right before I go shoving my big foot in my mouth."

"No." Jake shook his head reassuringly. "You're fine. We're figuring some things out."

Emma finally seemed to snap out of the trance she'd been in. "We didn't exactly part on the best of terms the first time around. Which is why we've kept that part to ourselves."

Gloria nodded vigorously in understanding. "Say no more. I completely understand. We all have a past. Again, I am so sorry to have eavesdropped. It wasn't intentional. And don't worry—I won't say a word." She walked over to give Emma a quick hug. "Smart thinking keeping this under wraps. Frankly, I make a point to never let the town biddies know any of my business." She made a zipping motion over her lips. "My lips are sealed."

Gloria checked her watch and then started hustling back over to her car. "I gotta run to open up the center. Jake, it was great meeting you. Emma, thanks again so much for baking even with all the repairs and things. I swear, some of these kids come to the center *just* to eat your cookies."

Emma managed a smile for Gloria as she sped away.

After they were alone again, Jake came up behind Emma and put a hand on her shoulder, squeezing gently. "Are you okay?"

She nodded faintly. "I'm fine. I wasn't prepared is all. But you handled it great. Thank you for jumping in."

"No worries. Gloria seems nice."

She still wouldn't meet his gaze. "Yeah, Gloria's great. And we can trust her not to talk about us."

"Do you want to?" he asked, smoothing a thumb over her jawline. "Talk about us, I mean? Or talk about anything?"

Please. Please let us talk. Really talk.

Though there was more hesitation than she'd ever displayed before, eventually a quick head shake and a plastered-on smile were Emma's reply. "It's all good. We're good." He could tell she was focusing her eyes on a spot somewhere next to his head.

It was all he could do not to drag her into his arms and just hold her. She looked lost. Not even her grip on her three floral pendants seemed to be grounding her on this one.

He was afraid the reality of their past colliding into their present may have very well broken her. Broken any chance he'd thought they'd had to move forward. "Talk to me, Emma. We can go right back to being Jake and Emma 2.0 afterward I swear. But just talk to me."

Every second of silence that followed deflated his hope.

A full minute passed.

And then . . . "Do you want to know why I always have Gloria pick up the cookies from me?" she asked softly, catching him by surprise. "I could just as easily drop the box off to her, but I arranged to have her pick it up instead. Do you want to know why?"

He'd figured it was just because she was busy with the bakery in the mornings, but clearly there was something more. "Only if you want to tell me."

"I started doing the cookie thing years ago. And in the beginning, when I'd go to drop off the box, with all the kids at the center, every once in a while, I'd see a boy there who I would swear on my own life was Peyton. Or an older boy, who looked just how I imagined Peyton would look at that age." She rubbed her hands over her arms, shaking her head when he offered her his jacket. "I'm not cold." Even as she said it a shiver quaked across her frame.

Jake didn't push. He knew all too well what that was like, enduring the bad side effects that came with the memories. On his part, it would feel a bit like penance at times. A toll fee at others. He'd found over the years that the memories never came without some price.

When her body finally stopped trembling, she continued. "I wouldn't see Peyton all the time. But when I did, it would take every bit of restraint I had to convince myself the mirage wasn't real. That it wouldn't be okay for me to run up to that random kid and hug him like he was my dead brother brought back to life."

"*Emma—*"

She shook her head again. *Right. No comfort. The price to pay.*

"But that's not even the worst part," she whispered. "Do you want to know what is?"

He was certain it would be worse than he could ever have imagined. But he asked anyway, for her. "What was the worst part?"

"That in the moment when I'd first see Peyton again, for the briefest of seconds, I'd be so happy, so relieved that he made it out of that fire alive."

He frowned. "Of course you would. Sweetheart, anyone would."

She simply shook her head. Over and over again. "Don't you see? If Peyton had survived, then that means *Megan* would be the one lying in the grave right now."

That blow coldcocked him out of nowhere. *Jesus Christ. Is this what she's been carrying around for all these years?*

Her voice cracked and withered. "So it's not okay for me to feel that way." The tears broke free, and shame filled her features. "That's why I stopped letting myself. I trained myself not to feel. If ever I'd see Peyton's little face among those kids, I'd *make* myself not be happy. Not be relieved. Not even for a second." She stared at the ground, shoulders sagging from the weight of that, a weight she should never have had to bear. "After a while, it just got too hard, so I stopped going to the center. And that's when I asked Gloria to start picking up the cookies."

"Emma." He speared his hands through her hair and gently tilted her face up to his. "Honey, I know it seems like that's the way you should feel, but it's not. It's okay to want your brother to have survived that fire. That doesn't mean you think, for even a second, that the opposite scenario between your siblings is even remotely okay."

He could see she didn't believe him. He wondered if she could even hear him right now. She looked as if she were drowning in her grief right before his eyes.

"Have you talked to Megan about this?"

That jolted her back to awareness. She tore herself out of his grasp. "Of course not. How can I possibly tell her any of this? I'm all she has, Jake. At least Peyton had his mom. So Megan needs me not to feel that way for even a second. Because Peyton had his mom wishing, out loud, that it had been Megan and not Peyton who'd died in that fire."

A horrified sound broke out of his chest. *"What?"*

Emma blinked, startled over the vehemence in his growl. She took a step back. He followed.

"Emma, did your stepmom do that? Say that to you? Or to Megan?"

A mask fell over her face. And she retreated behind a wall he couldn't breach.

"Emma, tell me. Did she? Did you hear your stepmom say that?"

"Yes." Eyes dull with pain met his. "She used to tell me that it was all my fault, that I killed her son. And she used to say it should've been Megan and not Peyton. She never told Megan that, but she told me. Over and over."

"She was wrong." He could barely keep the rage out of his voice. His dad may have sent him to juvie, but he never did anything like this. What Emma's stepmother had done, even if it had been done out of sadness and anguish, was cruel. Abusive. "She should never have said that to you, Emma. That woman had no right to say those things to you."

"She said them about you, too," she whispered. "Over. And over."

Jake backed up a step, forgetting for maybe the first time in his life the path he'd chosen, the burden he'd taken on when he'd falsified that confession. "Maybe I deserve her saying that about me. But not you. Never you. You did nothing wrong, Emma. And Megan's life should never have been talked about so callously. I don't care how much that woman was grieving. No one's life is expendable for another's."

The uncanny parallels between their situations wasn't lost on him. That this was a thousand times worse than anything he'd been made to endure slayed him.

"I didn't tell you all this so you'd feel sorry for me, Jake. Or so you'd try to fix me." She took in a deep breath. Then another. Soon the color returned to her face, as did the life to her eyes. But along with it came new, stronger, hundred-foot-tall walls between them.

"I told you all this so you would understand why I *need* to keep to our Jake and Emma 2.0 arrangement. Why I can't let the past seep into my present." Her voice hitched, but she finished firm. "Not even for the briefest second."

That single resolute statement shifted the ground under him. Almost sent him to his knees. Yes, he did understand now.

"You promised me we could go back to our arrangement after I talked," she whispered softly. "Did you mean that? Can we go back to being the two strangers who don't have all this behind us?"

She spared him the pain of asking him outright if he could keep his promise this time.

Unlike that night.

"Of course, Emma. We're right back where we were before you told me all that."

She looked at him as if measuring his level of honesty, her level of trust. "Good," she said after a few long beats. "Then we should probably get started with our day."

Just like that.

When they both stepped forward to head toward the bakery, Emma halted and made a quick snapping motion as if she'd just remembered something. "You know what? Paul mentioned he's ready for you to start ordering supplies for the library." Casual and breezy. She was pulling it off well. "Since you worked all night on the floors, why don't you take the morning off and head over to the library? I'm not going to be here anyway."

It was a flimsy way to put some space between them and they both knew it, but this was the first time the fire had come up since he'd started working here. There was no manual for this sort of thing. He wanted to give her time. Space.

Didn't mean he couldn't hate it.

He studied her distant expression, *willed* her to look up at him.

She wouldn't.

"You sure you don't want me in the bakery this morning?"

He'd chosen his words carefully. Want, not need. He didn't want her to just need him there; he needed her to *want* him there, too.

"I'm sure. Go make brilliant plans and order fabulous things at the library. I'll see you after lunch." Her new smile, though dim and fading, was at least genuine.

"Okay," he said softly, squeezing her shoulder one more time. "I'll check in at the library and then be back in a few hours."

They split off to head in different directions.

In more ways than one.

Chapter Sixteen

Emma glanced at the clock again. Then checked her phone. Again.

He'd been gone almost six hours now.

The incident earlier had been bad, yes, but she hadn't expected Jake to plumb not return. Even the mere thought that he was purposefully staying away was a blow to the gut. They were supposed to be able to bounce back to being Jake and Emma 2.0.

He promised.

Unable to stop herself, she quickly locked up and jogged over to the library with a Ziploc bag of cookies for Megan as her lame excuse, even though she knew Megan wouldn't be at the construction site since she was at a book fair talking to some local authors.

"Hey, Emma," called out one of the construction guys, whose kid brother, Timmy, loved coming in with his friends to window-shop and taste samples. Unlike his friends, though, Nick's little brother would gather up his coins to buy a cupcake every so often. When his friends weren't with him. She suspected there was a girl Timmy was sweet on, and he didn't want his third-grade classmates to tease him.

Nick hopped off the bed of a pickup truck as it backed into a stall in front of the library. A few other guys from Paul's crew jumped out, as well, and waved.

"Hey, Nick." She gave him an affectionate hug and ruffled his hair. "Jeez, when are you going to stop growing? I swear you're at least another foot taller than you were in high school."

"Don't remind me. I was also like forty pounds heavier." He flexed an arm and patted his abs proudly. "Working on Paul's crew for the past two years, I'm in better shape now than when I was playing football."

While his three buddies began ribbing him about still being the runt of their crew, Emma peered through the windows of the library, trying to see if she could spot Jake. "Hey, do you know if Jake is still around? He was supposed to come back to the bakery a while ago. I know he and Paul were going to work on a supplies list, though, so I wasn't sure if he was here or over at the lumberyard or something."

Nick shrugged. "Don't know. I actually just got here myself. Me and a few of the other guys have been out prepping another job site. Want me to find him for you?" He pulled open the door to the library and paused to scan the area alongside her.

Emma noticed then how the banging and buzzing and chatter came to a slow halt.

Nick did, too. After exchanging a few silent looks with the guys on-site, he turned to try to usher Emma back out the door. "You know what? Why don't you wait outside where it's less crazy, and I'll track him down for you."

"What's going on, Nick?" She watched him pale a bit as one of the guys whispered something to him she couldn't hear. "Tell me. I won't leave until you do."

He exhaled heavily. "Okay, but I don't know all the details yet, so don't freak out. An ambulance came for Jake a little while ago."

Dread filled her veins with ice. "Wait, Jake got injured?" The room began spinning and shrinking all around her as panic clawed at her from the inside out. "What happened?" She very nearly decked the poor guy when he didn't answer quickly enough.

Steve, one of the old-timers on Paul's crew, stepped forward. "We'd been putting up a new structural support beam when one of the guys tore something pretty bad in his leg. He went down, and then it went like dominoes. The guy next to him got tipped over with the ladder, and that took out the guy holding up the center. It all went to shit from there. We lost control of the beam and the remaining guys couldn't stop it from crashing down onto Jake, who'd been off to the side helping us guide it up into the ceiling."

"*That* ceiling beam?" The exposed center wooden beam he was pointing at was at least three times thicker than the other ceiling joists around it and well over twenty feet long, spanning the entire length of the room.

She remembered when something about half that size was installed in her bakery, the guys had mentioned it weighing more than four hundred pounds. Blocking her mind's eye from visualizing that giant beam falling on Jake, she armed herself with questions. "Was he wearing a hard hat? What did the paramedics say? Where the heck is Paul?"

Steve was quick to reassure her. "He had on a hard hat the entire time he was here, Emma. But that beam took eight of us guys to carry it. When it fell on Jake, even with the hard hat and half of us still bearing some of the weight, it knocked him out cold. That was about two hours ago, and last we heard, he still hasn't woken up."

Oh God. "Which hospital is he in? Connelly Memorial?"

"Yeah. Paul's over there now if you want to call and get an update. You look shaken up. Why don't you let one of us drive you there—"

She was already out the door.

Please be okay. Please be okay. Please be okay.

Emma wasn't sure if she pressed on the brakes once in the entire twenty-minute drive to the hospital. She definitely had no clue which lot she'd parked her car in. And it was possible that her ears were ringing right now because she'd been shouting so loudly at the folks manning the ER after they'd informed her that Jake was being transported between floors so his room information wasn't updated.

It wasn't until Paul finally found her and brought her to Jake's bedside that she felt her lungs fill with air again, her brain registering coherent thought.

"There's blood," she gasped, seeing Jake's unconscious form lying there with patches of dry blood marring his neck and parts of the hospital gown he'd been dressed in. "Why is there blood? Steve said Jake had a hard hat on."

She had no idea why she was fixating on that. She knew the hard hat wasn't some magical force field, but for some reason, she was clinging to the hope that in this situation, for this man, it was.

Paul squeezed her shoulder and tried to get her to sit down. "He did. But the corner of the beam nicked his ear and scraped up the side of his face some. All minor. They just haven't had a chance to clean him up yet because they were running MRIs and some other brain scans."

Brain scans.

She felt her stomach drop to her feet and her heart crack wide-open in undiluted panic. "Were the test results okay? What did the doctors say?" She stared at Jake's rugged face, seeing now the bruise forming along his jawline and the small bandage covering the tip of his right ear.

"It's a concussion for sure, but no skull fracture, and no brain bleeding or swelling. They also scanned his neck and spine and said they didn't find any damage."

"But they can't wake him up?"

"No. They say his brain needs time to recover from the trauma. Some folks wake up in a few hours, others in a few days. We just have to let him rest and heal. But the doctors are pretty confident that he'll be just fine."

Emma was having a hard time hearing anything beyond the scariest parts of that explanation. Trauma. Days to wake up.

What if he doesn't wake up at all?

She finally took Paul's offer to sit. Or rather, she pretty much fell back into the chair he'd slid under her. She scooted the seat as close to Jake's bed as possible and closed her hand over his. "You better hope you're in that first category and not the second," she whispered fiercely, even as she found herself begging the universe to be merciful rather than raging at it as she had for so many years after the fire. *Prayer, confession, whatever it takes,* she silently promised whatever higher power was listening in.

All the while she kept her voice strong and steady for Jake's ears. "If you stay asleep for a few days, I'll kick your butt when you wake up, banged up noggin or not." When he didn't crack open those beautiful sage-green eyes of his and smile at her only partly real threat, she put her head down against his shoulder lightly and closed her eyes.

Not really sure she'd be good at the praying thing, she tried confession instead.

I can't lose him again.

Over the next few hours, she heard nurses and some of the guys on Paul's crew filing in and out of the room. She even heard Megan calling her name. But Emma couldn't bring herself to lift her eyelids. The warmth of his body under the blanket and the slow rise and fall of his chest were the only two things her brain wanted to process. Nothing else around her mattered.

She eventually fell asleep that way, refusing to let go of his hand regardless of how many people tried to pull her away from him.

Emma remembered what it was like, how scared and confused she'd been waking up alone in the hospital after the fire. Nothing around her made sense; the only thing she had with her in that cold, empty room to ground her were her jumbled memories of what had happened before she lost consciousness.

The more awake she got, the faster the flashes of chaotic images from the fire came. And with them came longer stretches of nothingness where memories *should* have been.

She remembered how those void-filled pockets in her brain had been even scarier than the horrifying images.

Her own voice had been the only thing that sounded remotely familiar. And even that voice had been jagged and out of sorts when she'd called out to the nurses she could see through the glass-paneled walls of her room.

She had always thought it was so strange when movie characters in hospital scenes would wake up and call out, "Hello?" As if they were strangers knocking on an open door and announcing their presence. Or aliens arriving on a new planet.

But that night in that hospital bed, with nothing and no one around her that she recognized, she'd been unable to come up with a better first word to utter, either.

She didn't care how long he took to come to; she wasn't leaving his side. She was *going* to be there when Jake finally woke up and felt that strange urge to call out, "Hello?"

So she could say hi back.

Jake woke up feeling like a wrecking ball had smashed into his head.

But judging by the sight of Emma fast asleep in a chair beside his hospital bed, her head lying across his stomach, one hand clutching her talisman-like pendants, one hand holding his, he'd say the wrecking ball had been worth it.

Even though the sluggish feelings in his body told him he was on some kind of pain meds, his head still hurt like crazy. *Must be a concussion.*

It wasn't his first, so he knew to run through his memories to see if there were any holes. Thankfully there weren't. As soon as he determined that, he quit thinking about the past and focused on the present with Emma here *almost* in his arms.

What was that saying about gifts in the present?

He blinked through his pain-med fog and gave up trying to be all philosophical. Instead he just slid his fingers through that soft, glossy hair of hers, marveling over seeing it spread across his hospital bed, out of the ponytail or French braid she usually had it in.

He still remembered the one and only time he'd seen her hair down back when they were teens. She'd been sitting out on her back porch taming all that naturally sun-kissed caramel-brown hair into a long braid that went down to her waist.

He'd waited until she was done before going over to introduce himself.

Funny how it had taken fourteen years *and a concussion* for him to see it wild and free again. Again, totally worth it.

The nurse and doctor on duty came in shortly after to confirm the concussion theory and give him a quick once-over. All the while, Emma slept on.

"She didn't leave your side once," said the nurse softly as she brought him some much-appreciated water for his parched throat. "She's a fierce little sweetheart."

Yeah, that sounds about right.

Two more nurse check-ins and one muted basketball game later, Emma woke with a start.

She gasped. "Your eyes are open."

Even through the pain, he managed to smile at her reverent murmur. "So are yours. Been waiting to see those beautiful baby blues for a while now."

She blinked and looked out the window.

"How long have you been awake? Should I call the nurse?"

"Settle down, sweetheart. She came in already. They actually managed to check me out while you were sleeping—apparently you gave them a lot of practice doing that yesterday. Something about you being glued to my side all day and all night?"

She pointedly ignored his question and returned with one of her own. "Why don't you have any contact info for your siblings? We tried to look through your phone to find them, but there weren't any listings for a Daryn or a Haley."

"Haley doesn't have a phone. She's kind of like a modern-day gypsy. She buys prepaid phones whenever she travels, which she is right now. Sometimes she'll settle down for long enough to get a more expensive prepaid phone with Internet and stuff, but that only happened twice in the past five years. Other than that, if I need to get in contact with her, I usually just call her apartment super."

"What about Daryn?"

"Daryn's in my phone. Did you look his name up correctly?"

"There was only one Daryn, and I checked his number three times."

He frowned. "That's odd." He flipped through his call log and saw that she had in fact called the right Daryn. "It's this one. Did he not answer?"

"Nope. A girl answered. She was a little peculiar sounding. Superintense. Asking me all sorts of questions. She told me there was a Daryn that used to live there but didn't anymore, so to never call back again."

Jake sighed. "You had the right Daryn. That woman you talked to is his . . . friend, for lack of a better term. It's complicated. Basically, when she's off her meds, she gets a little confused. I'm sure Daryn didn't even know she had his phone; I'll be sure to tell him."

At her unwavering scowl, he squeezed her hand gently. "What's wrong?"

"I'm still mad at them. They're your siblings. They should've been here the whole time. They should've been at a phone where I could call them and tell them about what happened to you. They should've rushed their butts over here so you could hear their voices, and—"

166

"Hey, hey. Calm down. It's all right. Now you know it wasn't their fault. Trust me—they would've come down here if they'd known. They would've been glued to the seats next to you."

That seemed to work at slowing her breathing. "I just . . . didn't want you to be alone." Unshed tears filled her eyes. "What if you—"

"But I didn't," he interrupted quickly. "I'm fine. And I got to wake up to see a real live angel sleeping beside me. So I think I'm better than fine."

"Good news," boomed a voice shortly before the curtain in front of his door slid open. "We're probably going to be able to discharge you today." The loud, friendly nurse he'd met earlier when she'd come in to do some blood tests scribbled something on his chart and checked his blood pressure. "Just got your blood work back; all your numbers look great. The doctor will be by to chat with you in a bit, but in the meantime, I'm just going to go over some discharge info with you."

She began ticking through her list. "You'll need to take it easy for the next twenty-four hours. No going back to work, and no driving for the next forty-eight hours. I know you're a carpenter, but no returning to any sort of heavy lifting or strenuous work until next week. Period. Do you have someone to drive you home?"

"He's going to stay in my apartment with me," replied Emma without even a moment's hesitation. "So I'll drive him."

He raised a shocked brow at her but kept quiet as the nurse proceeded to tell Emma about his home care for the next two days. Emma listened carefully and took notes on her phone the entire time.

The sweet woman was going to have his head woozy all over again.

As soon as the nurse left, Emma plumped his pillows and said matter-of-factly, "My sofa pulls out into a bed. It's actually really comfortable. I can sleep there, and you can take my bed."

"I'm not kicking you out of your own bed, sweetheart."

"No. You need the bed. You need to rest."

"I don't want to inconvenience you. I'm sure you have a ton of things to do with your bakery reopening just around the corner."

"No arguments. You're staying at my place, and that's all there is to it."

He grinned. "Is that so?"

Her lower lip trembled. "This is all my fault, Jake. I told you to go to the library because I couldn't deal with everything we'd talked about after Gloria left. If I hadn't done that, you wouldn't be in here right now and—"

"Stop." He gave her a hardened look. "I don't ever want to hear you say that. This was an accident."

God, the irony.

"But you got hurt because of me."

"Emma, I'm not sure about how the world works, and I'm not nearly as existentially grounded when it comes to life and fate as my sister, Haley, is, but I do believe that even if I hadn't gone to the library today and gotten hit by a beam when I did, then I would've maybe . . . I don't know, fell on my ass in a public restroom and knocked myself out on a filthy toilet."

Her lips twitched. "Don't try to make me feel better."

"I'm being serious. Either way, I would've ended up here with head trauma—I'm pretty sure that's how the universe works. This means you very likely redirected my course away from being found ass-up with my head in a toilet by a big, tatted biker dude named Python."

A reluctant giggle escaped her lips.

"This had nothing to do with you, honey. I didn't have to be in that part of the library helping with the beam. I actually shouldn't have gone over to assist at all since I'm not even on Paul's crew. That was my own dumb fault."

Emma didn't reply, but he could see she still wasn't letting it go.

So he went with the obvious move.

"Anyway, I maintain that I'm not going to stay at your place unless you let me have your sofa." At her mutinous pout, he tossed out, "If that's not cool with you, I can always just catch a cab all the way back to my lonely apartment. Or maybe see if I can try to find which state Haley's in right now—I'm sure it's not far. And if all else fails, I'm sure Daryn and his—"

"Fine! I won't give up the bed."

Ah, that temper of hers. Worked every time.

She chewed on her lip for a bit before suggesting softly, "I do have a king-size bed that's kind of ginormous. There's no reason we can't *both* sleep in it."

Holy hell.

"That's probably better," she reasoned. "Because if something happens, I'll be right there. If you're all the way over on the sofa, I might not get to you in time to help."

He'd been up to her apartment repairing the subfloor after the flood. She was right; those twenty or so steps from her bed to the sofa were a pretty long and treacherous trek.

"I mean, it's just for one or two nights. I was pretty much lying half on top of you last night in this bed and it was no big deal."

"True." Was she really expecting him to object to having her in his arms? *Silly rabbit.*

"And from what I gathered, you don't snore."

"And on my part, I could probably just get some earplugs," he teased.

She whacked him. "I don't snore!"

He chuckled. She actually did. Just a tiny bit. Kind of like a soft kitten purr. But he kept that to himself.

"Okay," he conceded magnanimously. "I'll sleep in your bed with you, since you insist."

A riled-up little pout scrunched her nose.

"One thing, though, in case you find yourself half on top of me like you did last night, could you maybe sleep on my chest instead of my stomach?"

She gasped and ran her hand along his abs. "Oh my God, I'm so sorry. Is it painful? Is my head heavy?"

Something was getting a little painful. And heavy, for that matter. Maybe a solid seven or eight on the scale of one to blue.

Thank goodness the meds they'd given him earlier were starting to kick in. If they were effective with head issues at command central north, they had to work some on command central south, right? A tiny bit sluggish now—though only physically because mentally, he was clearly razor-sharp—he grabbed her hands to stop her from continuing to pet his abs in apology.

About two seconds too late.

"Oh!" Emma jumped back, staring at the front of his hospital gown as if it were going to bite her. But not necessarily in a bad way. He made a drowsy mental note to revisit that.

"Yeah. That's why I figure it'd be better if you sleep on my chest. So it won't be as . . . hard on me." He grinned muzzily.

She rolled her eyes in amazement. "You are such a perv. How can you even get it up when you were basically knocked out cold for almost two days?"

"I don't get this way on my own, missy." His voice felt thick as a fast-approaching sleepy haze started to fuzz all around him. Shifting his head to that perfect pocket he'd found in the pillow earlier, he blinked at her as the room got blurrier. "Whenever you're around, I'm never far from the corner of hot and bothered."

He'd been hoping for a blush, but her pleased smile was even better.

Eventually he had to close his eyes for a bit again. Having Emma around definitely helped with the pain, but he had to admit, his head felt as if it were twice its normal size. Without thinking much about it—or anything for that matter—he intertwined his fingers with hers, finding a nice little pocket fit there, as well.

After finding that comfy docking station for his hand, his subsequent blink turned into a failed mission; it simply felt like way too much work to lift his eyelids back up.

Before he knew it, he was out like a light.

The next time he woke, the sun was coming in stronger through the window blinds, and Emma had her head against his chest. Wide-awake.

"Hello," he murmured, rubbing his calloused thumb across her soft cheek.

For some reason that made her look up at him and gift him with a smile so radiant it warmed the entire room. "Hi."

Chapter Seventeen

Two nights later Emma climbed into her comfy king bed . . . and immediately felt Jake snuggle in behind her under the covers.

While this broke at least a dozen different boundary rules, she couldn't help but smile. "So you aren't even going to *pretend* to stay on your side of the bed tonight?"

"Really, don't we pretend enough as it is?"

Her brows shot up to her hairline. He was in it to win it tonight. "Well played."

"Thanks."

She *felt* that sexy grin of his against her shoulder and instantly her resolve dissolved like sugar in water. Seeing the man's rugged beard when he smiled was bad enough. But *feeling* that masculine pelt rubbing against her skin was worse. Panties-catching-on-fire worse.

They really shouldn't be doing this. Pretending not to have a shared past was one thing. Playing house and sleeping—just sleeping—in the same bed was a whole different, far more dangerous thing. She had to be strong. "Maybe you should take the futon sofa tonight."

He made a rumbling noise in his throat that sounded like a cross between an incredulous scoff and an indignant grunt. "That lasted all of twenty minutes last night." The next sound was definitely more of a grumbling rumble. "Twenty minutes we could've spent cuddling."

Had it been that long?

"Okay, it was more like ten minutes," he amended.

She grinned.

"Ten minutes before you broke down and threw yourself at me," he clarified, lips brushing against the back of her neck with every word.

Took her a while to get all the tingling to simmer down enough for her to fully register what he'd just said.

"I did no such thing!" She elbowed him in the stomach.

He scored her earlobe with his teeth.

She fitted every inch of her back against his front and gave him a full-body cat stretch.

He groaned, long and low. "Damn, woman, you fight dirty."

"Let that be a lesson to you."

"Lesson learned." The two words were whisper-weapons wielded against her skin, joined by the sliding of his calloused hand over her belly. But he didn't stop there. His warm, rough fingers continued its journey and splayed out wide, his thumb just barely skimming below the hem of her tank top. Not enough for her to call him on it. But definitely enough to distract her beyond saving.

"Touché," she muttered.

His lips curved up and slid over her hair in a barely there kiss. "Go to sleep. The longer you stay up, the longer I do." He shifted his hips against hers to demonstrate his point.

Why was this a bad idea again?

In slow increments, she let her body relax and melt against him like molasses. Dammit, why did he have to be such a perfect fit? She'd never, in her whole life, slept better than she had last night in his arms. If she wasn't careful, she'd get addicted to it. Start craving it. Needing it.

She might never be able to sleep without his arms around her again.

Maybe that was the evil genius's plan all along.

"You do know that after the doctor clears you, we're going to go back to how things were prior to you sleeping in my bed, right?" she asked, trying her best to keep them both hitched to the reality of the situation before she went and did something crazy.

Like break down and throw herself at him.

Because truth be told, last night if he hadn't made the first move and slipped under the covers to pull her into his arms, she would've joined him on the futon and done the same.

He just broke first.

When he ignored her question and continued to draw in slow, deep breaths to try to get to sleep, she pressed on. "Jake, you know this is just during your recovery—"

"Shhh," he interrupted.

She snapped her mouth shut. And then turned to him in disbelief. "I can't believe you just shushed me."

"It was either that or kiss you silent."

Was it wrong that she was wholly disappointed he hadn't chosen the latter?

"Are we not going to talk about it?"

"We can definitely talk about it," he murmured, his voice no longer teasing. "Or rather, the Jake and Emma who didn't just meet the other week can."

Fair enough. She turned over and put her hands over his when he wrapped his arms around her.

Even though he didn't push, she felt the tension still vibrating through his frame.

"I would've kissed you back if you'd kissed me," she admitted quietly.

"I know, sweetheart." His arms finally started relaxing around her, before flexing to pull her in closer. "That's why I shushed you instead."

For Jake, resting and recuperating for two whole days—the first time he'd really slowed down in working memory—had been great. Especially the part where he'd been able to hold Emma in his arms each night.

But by the next day, he had to return to reality, and his apartment, for one very basic reason. His siblings had all seemingly lost their damn minds.

After eventually learning about Emma's call from the hospital, Daryn had apparently been searching for Jake ever since. The only problem was that Jake just plain hadn't noticed his cell phone was dead until yesterday; it was not as if he got a lot of calls usually. When he finally did notice, he'd of course gone out to his truck to recharge the phone, and that was when he heard the eleventy million voice mails from all three of his siblings.

Yes, he was now officially including Carter in that bunch.

But that was a can of wormlike emotions he was saving for a rainy day to open.

By the time he got to the last message, he heard his baby sister threatening to order an APB out on his ass if he didn't call one of them back. Taking a shot in the dark, he'd called his own apartment first. Sure enough, he'd found a hysterical Haley there to answer.

Next came his call to Daryn to cancel the panicked missing persons report they'd filed.

Then Jake spent most of the three-hour drive home back on the phone with Haley, who launched a full-tactical interrogation about Emma, interspersed with verbal slaps upside his head for—irony of ironies—going off the grid without a way for anyone to contact him. After that, he and Haley had a fun night eating takeout and catching up while he repaired the two gaping holes she had made in the drywall next to his front door to break into his apartment. He didn't ask for details on why his baby sis knew to do that, or how she managed to accomplish it without any obvious tools; suffice it to say that for a girl who lived the modern hippie-gypsy lifestyle, she'd always been viciously protective of her brothers.

Good times.

The next morning, with three finally calm siblings, a just-acquired clean bill of health from his doctor, and no more than a mild lingering headache, Jake drove back down to Juniper Hills at around ten with grand plans for an excitement-free day finishing up the last of the repair work on the bakery . . . which he bid a quick farewell to the second he saw Emma zipping around in the middle of what looked like some sort of baking meltdown.

While five men and one woman he recognized from around town watched her in visibly concerned silence.

"Ohmigod, ohmigod. We're not going to finish in time!" cried out Emma while simultaneously popping a miniature cake the size of a softball out of a baking tin with one hand and mixing up more cake batter with the other.

The guys had their hands up in the ready position as if they were waiting for the kickoff in a touch football game, while the woman was slowly inching her way out of the kitchen.

"What's all this?" Jake walked over to Charlie, the single dad who ran the hardware store in town, since he knew him best. Before Charlie could reply, they both ducked to avoid a blob of bright-blue frosting flying right past their heads.

"The party! The girls! They're so looking forward to this!" Emma's frenzied answer to his question sounded strung together by a thin cord of sanity. "Anabelle already told all her little friends that they're each getting personalized cakes designed to match the Disney princess they're coming dressed up as!"

Judging by the double-oven door hanging on its hinge, the dozen or so ruined cakes in the sink, and all the bright-colored frosting decorating her hair and the tip of her nose, he was going to assume she'd had a rough morning.

"Honey. Breathe." He edged over to her like he would a manic wild animal doing somersaults from tree to tree. "Just take a deep breath and tell me what's going on. From the beginning, so I can catch up."

The closer he got to her, the more vigorously the five men in the room shook their heads to warn him. The woman just held her hand over her eyes as if expecting a massacre.

Seriously, what the hell happened here this morning?

As if hearing his unspoken question, Emma began talking at a mile-a-minute speed. He got a few face splatters of cake batter and frosting during her animated retelling of the morning's events surrounding her now-broken double oven, a bunch of supertechnical baking reasons why her big industrial oven and the space-age silver monstrosity she called her pie oven weren't suited for smaller cakes, and how she was nowhere near finished baking the thirty minicakes she needed to have ready by noon for a five-year-old's birthday party.

"Sweetheart, I don't understand. I thought you weren't cleared to cater yet. Did you get an early building inspection or something?"

"This isn't a catering job. We're all doing this for Megan's boss."

At her use of "all," the men's football-ready hands instantly flattened out to look more like they were being held hostage in a stickup.

Jake looked over at Charlie again questioningly.

"Dennis and his wife are throwing a birthday party for their daughter, Anabelle, and her friends today, but the forty minicakes they'd ordered didn't get delivered," explained Charlie.

"That baker should be strung up by her apron strings!" called out Emma.

Whoa.

While it was admittedly cute to hear her still be so adorably PG even when she was viciously pissed, Jake wasn't foolish enough to smile. He just nodded in agreement instead.

"Dennis was one of our very first friends when we moved into town, Jake, not to mention the one who'd first given Megan a part-time

177

job back when she was barely speaking in public, and also the one who started her on the road to her dream career as a librarian in the first place."

She did a track-star-worthy hurdle over some broken oven parts to get to what looked like a giant toaster oven to slide another two mini-cake tins out. "Even if I didn't owe him literally everything for what he's done for Megan, I just hate letting my friends down," she exclaimed as she used a giant cookie pan to fan the pint-size cake. "Did I mention Megan and I are little Anabelle's godmothers? And that Megan's boss and his wife had tried to get pregnant for *ten* years before they were finally blessed with Anabelle?"

She scurried over to the counter to whip up two bowls of frosting, one purple and one pink, before rolling flat a white Play-Doh-looking ball and quickly using a cookie cutter to make a bunch of tiny flower cutouts. "Worst of all, a little girl's dream princess party is hanging in the balance if I don't finish these cakes!"

Jake calmly walked over to the sink and washed his hands. Then he put on a frilly apron and grabbed a bunch of kitchen utensils that looked sort of like the long putty knives he used to spackle holes in the walls on job sites.

He started passing them out to the guys.

Emma screeched to a halt and gaped at him. "What are you doing?"

"Helping." He spun the two putty knives in his hands like an old Western gunslinger. "You and Marie over there can focus on baking the last of the cakes, and the guys and I will take care of the frosting—looks as straightforward as mixing grout or mortar. We'll just lay the foundation and spackle it on the cakes for you before you finish 'em up all pretty."

Shoulders sagging in both disbelief and relief, she blinked at him. "Ohmigod, that might actually work."

"Of course it will."

"Uh . . ." voiced Marie from about as far away as she could be while still technically in the kitchen. "I'm not so sure you want me around the cakes. Tried-and-true recipes and even the simplest dishes seem to have mysteriously tragic outcomes around me. There's a reason why my husband does all the cooking."

Jake liked Marie's husband. He was a good guy. Fantastic with Marie's two girls from her first marriage.

"Not just that." Marie pointed at herself and the other five guys. "We weren't sent here because we're the best suited for the job. We're all the rejects from the party. All the other parents have mad skills with crafts and face painting and balloon animals and stuff."

"Yup." Charlie nodded. "We have no skills. The party is starting soon, so all the other parents have their big, important jobs. We were the only ones who could be spared."

"I usually have one job at these parties, and that's to keep an even variety of Capri Sun juice packs in the cooler throughout the day," added Zeb, the oldest in the bunch, who had three daughters, if memory served. "As soon as the cake fiasco was announced, my wife dumped all the juice packs in a kiddie pool with ice and told me my job wasn't a real thing before shoving me out the door with strict instructions to help but don't touch anything."

"Hey, my wife told me the same thing," chimed in Dominic, a funny dude Jake hadn't had a chance to get to talk to more than a few times. "Then she went and assigned my six-year-old nephew my usual party task . . . as if I hadn't been voted the best gift-table present stacker ever at the last party."

The remaining two guys praised them for having had roles instead of sitting on the sidelines like they'd done at the last couple of parties.

These guys were a freaking hoot.

Jake wasn't much for making friends outside his construction circle, especially not with the dad group. But he could see himself hanging out with these guys.

One day.

When he had a kid and wife so he could join the club.

His eyes strayed over to Emma. The woman was *made* to be a mom. A great mom. The kind who would run herself ragged to single-handedly make cakes for forty girls, even if she ended up destroying her entire kitchen in the process.

Jake turned back to the motley crew before him. "Well, come on then. Let's get in there and save the day."

Marie shook her head soberly. "All kidding aside, our spouses are right. We really should be sticking to the more hands-*off* helping."

"I disagree," Jake informed them with a smile as he handed Marie a piping bag. "You can handle the writing of all the girls' names on the cakes."

Marie paled and gave him a hell-no head shake. "Emma should handle that."

He raised a pointed brow over at the two finished two-tier cakes decorated like colorful little ball gowns. "Unless those first two party guests really are named Jamio and Biamca, I think you would definitely be helping Emma out there."

Emma gave him a huffy scowl. "My hands shake when I'm on adrenaline overload—so sue me."

Leaning in to whisper so only she could hear, he teased with a hidden grin. "What a coincidence—your hands shake when you're curled up in bed with me, too. Interesting."

He sidestepped to avoid getting clocked in the head with a batter-covered whisk.

While the now not-quite-as-stressed-looking Emma (thank you very much) was busy blushing and glaring, Jake grabbed the cookie pan she'd used to fan the cakes earlier. "Trent, I've seen you do those weighted rope workouts like a champ. You handle this cake fanning." He turned to Charlie next. "You can take care of adding the food coloring to the frosting to make the colors Emma needs; it's just like mixing latex paint colors at your shop."

It wasn't at all the same, but Charlie looked loads more confident after hearing that.

Jake winked at Emma. "Don't worry, babe. We've got your back on this."

For the next two hours, they all got into a synchronized-swimming-like rhythm, where Emma took care of baking the minicakes to perfection and doing the fancy decorations, while the others did their assigned tasks that helped keep them all churning 'em out.

Zeb ended up being a surprise star in the cake assembly, using his experience laying brick and tile to mortar and grout the cake layers like a pro.

And at the end of the assembly line was Jake, who used his make-Martha-Stewart-proud, two-putty-knife technique to spackle the frosting on nearly as prettily as Emma did.

And in between cakes, he took care of his other job, which was calming Emma down with inappropriate jokes, all in the name of getting her to blush harder than she was freaking out.

At a quarter after noon, they were officially done.

He and Emma collapsed onto the nearest bench in exhaustion, shortly after Marie and the guys transported the finished cakes back to the party.

After a few minutes of satisfying silence, she lifted her head sluggishly off his shoulder and murmured gratefully, "You were amazing today, Jake. There's no way we would have finished without you taking control of the situation. Seriously, I don't know how to thank you."

"Group effort all the way." He turned to press a kiss to her forehead. "We make a pretty good team."

That was as effective as a butt pinch in getting her back up on her feet. Seconds later she was briskly tidying up the kitchen like it owed her money. Sighing, he got up and joined in the cleaning extravaganza.

"So I heard the guys invite you to the birthday party." She said it so casually, he almost missed the nervous wobble in her voice toward the end. "Were you thinking of heading down?"

She quickly ducked low to put something away. "Because," she continued, her now noticeably shy voice floating up from the kitchen island, "if you were, maybe we could go together?"

"Took the words right out of my mouth, sweetheart."

She popped her head up like a prairie dog. "Yeah?"

He gazed at her and fought the urge to drag her into his arms so he could taste if that bit of frosting at the corner of her lips was as sweet as she was. "Yep. It'll be my first kid's party, though, so I'll of course need you to show me all the proper etiquette and stuff."

Emma smiled, no longer quite so nervous-looking, as she untied her apron and rinsed off her hands. "I'm sure the other dads will show you the ropes."

She immediately pursed her mouth shut, but she didn't call back the words. Probably hoping he hadn't heard her fully.

Oh, he'd heard it all right.

Other dads.

Damn, the meaning embedded there had a nice ring to it. Especially coming from Emma's lips. And directed at him.

While he wanted nothing more than to ask her why she looked so panicked—or, better yet, why her eyes had softened before the panic had hit—since she seemed ready to bolt, he pivoted and headed to the bathroom to wash up instead. "I'll be right back. Just going to clean up and make myself a bit more presentable."

Sometime between her saying what she'd said and his replaying it a few more times in his head on the way to the bathroom, he knew.

He'd gone and fallen head over heels for his girl next door all over again.

And the chances of his getting his heart ripped out of his chest again were even higher this time around.

Chapter Eighteen

"I think we should go out on a date," announced Jake, clanging in through the front door of the bakery.

"You wha—" Emma lost her footing on the stepladder she was standing on and went windmilling backward into an oh-so-graceful ass-first dismount.

Luckily Jake shot forward to catch her so she could stick the landing. He shook his head. "I swear—I can't leave you alone here for a second, can I?"

No. No, you can't. From now on, no more leaving me alone.

Huh, her inner Jezebel Cricket had certainly gotten needier since he'd finished up the last of the bakery repairs the other day and started his contract over at the library.

For once she and Emma were on the exact same page. They both missed having their resident sexy lumberjack in the shop every day.

Instead of telling him that, however, she went with the more Emma-esque response: "Did you hit your head at the job site again?"

He chuckled. "Nope. My noggin is just fine today."

Yeah, she wasn't so sure. "Yet here you are asking me out on a date."

"No, here I am telling you that we *should*. Go out on a date." Said it with a persuasive-as-hell double-brow-raise execution and everything. The triple-dog dare of facial expressions.

The man wasn't messing around today.

"But—"

"Now before you say no, I checked the bylaws of our Jake and Emma 2.0 agreement and found no restrictions on us dating."

Okay, so she hadn't put in a clause about that—

"And if you really think about it," he pushed on, "we've pretty much been going out on unofficial dates for the past few weeks. Successfully, I might add."

Well, sure, if you squinted your eyes just so and looked at their lunch and dinner and art show and barbecue and kids' party outings with a convoluted magnifying glass—

"So you agree."

Crap, had she been nodding her head this whole time? *Quit it.* She stopped doing her impressive imitation of a bobblehead figurine. "I don't think that's such a good idea."

Uh-oh. He didn't look fazed one bit by that.

"Okay." He shrugged.

That's it? "Wait. You're dropping it, just like that?"

He gave her an are-you-nuts look. "Of course not. I'll be back here again same time tomorrow. And the next. And if you're feeling *exceptionally* stubborn, the day after that."

Good lord, the man was charm personified. *Don't you dare smile, Stevens.*

She didn't. Just barely. "So you're saying that if I don't agree to your crazy idea, you're going to keep coming back in to revisit the topic?"

"For as long as it takes," he confirmed.

Funny, in all her wildest fantasies from her teen years to, yes, even now, she'd imagined him asking her out a million times, and never once did she picture him wearing a neon-bright, high-contrast commercial construction job site T-shirt while he did it.

That alpha, we're-going-out-and-that's-all-there-is-to-it gleam in his eyes, on the other hand? Oh yeah, that was consistent with her imagination.

"But you're not actually asking me out. Yet. You're just here to *warn* me that you're going to ask me out?"

"Warn? You make it sound like some sort of Doppler radar alert."

Yep. That's exactly what this was, a siren-blazing weather warning for an incoming hurricane. Category five at least.

As if he could hear her thoughts, he gave her a toothy grin.

The sound of a child's panicked screech and a subsequent collision outside put a swift end to their banter.

Jake ran to the front door with Emma right on his heels.

It was four-year-old Carly, the Jorgensons' youngest, and her best friend, Miley, in a two-trike pileup on the sidewalk.

Jake knelt down and picked both girls up, one on each hip. "Well, hello again, Miss Carly. I see you have a schnazzy new ride."

Giant eyes filling with imminent tears grew wider and wider before Carly tipped her head back and sobbed, "I *crashed* it."

Since this sort of thing was often quite contagious, it was no surprise when Miley joined in a second later, until the two were crying uncontrollably in stereo.

"Hey, hey. None of that. We can fix these bikes up good as new."

Both girls sniffled and stared up at Jake like the dragon slayer he was. "You can fix it? Honest?" asked Carly, wiping her nose with her jacket sleeve.

"I'll do you one better," countered Jake. "I'll teach *you two* how to fix it and even add a few aftermarket upgrades—something along the lines of rainbow streamers and a bigger basket for your toys? What do you girls think of that?"

Twin pint-size cries of delight brought a ripple of approving smiles from the small crowd that had gathered.

Jake walked back over to Emma, with both girls still perched at his sides. "Rain check on what we were talking about?"

No rain check needed. *Tell him. Just tell the man "Hell, yes" to his crazy idea so you can move on to the dating portion.*

Never one to be impulsive, she swam out halfway. "Same time, same place?"

His lips curved up in surprise.

Then he went and wobbled her knees even more.

"Did you hear that?" he asked the girls in a stage whisper. "I might just be getting a date soon with the prettiest girl in town—well, next to you two beauties, of course. If she says yes, will you two help me pick some wildflowers so I can impress her on our date?"

The twin squeals of excitement from the girls sounded markedly similar to the one echoing in her head from a very tickled-pink cricket.

As the trio went over to his truck to grab his tools to fix their trikes, Emma heard a sage voice caution, "Don't play hard to get *too* long with that one, dear."

Emma turned to find Mrs. Taylor in her new motorized scooter pointing over at Jake. "A man like that won't stay single forever."

"Oh." Emma shook her head. "Jake and I are just friends." No need to have the reigning monarch of the Old Biddy Brigade thinking otherwise.

"Oh pish posh, you can't fool me. I've seen the way you two look at each other." She gave Jake a longing look. "He reminds me of my Carl. So dashing, so kind." With a firm finger wag, she scolded lightly. "Now I know it's normal for you kids to 'play the field' nowadays, but trust me when I tell you that you don't want to waste your time if that boy is the one for you. You're going to want every possible minute you can have with him."

Emma wasn't sure what to say to that.

"He's one of the good ones, you know."

That one was easier. "That he is."

"Did you hear how he built a pottery shed for Sharon and Steve the other week? It was a beaut. And the only payment he took for all his hard work was a handmade quilt and some fresh deer jerky. Can you believe it?"

Yep, she could at that.

Stories of Jake's side jobs had been circulating around town for weeks. Each story sweeter than the last. The most recent she'd heard about was a job he did for the steep price of twenty finger-painting masterpieces courtesy of the toddler day-care center over by the lake.

Seriously, how many other carpenters would spend their entire day off building an awesome new playground obstacle course for the cost of supplies and twenty toddler paintings?

"Jake's a keeper, Emma. The only reason us old biddies in town haven't tried to marry him off to one of our daughters and nieces yet is because that boy is head over heels for you. But if you don't do right by him soon, I promise you we can find a dozen women who would jump at that chance."

She felt the threat of that like a bullet to her heart.

Mrs. Taylor gave her a knowing grin. "Mmm-hmm. Think *that* hurts? Wait too long and you'll feel a lot more pain than that. Trust me—I know. Carl and I had let society norms and other silly things get in the way of our relationship when we were young enough and stupid enough to ignore our hearts. Thank the lord we found each other again after his Maggie and my Stanley both passed, God rest them both."

She patted Emma's hand gently. "Just some friendly advice from an old lady, dear. That saying about taking chances isn't just talking about the risk involved if you do it. There's also a risk if you don't. Second chances don't always come around. I know far too many friends who found that out the hard way."

Mrs. Taylor honked her good-bye and zipped off after dropping that nuclear bomb of sage wisdom. The fact that this right here *was* Jake and Emma's second chance—something Mrs. Taylor couldn't possibly have known—made that risk factor involved so much higher. On so many levels.

So now the only question was, which risk was she more afraid of?

Losing her heart?

Or losing Jake?

The next day Jake showed up for his "same time, same place" appointment at Emma's bakery. Pushing through the clanging front door of the bakery, he went straight to the back, knowing he'd find Emma busy in the kitchen, now that the town building inspection of all the repairs was approved and filed.

When he found her, he took a few seconds to just lean against the wall and watch with a doting smile as Emma whistled and pranced around the kitchen like a culinary nymph, sprinkling flour like fairy dust all over a ball of dough bigger than her head on the new and improved butcher-block island he'd built for her.

"Jake, hi! I thought you were Megan."

"You know, I get that *all* the time. I think it's the beard."

She giggled and waved her floured rolling pin like a wand at the bakery display cases that were now no longer empty. "Did you hear? We breezed through the inspections yesterday afternoon, and we're officially cleared for business again."

"I heard. Congratulations." He nodded over at the twenty or so pie and tart pans she had stacked up beside her. "Is that all for tomorrow's reopening?"

"Yep. My version of flowing champagne for all my returning customers. And don't worry—I'm making an extra bourbon pecan pie."

His favorite. "You spoil me."

"Well, you deserve it. You did such an amazing job in here, Jake, really. I can't thank you enough."

"It was my pleasure, sweetheart."

Reaching over to brush some flour off her cheek, he crowded her space slowly, purposefully. "So . . ." He tipped her chin up and snagged her shy gaze completely to make sure he had her full and undivided attention. "Now that the inspections are done, I believe our working contract is now officially completed. Agreed?"

Wide blue eyes locked on his as he slowly backed them up against the commercial fridge. At least it would cool one of them down.

Belatedly, she nodded in response to his question.

And the temperature in the room spiked another ten degrees.

"You and me. First official date. What do you say?"

"A-are you asking this time? Or is this just another Hurricane Jake watch?"

The woman was forever entertaining him with her crazy thoughts. "I'm asking."

Though she tried so hard to hide it, he saw the flash of fear in her eyes. That she was fighting to temper it brought them one step closer. "We can still keep being Jake and Emma 2.0, baby—I promise." To be honest, he didn't know if *he* could survive seeing her deal with the collision of her past and present again. "Us dating doesn't have to open up floodgates to everything in our pasts."

Just a tiny bit more hope brightened her blue eyes. "Are you sure we can?"

Was he? No. And he told her as much. "I can't guarantee that we won't take a few hits along the way. You know how the universe likes to get paid when it comes to that sort of thing with us. But do you trust me when I say that if that does happen, I'll be right here beside you doing my damnedest to eclipse the bad with the good? Because there is so much good in our history, too, Emma. I know it's hard to remember it sometimes, but it's there. And the more time we spend together, the easier it's been for me to find those good memories."

She took in a few deep breaths.

Meanwhile he couldn't remember the last time he'd exhaled.

At the myriad of expressions racing across her face, he tried a different tactic to ease her fears. "We'll keep it totally casual. I won't even feed you if that whole first-date-at-a-restaurant thing is what's freaking you out," he cajoled. "You won't even have to change after work. In fact, I kind of hope you don't because those frilly little aprons of yours are all kinds of sexy."

Damn, he loved making her freckles pink up like that. "You will need comfortable shoes, though. Probably not the same ones you wear in the bakery."

She blinked in surprise. "Sounds like you have it all planned."

"Honey, I started thinking about our first date fourteen years ago. Safe to say I have a few ideas. Laid-back ones, but plans nonetheless." Suddenly doubt crept up his spine, and he backtracked, called himself a fool a dozen different ways. The plans he was thinking of were probably more catered to the Emma from Riverside. A grown-ass woman probably wanted to be wined and dined. *Crap, way to screw this one up already, Jake.* "But we don't have to do laid-back. We can definitely do something fancier. There are a ton of great restaurants in the city—"

She quickly shook her head. "Laid-back sounds perfect."

Whew. So he didn't get that detail wrong. "So is that a yes? No rush on scheduling it, of course. I know you're busy with the reopening. We could wait until after you get back into the groove of things here. Maybe in a few weeks?"

After a brief pause, she replied with a firm "No."

He felt his heart drop like a stone to the pit of his stomach.

Her flour-covered hands flew up and clouded the air in a frantic puff of white dust. "No, no! Jake, I meant, no on the waiting until after things settle down here." She chewed on her lip shyly. "I . . . don't want to wait that long."

"Oh." And his heart was back in his chest again, beating overtime. "Hell. So that's a yes then?" He really needed to hear her say the words.

She nodded, and then said the fourteen-years-in-the-making response aloud seemingly as much for her own ears as for his. "That's a yes. Yes to the first date." She gazed at him unwaveringly. "Yes to us."

∽

"So you're not going to give me even a *tiny* clue where we're going on this date?"

Jake smiled at Emma's cute little pout as she buckled into the passenger seat of his truck. While normally that totally would've worked on him, his wanting to keep this first date as a true surprise managed to win out. "Nope."

She sighed and then redirected her curious focus elsewhere. Namely, to snooping around for clues. "Aha!" She reached for the brown paper bag tucked under her seat.

But he snatched it away before she could get a peek. "Just be patient, woman. You'll find out what we're doing on this date in less than an hour, so just relax. Enjoy the sunset."

She sat in silence for a good ten seconds before breaking. "Are you going to start the engine anytime soon?"

Laughing softly over her having lasted even that long, seeing as they'd been sitting outside her shop for a good few minutes, he turned on his engine to at least get some music going, but he kept the truck in park. When he still didn't drive out of his parking spot, she looked over at him quizzically. But then her eyes popped wide-open in delight when he rolled down his window to wave over the delivery man carrying the box of pizza he'd ordered for them.

He wasn't sure if they'd let him request a delivery for "the truck outside Emma's bakery," but the restaurant folks didn't even hesitate. Man, he really loved this town.

Her eyes rounded at the logo on the box. "Moretti's pizza? Wow, Megan's been giving you some good intel."

"I told you—I've been thinking about this date for a while. So of course I deployed all the spies I could." He handed her a napkin and served her a piping-hot slice before putting the car into gear. "Eat up. We're going to stop at your favorite malt shake place next."

As he rolled his truck into gear and headed for the freeway, he was surprised to find the first slice of pizza from the box hovering in front of his mouth.

"You first," she prodded. "You always manage to make food taste ten times better with all your sex noises."

That *was* his gift. Might as well share it. He took a big bite and then directed the slice back over to her. It wasn't until he heard her take a bite, as well, that the flavors in his mouth truly hit him.

Jaysus. That was one mean slice of pizza.

And this time he wasn't the only one making sex noises in between chewing.

The next twenty minutes for them thus consisted of a comfortable silence, punctuated with the occasional blissful pizza moan as they took turns taking bites, then sharing a malt shake as they chased the setting sun over to the surprise he had in store.

Her startled, delighted laugh when he turned into a long dirt driveway just as dusk was settling in across the colorful sky told him he'd chosen well.

"You brought me to a farm."

"I brought you to a *baby* animal farm."

Her gaze shot up to meet his. "Really?"

His eyes ran over her face, watching the surprised pleasure light up her features. "I remembered once when we'd been talking over the fence between our yards, you mentioned wanting to live on a farm of just baby animals."

"Like those county fair petting zoos," they said in unison.

She laughed and shook her head. "You probably thought I was nuts."

"Hardly. If memory serves, I'm pretty sure I spent that night on the computer researching which baby animals could be kept on farms in the Midwest."

Quickly turning her head to hide her smile, Emma looked over at the little farmhouse with the sweet elderly couple sitting on the porch swing waving at them. "So you actually managed to find one? A farm of just baby animals?"

"They have a few mama and papa animals, as well," he disclosed with an indulgent grin. "But, yes, they continually raise baby farm animals and run a petting zoo for kids all year-round."

When he turned back to look at her, he saw her tongue swipe at her lower lip to wet it unconsciously. "Well, what are we waiting for?"

What indeed? He cleared his suddenly dry throat, and averted his eyes from what could be the most kissable mouth he'd ever seen. Hopping out of his truck, he managed to get his focus back on the date at hand when Emma quickly scrambled out of her side in sheer excitement before he could open her door for her.

Waving at the couple on the porch, Jake explained. "Normally, the petting zoo is during the day, but I asked them to make an exception for a woman who's waited a long time for this."

Her gaze caught and held his. "You're right," she said softly. "I've been waiting for this for quite some time. Not just this mythical farm but this date, too."

Jake reached back into the truck to grab the brown paper bag filled with fresh carrots, celery, and lettuce, then slipped her hand in his.

"I have, too, sweetheart."

Chapter Nineteen

Huh, maybe I've stumbled through a wormhole into an alternate universe.

That was the only thing that could explain why Jake was currently hitting "Send" on the e-mail reply for a possible kitchen remodel that he was going to check out and bid on this weekend.

This was the *third* e-mail inquiry he'd received this weekend, which was 300 percent more non-good-deeds-related project inquiries than he'd had all year. And they weren't little side jobs, either. They were substantial projects that would cover his food and rent for months. More even.

Closing the e-mail program on his phone, Jake hopped out of his truck and made his way over to the library, still wondering what could possibly be going on. Carter didn't seem to have had a hand in this. And Paul was so busy on the other project, Jake doubted he had anything to do with it, either.

He was almost at the library entrance when he got practically *run over* by Sally from Sally's Diner.

"Jake! Just the person I was looking for. I need to see if you're available later in the spring for an expansion I'm planning for the diner. I want to make a covered pavilion with outdoor seating to accommodate more diners." She quickly sped through a million more details in a few seconds flat.

Jake blinked. Definitely an alternate universe. What Sally was describing was another really big job. "Sure, sounds like fun," he interjected quickly when she took what seemed like her first breath of air since she'd run up to him. "Just let me know the details. I'll stop by sometime this week to take a look at the space and put in a bid."

"Perfect, but you have to promise me that you'll come to my diner before you go to Kim's Sandwich Shop."

What?

"No need to play dumb, Jake."

He wasn't playing.

She rolled her eyes. "I know Emma recommended you for the secret expansion project Kim's planning, as well. Everyone knows I love Kim like a sister, but I'm supercompetitive. And that shop is my diner's direct competition during the daytime hours. I *won't* be outdone by her."

"Well, seeing as how I haven't talked to Kim yet, it's safe to say I'll be checking out your project first."

Sally clucked her tongue. "Oh, don't be so sure. That Kim is a crafty one. Yesterday Emma planted the seed in Kim's head about having you build her a small play area like those big fast-food joints have. Frankly I'm surprised I beat her to you. But no matter. Verbal agreements are binding. You're going to bid on my project first." She let out a triumphant hoot. "Can't wait to go rub that in Kim's face when I meet up with her for our normal Sunday brunch date."

Oh, good lord.

It was Emma.

She was the wormhole working magic on his career.

"Between you and me," confided Sally, "Emma's idea is freakin' brilliant, so I just know Kim's going to do it. Kim and I talk almost every day, and she wasn't shy about the idea yesterday, so I checked with Emma late last night to see if she had any cool additional ideas that might help out my business."

Sally smacked him on the shoulder excitedly. "Get this. Emma suggested that I talk to the head of the town board—aka my uncle Phil—about possibly hiring you to transform the abandoned lot right next to the area I'm planning for the pavilion into a small skateboard park." She made dramatic firework gestures with her hand next to her temples. "Seriously. Mind *blown*. That'll get me the teen crowd, but it'll also be great for the older kids in town to have a safe, local place to skateboard and hang out. Kim will *never* be able to top this!"

It was tough, but Jake managed to smother back a smile. Emma was single-handedly creating competition between the women to drum up amazing new work for him that would keep him busy for a full year after the library job.

She was unbelievable.

It had been hard enough for Jake to drop Emma off at the end of the date with just a chaste, respectful peck on her cheek. Hell, the entire time they'd been playing with the animals at the farm, he'd had to fight the urge to drag her into his arms, soak in the smiles, and drink in the laughter.

Since he'd had a busy day today working by himself in the library to get some stuff ready for the guys this week, he'd figured he'd be able to not spend all his time daydreaming about the woman for at least the waking hours today.

Then she goes and does something this extraordinary.

All last week his phone had been ringing off the hook with local Juniper Hills residents calling him for small jobs here and there. He hadn't thought much about it at the time, figuring it was because they knew he'd worked on the bakery and was now working on the library. But he wouldn't be surprised if Emma was responsible for those job inquiries, as well.

His carpentry business had new life.

Only that didn't really explain all the calls he'd been getting for jobs outside Juniper Hills. *Maybe the Internet has crashed or something.* After waving good-bye to an over-the-moon Sally, Jake took out his phone to pull up Google and do a standard search for his name.

Turned out the Internet was working just fine. And what he found was something far more amazing.

She'd submitted a review and comment to each and every forum.

Every online forum that home and business owners frequented to vet folks in the trades now had a *glowing* review for him and his business. Not only that but Emma had also left comments on the online forum his reputation had been tarnished on. She'd explained how much of a bang-up job he'd done on the bakery *and* described how he'd been doing some odds-and-ends jobs around town in exchange for jars of jellies, coolers of freshly caught fish, and other nonmonetary things that the hardworking folks he'd been helping out the past few weeks had been able to barter for his services. Jake knew how important pride was when the universe kicked you in the nuts and left you little else.

Those comments had garnered the most interest and follow-up responses. There were at least a dozen comments from strangers writing that they were definitely going to keep him in mind for their next project because they wanted a guy like him to be working on their homes and places of business.

A guy like him.

This was the first time that statement was uttered about him in a *positive* light.

And if all that weren't more than enough already, Jake quickly discovered that Emma had posted pictures of his work on every single site that would allow it.

Since photos were fodder for search engines, the photos of all his work on the bakery were now defaulting on the search hits for his name on *every* home-improvement and small-business forum indexed by Google.

It was too much.

Suddenly he found his feet pivoting away from the library and heading straight over to the bakery.

With a brief nod at the part-timer running the cash register, he went right on back to the kitchen and kept on going until he was within breathing distance of Emma.

Damn, she smelled good. Like scones, sun-warmed skin, and sweetness.

Eyes wide, she shot him a puzzled grin before rising up on her tip-toes to give him a hug. "Hey. What's going on? You okay?"

He planted both hands on either side of her on the butcher block and caged her in. "No, not okay."

She frowned worriedly. "What's wrong?"

"You didn't let me finish. I'm *better* than just okay."

Her brilliant smile was back. "Yeah? Something good happen today?"

"Something great. And mysterious."

"Sounds intriguing."

"It is. Did you know that there's someone going around writing some amazing things about me on the Internet?"

Her face became an innocent mask. "You don't say?"

"Mmm-hmm," he murmured, leaning in closer. "Any ideas on who that person could be?"

She shuddered when he whispered the last question bare millimeters from her ear, then replied breathily, "Sounds like super-meddle-some pod people." Her hands flexed against his sides when his teeth nipped at her earlobe. "Gremlins are another strong possibility I'd put on the suspect list."

God, the woman drove him crazy. In all the best possible ways.

Leaning forward swiftly, he captured her chin and angled her face up to his, taking *possession* of her lips, in a deep, sinking, melt-your-bones way, until a small sound rumbled out of his chest.

He had no idea how long the kiss lasted, but by the time he released her and put at least a foot between them, he was sucking wind as if he'd sprinted a few miles. Her reddened lips and bedroom eyes were effectively sending what little blood he had left in his brain due south.

"I'm sorry," he apologized. Not for the kiss itself but because he'd been seconds from throwing her on the butcher block and going a lot further than a kiss . . . in her place of business with at least a dozen curious folks on just the other side of the kitchen wall. "This probably wasn't the right time for—"

"No, don't apologize," she replied, gazing up at him with heated eyes. "I'm actually due for a break. We could go upstairs and—"

Holy hell. He yanked her into another kiss before she could finish that dangerous suggestion, which she gave back as good as she got, in classic Emma style. Arguing with him, driving him crazy. Only this time with just her lips.

And tongue.

And good lord, her teeth.

Breathing hard, and just plain hard everywhere else, he somehow managed to tear himself away to say the one thing he'd come here to say. "Second official date. Tonight."

She just nodded mutely, a dazed look on her face as she touched her lips lightly with her fingers in wonder.

"And thank you, sweetheart. For everything you did online, and with Sally, and Kim."

She shook her head. "It's no big deal."

"It's a very big deal. You're incredible, Emma Stevens." His voice grew thick with emotion. "No one's ever done for me what you did."

"Gush about you like you're the best thing since sliced bread?" she asked, eyes crinkling at the corners.

He shook his head. "You defended me. Protected me. *Fought* for me. Despite everything in our past, despite having every reason not to, you continue to choose to believe I'm worth all of that. Unconditionally. Based on blind faith alone. I've never had that before."

In fact, he'd never felt he even *deserved* any of that before today.

Before Emma.

Chapter Twenty

Emma peeked through her window and frowned at the sight of Jake rolling out his sleeping bag in the back of his truck.

The most stubborn, *sweetest* man alive, ladies and gentlemen.

With his living a few hours away, their staying out late tonight meant he'd get only an hour or so of sleep before having to turn right back around to make it to work at the library in the morning. But there'd been a perfectly great solution to that problem . . .

She sighed as she looked back at her empty bed. It made no sense at all that there wasn't a warm, slumbering lumberjack in it right now.

Tonight had been their third date—*the* third date. And at the end of it, when he didn't catch any of her subtle hints, she'd actually flat-out *asked* him to stay over. Not because of some arbitrary third-date expectations set by society. Nope, these were 100 percent personal reasons through and through. She didn't need society to tell her she wanted the man. Bad.

But aside from one hungry look of pure, intense temptation, he'd declined. With a gruff single head shake . . . shortly before he'd sunk his fingers in her hair and imprinted her body with a near-savage kiss as a rather spectacular thank-you for the offer.

And now here he was camping in a sleeping bag in the back of his truck.

Dang it, he was just such a good guy. How many men would do this after a date to ensure he got enough shut-eye for a grueling shift of work the next day?

None that she knew.

Which was precisely why she found herself standing beside his truck in the middle of the night, staring at his handsome sleeping face.

Climbing up onto the tire quietly, she eased herself into the bed carefully, not wanting to accidentally step on something vital.

He didn't stir. He'd been like that the few nights he'd slept at her place after his coma; she'd actually nudged him a few times to make sure he was still responsive.

Tonight she didn't need to check. He was quite obviously *very* responsive at the moment, if the fit of his jeans was any indication. Even with the lack of visibility from the soft streetlight above, she could clearly see that the sweet, handsome, honk-your-tractor-if-you're-from-Kansas farm boy had definitely grown up.

"Into freaking Superman with a hammer," she murmured with no small amount of awe and appreciation.

"You mean Thor," he rumbled sleepily.

She froze in her pervy perusal and played possum.

At her continued silence, he peeked a heavy eyelid open a fraction. "You said Superman with a hammer. Superman doesn't have a hammer."

She glanced down and exhaled slowly, whispering under her breath, "Oh, yes, he does."

That's when she felt every muscle in his body harden alongside her and his arms snap around her like steel bands. She gasped. But not in fear.

"Emma?"

"Yes?"

"Do me a favor?"

"Sure."

"Don't move."

"Okay."

It took a few shuddering breaths for his body to relax. Another few seconds and he was turning to face her. "If I open my eyes again, will you be looking at my, uh, 'hammer,' again?"

Oh God. Hearing her words in his voice was a thousand times worse. Thank goodness it was dark enough he couldn't see her face on fire.

"You're blushing," he marveled, sounding pleased as punch.

Dammit!

"You're practically burning up next to me." His lips curved up at the corners. "So I take it that means you're still perving on my package?"

She whacked him. "I haven't been *perving* on anything."

He opened his eyes, one brow raised to call her on her fib. "I have excellent night vision, sweets."

"Fine. I may have . . . glanced in that direction." She blinked innocently. "But that was only because it was practically saluting me."

He chuckled. "Yeah well, you can thank yourself for that. I can't seem to keep him from 'saluting' whenever you're nearby smelling like . . ." Nuzzling closer to her neck, he murmured appreciatively, "Sugar and sass."

She found the hem of his shirt and slipped her hands underneath, nipping at his lip in a pure feral response when she finally felt all those glorious muscles she'd been seeing for weeks now. Beneath her palms, his stomach tightened as his similarly roaming hands made a discovery of their own.

"You're not wearing any shorts under this T-shirt," he rumbled from somewhere deep in his chest. "Or a bra."

"I was getting ready for bed." She began tracing the ripped muscles across his back, her fingertips practically humming in appreciation.

"You walked outside practically naked."

"I wanted to talk to you."

He tensed. "You climbed *into my truck bed* practically naked."

She took a deep breath and inhaled a lungful of lust to bolster her courage. "Okay, so maybe I wanted to do more than talk."

"Good lord, woman. I'm trying to be a good guy here. Just because it's our third date doesn't mean we have to have sex."

"True. But you said it yourself—we've basically been dating for a few months, just without the official labels."

He had no comeback for that. *Excellent.* She was wearing him down. "Jake?"

"Yeah?"

She decided to go with honesty. "What if I tell you that yes, I want to have sex with you, but even if you want to wait, what I had come out here to ask you was if you would like to come up to my bed and cuddle with me again. Only . . . this time with some kissing involved? Those two nights you slept in my bed, all I could think about was how you felt next to me, how much I wanted you to kiss me—"

She'd never seen a human move so quickly.

He had her scooped her up in his arms within the blink of an eye, shortly before he hopped over the side of his truck in a single bound.

"I think you might actually *be* Superman."

His arms tightened around her as he got them to her shop in two long strides, inside the bakery with the door locked behind them in under a second. "Stop with the superhero compliments, woman. Or I won't be able to make it up the stairs."

"Frankly, I don't see how you can walk with that giant thing at all." She wriggled in his arms, enjoying having the upper hand for once. "Is that why they call you the man of steel?"

Growling softly, he stopped his staircase climb a few steps from the top landing and set her down gently . . . before pinning her back against the landing and caging her in with his arms.

His lips were on hers an instant later.

Suddenly all jokes disappeared from her brain, along with almost every other coherent thought she possessed.

He'd been holding back before. That much was clear. With just his lips, teeth, and tongue, he was already bringing her close to the edge. *"Jake."*

He yanked himself back and stared down into her eyes. "Too fast?"

She shook her head.

"Do you want me to stop?"

Her hands flexed against his sides in alarm as she shook her head again adamantly, almost violently this time.

"Words, baby. Use your words."

"Don't stop."

He exhaled harshly and crushed his lips to hers again. God she loved it. Loved feeling him lose control. Loved losing control along with him.

Shaking his head, he dropped down to his elbows and speared his hands through her hair. "You could try the patience of the pope."

"And you could tempt a pair of panties off a mannequin. I thought we were going to stop with the superhero compliments."

Grinning now in that wicked, wicked way he did sometimes, he dropped down one step lower and leaned back so he could run his eyes over her body slowly. Very slowly. She felt like prey. Well, prey that was about ready to ambush her predator.

"You're absolutely right, sweetheart." He slid his rough palms up her thighs. "You're dangerous to my control when you speak."

"To be fair, I stopped making references to anything related to your pitching a tent," she argued innocently.

"No more dirty talking from you." He pulled her flush against him and quickly fastened his lips on hers. A nanosecond later, he slipped his hands under her shirt and stole her ability to speak completely.

Emma didn't know which delicious sensation to focus on more, his palms smoothing up over her rib cage or his lips dropping soft kisses down her belly.

"It's too dark here to see if these panties are pink."

Or she could just lose herself in that deep, sexy voice of his and try to keep from orgasming.

His thumbs brushed over her nipples just as his thick beard rubbed over the sensitive crest of her hip bone. "Are they?" he breathed the question across the fabric he was so curious about. "Pink? Like the ones you were wearing the other night?"

Seriously, at this point, if he huff and puffed in *just* the right spot, he could blow her house down.

He smiled against her skin as if hearing her thoughts. "Quiet all of a sudden."

Did the man really expect her to be able to speak with his mouth rasping over her center? Close but not nearly close enough.

She was just about to take matters into her own hands—literally—when he dragged her curious fingers away from the front of his jeans and threaded their hands together . . . behind the small of her back.

Though he was more holding her, rather than restraining her, the alpha-sexiness of it all was enough to flood her with an arousal so close to the edge, she lifted her hips in a silent plea.

Which he answered by dipping his head down and tracing his tongue over the seam of her sex.

"Jake," she gasped, her body practically vibrating with need.

The breathy, uninhibited utterance earned her a brief moment of freedom, before he gently manacled both her wrists with one hand, and used the other to—swear to God—rip her panties from her body.

She was halfway past detonation and strung out with pleasure when she felt him slip two thick fingers inside her as he fastened his mouth over her core.

It didn't take much more after that.

More hot, wet suction.

His fingertips curling over a magical spot she'd always thought was missing in her anatomical makeup.

His eyes locking on hers in a silent promise of even more *unspeakably* dirty things.

Then his teeth grazing over her until she cried out.

She was a goner.

By the time he slid his tongue in deep, she was spiraling over the edge, his rough, ragged growl against her sensitive flesh sending her shattering, scattering into a thousand cataclysmic pieces.

And somehow she never felt more whole, and more inexplicably tethered, than she did in that one turbulent, riotous moment.

Holy hell.

Jake had barely managed to keep himself from coming right alongside her and making a mess of his jeans. He placed one last kiss on her soft belly before gently scooping her up into his arms. "Dammit, I can't believe I did this on the stairs. I'm sorry, baby."

Thank God he'd at least been able to control himself enough to take her to the top of the stairs before, well, taking her. The street was a ghost town at night, and the stairs were situated behind a curtain and far enough back behind the bakery counter that no one outside could really see up the stairwell, but still. The idea of anyone else seeing Emma's lush body made him a little crazy.

He looked down into her dazed eyes and couldn't help but smile. It was a good look on her he intended to draw out again, but on top of a proper bed this time.

After laying her down on top of her comforters, he debated whether he should keep his jeans on or not.

Clearly Emma was thinking "or not."

He hissed when he felt her hand undo the fly of his jeans. She demanded, "Why are all your clothes still on?"

God, he loved it when she used that bossy tone. He looked up at her, and, sure enough, her cheeks were flushed. Freckles on full deployment.

He had every intention of finding every last freckle on her body and kissing each one before the night was through.

Damn. If possible, he'd just grown another hard inch. And her muffled murmur of appreciation wasn't helping. Neither were the soft kisses she was placing along his one-slight-breeze-away-from-bursting length.

A long few seconds later, he had to gently yank himself away from her. His entire body vibrated with the effort it took.

Jeans were definitely staying on.

"Sweetheart, we don't have to rush this. We've only had a few dates. Sex can wait. I want us to wait."

She gave him a dubious look. "And the stairs were . . ." Her expression hardened. "If you tell me that was a mistake, I'm switching you back to decaf."

He blanched. Well, that was *almost* enough to get his raging hard-on under control. "Woman, don't joke about that. I'm still traumatized from the last time."

Burying his lips against her neck as he dropped onto the bed beside her, he smiled when he heard her grouse that she wasn't joking.

"Of course I don't think it was a mistake. I didn't say we can't keep doing *that*. We're definitely doing more of that. Right now, in fact." He started sliding his palms down those sanity-stealing curves of hers.

Emma snapped her thighs closed—with his hand happily trapped—and, swear to God, he almost came just a little bit. "Wait a minute. You're saying it's okay for you to make me come all over the place, but you won't let me do the same for you?"

Good lord.

Raggedly he dropped his forehead down onto her chest, praying for strength when he saw how thin her shirt was. One good tug would shred the fabric and he'd be able to taste her soft skin.

Focus, Jake.

He forced his mouth away from the pebbled nipple tempting him.

Erection hard as a spike, he tried to stop all the rabid lust from coursing through his system. "I didn't say that. I said let's not rush having sex." He nibbled on the exposed skin at her shoulder and used his free hand to pull her shirt down just a tiny bit more—he was only human. "But other things, on my part, at least, I obviously want to keep doing. But you don't have to. I know not all women enjoy that."

"Jake, look at me."

He wasn't sure he had the strength.

But the stubborn woman wasn't taking no for an answer. Nor was she loosening her grip on his one trapped hand. Locking on to her cornflower-blue gaze, he prepared himself for a full-tactile assault of the Emma Stevens variety.

He got a soft sigh from her instead. "You make me crazy—you know that, right?"

He grinned. "Right back at you, babe."

She let his trapped hand free. "Do you really want to wait? Is it important to you? One thing I've learned about you is that you only get bullheaded about things when it's important." Her lips quirked up at the corner. "I'm not sure if you noticed, but I get bullheaded about stuff all the time."

No comment. He wasn't touching that one with a ten-foot pole.

"But you." She sighed again. "You're serious—aren't you? Waiting is important to you."

He loved that she got him. "It is."

"Can you tell me why?" She chewed on her lower lip nervously. "You're not . . . this isn't your first . . ."

He barked out a laugh. God, she was cute. "No. I'm not a virgin, sweetheart."

"Yeah, I didn't think so. Not with how hard you made me—" Her cheeks burned bright red.

"Woman, you need to stop deploying your freckles. I'm trying to dial it down a notch, remember?" He dropped a kiss onto each new freckle he found on her bare shoulder. Forget her bourbon pecan pudding, Emma's skin was his new favorite dessert.

"Jake. Focus."

"I would if you weren't so damn wet," he complained as his fingers slid up her thigh to find her even wetter, hotter than she'd been on the stairs.

"Jake." She grabbed his hand, then really got his attention by using the other hand to grab—

"Christ, Emma." He was a weak, weak man. And with each slow pump of her hand, he was getting weaker by the second. "You're going to make me come if you keep that up."

She stopped . . . only to slip her hand into his boxer briefs a moment later.

"Now do I have your attention?"

Hell, she could have anything she wanted at this point.

Rubbing her thumb over his feverishly hot, almost painfully hard, shaft slowly, she asked again, "Why do you want to wait, Jake?"

Wait? Wait for what? His lust-fogged brain could barely make sense of her words. He was T minus less than a minute from not waiting for anything.

She squeezed gently and lazily began sliding her hand down . . .

"Emma, stop." Those two words earned him some sainthood points for sure. Especially when she dragged his boxer briefs down completely and took him in both hands.

Holy hell, that feels good.

Jeez, focus *Jake.*

Only the woman had no intention of letting him focus. On anything other than the feel of her mouth on him.

She looked up at him through her lashes as she traced her tongue over his entire length.

"Sweetheart, you don't have to do this."

She closed her mouth over him fully and drew him to the back of her throat.

Yeah, she was right. He should stop talking.

A throttled groan rumbled out of his chest. It'd been a while, so he couldn't say with absolute certainty, but he was pretty sure that mind-erasing swivel move she was doing was brand-new in the world of blow jobs.

His hands slid into her hair, just to hold her, not guide her motions, because sweet lord, the woman was doing a bang-up job taking him from zero to sixty. Already he was starting to see colored spots in his vision, and his breathing was erratic at best, nonexistent at her *very* best.

Like now, for example. There was absolutely no oxygen going up to his brain, and his lungs were burning and demanding he take in a goddamn breath of air, but he didn't care. With each slow glide, her lips tightened over him and then relaxed each time she took him just a little bit deeper.

And the vicelike grip she maintained with both hands at his base as she stroked her tongue over his hard shaft made for a perfect trifecta.

He could feel his control slipping with each pulsing pass.

Then she took him as deep as she could go.

And swallowed.

"Baby, I'm going to come," he ground out the ragged warning through clenched teeth, sheer determination the only thing keeping him from spilling in her hot, wet mouth.

The stubborn little thing just took that warning as a signal to swallow him down again, and work him with her throat, and he was done for.

His vision darkened at the edges as the most violent orgasm of his life crashed over him and sucked him under the tide.

When he came to a long, blurry second later, he found Emma trailing gentle kisses up his abdomen.

He wanted to say something romantic. Or at least classy. But the best he could manage was, "Jesus Christ, Emma."

Her lips curled into a grin against his skin in response.

"Now." She sat up and locked on to his half-lidded gaze. "Tell me why you want to wait, Jake."

Whoa, the woman played hardball.

He sighed and tried to put his rationale into words. It had been hard enough without the post-orgasm haze. Now he'd be lucky if he could explain it without botching it up. He decided to just say what he'd been thinking ever since the possibility that something might be possible between the two of them first arose. "I know you don't like thinking about our past, Emma, but I think about it all the time."

Her smile faded. "Oh."

She stopped with the distracting kisses and gave him a little more room to think. *Whew.*

211

Knowing she was going to avoid his gaze, he gently gripped her chin to keep her eyes on his. "The reason why I want to wait is because, for me, this relationship started fourteen years ago. Just because we're now adults doesn't mean I want to rush what I'd wanted to start back then. Does that make sense?"

Unshed tears glistened in her eyes. "You think about that?"

"All the time, sweetheart. I told you—I've thought about our first date for years. Our second date almost as long."

"H-how many dates have you thought up for us?"

"Hundreds, at least. But the thing is, those were dates I'd planned for the teenage versions of us. I'm only now getting to know the adult version of you. And I want time to plan new dates for this version of you." He brushed his lips over hers. "Because I think she's pretty darn special."

"If you want me to stop deploying my freckles, you need to stop with all the sexy talk in that smoky voice of yours."

He smiled. "Sexy talk? I was just being honest."

"Exactly." She exhaled.

He rubbed his thumb over her heated cheeks. "If it helps, I can guarantee you'll be driving me more crazy than I'll be driving you."

"That does help, yes. Thank you."

He chuckled. "And I meant what I said about what we did on the stairs. We can, of course—"

"Oh, no, you don't." She pulled her shirt down and scooted up the mattress. "If you want to wait to have sex, then we're going to wait completely."

"So earlier, when you made me come so hard I almost blacked out—"

"You got to taste me once, so it was only fair I got to taste you once."

Jeez, he had to ask.

"But from now on, if you're going to wait, then so am I. A hundred percent."

Talk about being between a rock and a hard place.

"But—"

"Nope." She dragged a pillow over her lap. "Neither one of us is going to be revisiting tonight's festivities until you and I *both* decide we're ready for our relationship to have a *whole* lot of sex in it. Dirty, nonstop, do-it-on-every-available-surface sex. Sound like a plan?"

He groaned. "Why do I get the feeling I just armed you with a whole lot of ammo?"

Her only reply was a pair of innocently twinkling eyes.

Chapter Twenty-One

Jake couldn't believe he'd actually called up his *brother* to get his advice. Voluntarily. And not just any brother. Carter. The one whose philosophy in life basically whittled down to meddle until you can't meddle anymore, then find an app that'll make you an even more efficient meddler.

But at this point, Jake was ready to try just about anything to figure out what the hell he was supposed to do.

"Everything's just so . . . perfect with Emma." Jake cringed and rubbed his temples, knowing he sounded like a lunatic for having a problem with that. "That's the only way to describe it the past few weeks with Emma. No issues. No conflict. All the time."

"Gee, that sucks," replied a dry Carter, deadpan. "Are you also having a good hair day, too, man? Because I can find you a support group for that."

Jackass.

Unfortunately, the jackass had a point. Jake had yet to get to the root of the problem. And Carter was simply doing what he did best to get Jake to dig deeper.

The only problem was, Jake had no clue where to dig. Or what the heck he was looking for. Or why he was even burrowing into that hole to begin with.

The dates had all been perfect, yes. But Emma was still holding back. It was in the little things she did. Like when she'd stop herself from talking about the past too much. Or when she'd get uneasy and awkward when they were watching TV and the late-breaking news showed something about a big fire. Or when she'd immediately change the subject when folks around town would casually invite them to an event later in the year.

Or when she'd hold on to those pendants of hers and draw on some hidden well of strength . . . only to let go when she'd see him watching her.

Each were tiny but potent blows to his heart.

He didn't know what to do anymore. Which was why he'd turned to *Carter* for advice, as well as answers.

Jake wasn't stupid. He knew that Carter bought the library because it was Megan's one special haven.

Guilt could inspire a man to do crazy things. And it could also be the reason a man made excuses for far less than was advisable in a relationship with the girl of his dreams. Somewhere in the past few weeks, Jake had started feeling he was doing just that. Which was crazy, really. Jake would be the first person on the job site to tell his guys, if it ain't broke, don't fix it. On paper, sure, it looked as though nothing needed fixing between him and Emma. But their past was still broken, under the surface. *They* were still broken, under the surface.

He just didn't know how to fix it.

Exponentially so because Emma wanted to ignore that aspect of their relationship.

"Let's try to play devil's advocate," suggested Carter. "So your girl-friend wants to keep pretending you two only met a couple of months ago so you never have to deal with what happened. What's the big deal? Is that *so* bad?"

"Yes." Hell, yes, it was that bad.

"Why?"

215

Before Jake could answer, Carter followed up that question with one aimed well and aimed low. "Isn't that the same thing that you've been doing when it comes to us?"

Seriously, what had he been smoking when he'd had the brilliant idea to call up Carter tonight?

"It's not the same thing," argued Jake.

"Tell me why."

"Because." Shit, were they really going to get into this? "Because isn't it like the damn mantra of most self-help books that folks need to deal with their past crap before they can move forward?"

"You know what? I think I read that book."

His brother the friggin' comedian, ladies and gentleman.

"I repeat," pushed Carter. "What's the difference between your relationship with Emma and your relationship with me?"

"Because." Dammit, there was no way of saying it without hurting the guy's feelings. "Because truthfully, up until recently, I never really . . . thought you'd be a permanent fixture in my life, let alone my future."

Deafening silence resonated from Carter's end of the phone line.

"I'm sorry, man. You know I love you and all that. You're my big brother. Always will be. I'd give you a spare organ in a heartbeat. But I'm trying to be honest. Part of the reason why I never let you push me to deal with our effed-up past is because I figured you wouldn't be a permanent part of my future anyhow. Some part of me thought you'd one day give up on the bimonthly calls. Which would've made us working out our shit pointless."

"Do you still feel that way?" Carter asked quietly.

"No." And that was the God's honest truth. "Now I want us to work our shit out. For better or for worse."

"Is that the girlie version of you telling me you see me as a part of your life now? Your future?" His words were teasing, but his tone was anything but.

"*Or* I just finally realized you were more stubborn than a mule, so I should give up trying to keep you out," reasoned Jake, interrupting their Hallmark moment with a far more appropriate dude moment.

Carter chuckled. "I'll take it."

They basked in that for all of one second before Carter returned them both to the conversation at hand. "So by your logic, the reason why you're upset that Emma isn't wanting to deal with the past is because you . . . ? Fill in the blank here, buddy. Because I sure as hell won't do it for you."

"Because I want a future with her."

"Ding, ding, ding. Tell the contestant what he's won," bellowed Carter in his best game-show voice. "Jake, you just won yourself a *committed relationship*." Carter made comic whistling noises, presumably to give Jake some time to let that sink in.

Holy shit. The annoying asshat was right. He wanted Emma for the long haul. This wasn't a fling or a relationship they'd look back on as the one they couldn't make work. Nope, she was it for him, and he wanted a future with her.

Which wouldn't be possible if she didn't allow them to work out their past.

"Jake, let me fly out there and confess everything to Emma. I can take the first flight out tomorrow morning."

"No. No way, man. You're not confessing anything to anyone."

"But I don't want my actions, the ones you took the blame for, to be the reason why you and Emma can't be together."

"I agree. So by that logic, a confession from you shouldn't be the magical fix-all. If the sole reason why we can't make it work is *you*, then it clearly wasn't meant to be."

"That's a stretch, and you know it, Jake. Getting over something like a fire like that isn't a reasonable expectation, nor is it a fair test to a relationship. And I think you know that."

"I'm not using it as some big test of our relationship," Jake argued truthfully. "Frankly, the reality that it was you who set the fire that night can and should stay buried in the past. Taking the fall for you was a path *I chose* fourteen years ago. My going to juvie was a past I *chose* to have be a permanent part of my history. If Emma, or you, or anyone for that matter, can't come to terms with my past and accept that part of me fully, regardless if it's wholly factual in the legal chain of events sense, then really, we don't stand a chance in hell in having a future. It's who I am. And while our parents may not love or accept who I am, the woman I want to spend the rest of my life with should—don't you think? Don't I deserve at least that?"

"Of course you do, man. It's just . . . it might just be too big an expectation."

No. Hell, no. He wasn't going to live his life that way; he wasn't going to simply accept feeling like he didn't deserve it all, like he was somehow unworthy. He'd been made to feel that enough by his parents fourteen years ago. He wouldn't stand by and accept it ever again. Even if it meant losing the woman he wanted to be a part of his life for the long haul. Because what kind of life would that be? Conditional love and acceptance?

No. Just no.

"Jake, just let me talk to her—"

"Don't you dare interfere or confess or do anything stupid like that. I didn't go through juvie to have you make it all unnecessary by some grand gesture. Give me your word, right now. Swear to me that you won't tell Emma."

Silence. And then: "I swear I won't."

"Or Daryn and Haley, either."

Their siblings deserved not to have to discover that everything they thought they knew was wrong. God knew that fire affected their lives, too. Daryn, being not that much younger than him, had had to live in Jake's tarnished shadows all through high school. And Haley, the same age as Megan and Emma's deceased brother. She'd had it the roughest since her classmates had gotten killed and injured because of that fire.

Thankfully Carter had another call come in, saving Jake from having to talk about this more tonight. He wanted to focus on one issue at a time.

After hanging up, Jake tossed his phone on the dashboard and leaned his head against the seat. Since Emma and Megan were having a girls' night, he'd planned on doing a couple of weeks of piled-up laundry as his big evening activity, but the shoe shop owner next to Emma's bakery had needed some help with some new storage racks, which had ended up taking hours. With it being close to midnight now, he was beat, and *not* looking forward to the drive back to the city. *I'll just close my eyes for a few minutes* . . .

"So it *wasn't* you who caused the fire?" came a small voice from just outside his truck.

Holy shit.

Jake looked out of his partially open window.

And found Emma standing right outside on the dark, deserted sidewalk with a small box of cupcakes in her hands and a look of horrified confusion on her face.

Chapter Twenty-Two

"Don't." Emma held up her hand to stop Jake from explaining the second he hopped out of his truck. She'd heard only part of the conversation, but it was enough. "You don't need to tell me who that was. I actually don't want to know. Because I don't want to have hate for another person." She stared at his tortured expression. "And I would. Hate whoever you were just talking to. Whatever coward allowed you to suffer the punishments for actions that weren't yours."

"Emma, he didn't—"

She held up a second hand and just shut her eyes. Attempted to get her shaky breathing under control as she tried to process what she'd just overheard.

He wasn't the one responsible for that fire. *Jake had been innocent this entire time.*

Everyone involved had been condemning the wrong man all this time.

Even her.

There was only a single thought echoing a thousand times in her head in response, and it fell from her lips on a broken whisper. "I am so sorry, Jake."

She couldn't even begin to describe the expression twisting across Jake's features at the moment, but the resolute, almost horrified anguish in his voice was abundantly clear when he nearly shouted, "Don't ever, ever . . ." His jaw locked tight as a tremor shook his entire frame. "Emma, you have absolutely nothing to apologize for. I don't ever want to hear you say sorry to me. Not for that night."

"But you've been living with all of us blaming you for something you didn't even do."

"And that's a choice I made with my eyes wide-open, sweetheart."

She didn't want to ask. All the same she couldn't stop the question from tumbling out. "Why? I don't need or even want you to tell me who was on the other end of that call. But I don't know that I'll ever stop wondering why. Why you would put yourself through all that for someone else?"

Jake's wrecked gaze drifted back up to the sky.

"Were you . . . protecting that person?" Emma shook her head at the absurdity of her even asking that; of course he'd been protecting that other person.

While she'd long held the belief that Megan had the purest heart of anyone she knew, more and more she was realizing that Jake's was assuredly the strongest.

She'd mistaken that strength for kindness until now. But a kind person wouldn't put himself in the path of a bullet intended for another. A person who had Jake's type of strength, on the other hand, would. Because it took an indomitable strength to be able to hope for survival in even the most unlikely situations, to be able to believe that the person whose life you were sparing was destined to live that life to the fullest.

In this, Jake was so much stronger than she could ever hope to be. Not just because he'd taken the fall for someone else's crime, that life-altering bullet intended for another. But because he'd survived where others might not have.

Because he'd taken on an infinite load of suffering *so others didn't have to.*

She laid a gentle hand over his heart until he met her gaze again. "You didn't just do it to protect that one person." A look of surprise flickered in his eyes before a dark cloud fell over them, even stormier than before. "You did it to keep your father from dragging it out—didn't you? You absorbed the brunt of it so you could spare everyone around you. *Around me.*"

Another slow realization dawned on her.

"You've been punishing yourself. You're *still* punishing yourself."

He flinched. "Emma, you of all people know better than anyone the answer to that question. And just as important, you know the reason why."

She nodded. He took her hand and swiftly tugged her over to the bakery.

Without bothering to flip on the lights after she let them in, he turned to her and started in on the very conversation she'd been trying to avoid for the past few weeks.

"Then say it. Out loud, Emma. Say the words we both know to be true. Even though I didn't set the fire, even though you know that I didn't set the fire now, admit out loud that you still feel the same way you did that night."

Emma shook her head, not wanting to make that admission, even as she felt the helpless tears sliding down her cheeks.

Jake broke his gaze away and said it for them, in a tone bleeding with pain. "I may not have been responsible for the fire, but I was still responsible for your brother's death."

"I'm so sorry, Emma."

He'd never had a chance to tell her that back then. Neither of their families' lawyers would let him.

His apology now seemed insanely, insultingly inadequate. And it simply reminded him why he hadn't been able to say the words to her that night when she'd first figured out he hadn't been able to save her little brother. Why a thousand unmailed letters to her had sat under his mattress in juvie.

Why he had one more apology to give her now.

"I'm sorry for not being strong enough to stop what's been happening between us these past few weeks."

Her tear-filled gaze snapped up to his. "Don't say that. Don't ever say that. Because I'm not."

God, his heart wanted to believe that. More than it wanted its next heartbeat. "We have to talk about this."

"Why? Why do we have to? It's been fourteen years. And we're happy. You make me happier than I ever remember being."

"Sweetheart, you make me happier than I ever thought I *could* be." His words held such vehement truth, it sounded more like a whispered benediction than a mere statement.

Her tremulous smile tugged at the tangled chords of emotions in his chest until he couldn't feel one emotion without tripping over another. He wasn't sure if he could survive losing her again.

But he had to do what was right.

You save one, and I'll save the other.

Jake thought about that promise he'd made her that night.

That night had been the scariest of his life. Over the year, he'd replayed it over and over again. He'd asked the juvie shrink he'd been assigned to if he'd made the right decision. He'd asked the cop who'd taken his statement. He'd asked one of the firefighters who'd been called in to testify at his trial.

They'd all said the same thing.

They couldn't tell him if what he did was right or wrong. Just that what he did had saved two lives. They kept telling him to look at it that way: he'd saved two lives.

Not that he'd killed one in the process.

Jake had broken his promise to Emma that night. And her little brother, Peyton, had died as a result.

He constantly thought about that promise he'd made. Whenever anything bad happened, those words would resound in his head like a reminder of the biggest failure of his life. The most devastating.

That same reminder popped up even more so when something good happened.

And Emma was the *best* thing that had ever happened to him.

He shut his eyes for one more turbulent heartbeat, and every moment of their time together the past few weeks hit him square in the heart.

She was everything good in his life rolled into a beautiful gift he knew he didn't deserve. But he couldn't stop wanting her. Hoping beyond hope that he could keep her.

It was time.

"Those three floral pendants you wear. Can I ask you about them?" He nodded at the three dainty gold chains she always wore, each a different length and style, and each with a different floral pendant charm.

Sometimes he'd catch her staring off into space, thinking, and she'd reach up to touch one of the pendants. It would be as if she was seeking a specific one of the three. A calm look would then settle over her features when she found it.

And it drove him crazy every time.

"You always touch them when you're lost in thought," he continued. Just like she was doing now. "I've spent every spare minute I've had for weeks on end trying to figure out their significance, which was difficult because while I recognized the daffodil and the tulip pendants, I had no clue what the third flower was."

"Hyacinth," she said softly. "And the reason why I wear them is because all three flowers represent forgiveness. But in different ways. And for different stages in my life."

Her smile was filled with some emotion between happiness and sadness that he couldn't quite decipher. "I've had the charms for years now. I actually got the hyacinth first, not long after the fire, because I read somewhere that you give hyacinths when you want to tell someone you're sorry, because they represent sorrow and deep remorse." She touched the pendant on the shortest chain gently. "I hold this pendant whenever I think about Peyton. Sometimes I'll be out and about and I'll see something—a kid on a bike that reminds me of him, or a roly-poly puppy that I know Peyton would've loved. That's usually when you see me holding the pendant. Because I'm giving him a hyacinth in heaven. To seek forgiveness."

She held up the other two. "The daffodil and the tulip I actually got right after college. Here in Juniper Hills, in fact." She blinked in surprise. "I almost forgot about that. While I was out researching places that Megan and I could move to, I found this little town, and they were having a craft fair the day I visited. Turns out the designer of my hyacinth pendant had carved two others, as well. These two. And she told me all about them. How those flowers also represent forgiveness. Since I already had a pendant, I didn't buy the others. But after Megan and I moved here, I saw the jewelry artist again. And I bought both pendants."

Jake looked at the two pendants she was now holding. "One for you and one for Megan?"

Emma shook her head. "I think maybe at the time I may have bought them with that in mind. Three siblings, three pendants. But even from the beginning, when I started wearing all three pendants together, only the hyacinth represented a person for me." She chuckled. "I think the other two were just pretty."

"But they mean something to you now?"

"Over time. The tulip's significance sort of grew slowly for me. After the bakery was up and running and I was finally in the black. After I got settled here and really felt at home, that's when I thought more about what the jewelry artist had told me. About how the white tulip represented forgiveness, yes, but also a fresh start. So I guess the tulip sort of became my personal talisman after that."

Finally, she ran her thumb across the pendant on the longest gold chain. "This one . . . this one I didn't have any special attachments for until recently." Lifting her gaze up to meet his, she said softly, "Not until that first day I saw you standing in my bakery." With a shaky sigh, she admitted, "I think I kind of fought that one, frankly. Because it started happening unconsciously. I would think of you and then naturally reach for this pendant. I didn't even realize I was doing it until Megan pointed it out. That's when I began analyzing what might have been going on in my subconscious. And sometimes, especially when you were being particularly annoying, I'd purposely stop myself from holding the daffodil pendant."

Stunned, he stared at the pendant she was now affectionately tracing with her finger. "Are you saying that last pendant represents me?" That was the absolute last thing he'd expected to hear.

"Believe me—I was shocked, too. But the more I started thinking about how the jewelry artist had described the daffodil, I could see why my subconscious was linking you to it in my mind. It's actually pretty similar to the tulip in that it's a symbol of forgiveness and a sort of rebirth, but the woman had specifically told me that the daffodil has also long been thought to represent happiness and chivalry." She chewed on her bottom lip and shook her head slightly. "I think that's why I fought it in the beginning. Because it was almost . . . too perfect a fit. And it also scared me. To have you just waltz back into my life out of the clear blue sky fourteen years later, and then suddenly have this significant connection to one of my pendants. I reasoned that I couldn't allow the pendant to get attached to you because after you left, I'd never be able to wear it again."

Exhaling heavily, she added, "But I figured out soon enough that I was scared *I* was getting attached. Not just to you but to what you and that third pendant represented in my life, past and present." She released the dainty pendant and looked up at him again. "I just wasn't ready. And a part of me couldn't believe it was possible."

He didn't dare hope. But he couldn't simply hold his heart in his hand and wonder, either. "Do you forgive me, Emma?"

"Jake, stop," she begged.

"I have to know. We *both* do. Have you forgiven me for what happened that night?"

The look in her eyes gave him the answer before she uttered a word.

Emma wished so badly that she did forgive him, but she knew without a doubt in her mind that she didn't. She didn't, couldn't forgive him. She didn't blame him, of course, not for the fire, or even for Peyton dying. Not really.

But what she did blame him for was the real thing that had been torturing her heart all these years. The part of the night that even Megan didn't know about.

"I don't know that I *can* forgive you, Jake," she whispered raggedly.

She gripped his hand and held it firmly against her face, afraid the truth would steal him away from her.

But he didn't pull away. In fact, he pulled her closer, tugged her into his arms, and allowed her to collapse against him. His arms tightened like steel bands around her. And she clung to that, wished for it to be enough to keep all the rest of it away.

"It's okay, sweetheart. It's okay if you can't forgive me."

The weight of his words slammed into her like a punishing wave. "It isn't fair." She clutched his shirt in her hands, not wanting to let go.

A warm, calloused hand cupped her cheek, and she leaned into his touch, not wanting to lose it.

"You save one, and I'll save the other," he uttered in a raw, tortured whisper.

And just like that, she was back there in the fire that night. The night her home and family went up in flames. Emma staggered back a step and clutched at her heart.

"That's the promise I made you that night in the fire. The promise you trusted me to fulfill. The promise that made you make the hardest decision you'd ever had to make. That's what you can't forgive . . . isn't it?"

He was right.

Chapter Twenty-Three

It was the one thing he'd told her, *promised* her while the fire had blazed all around them that night. His words had been the one driving force that had finally propelled Emma to move her lead feet and go save her sister. Only she'd made that decision not knowing what Jake had already figured out.

That they'd be able to save only one of her siblings that night.

Emma felt the tremors shaking her limbs just like she had that night. That one broken promise.

Replaying it in her head could always bring her right back into that fire like nothing else could. Bring her back to the worst night of her life, where fire as far as the eye could see scorched the very air around her, broiled her alive. Coated every inch of her with fear, stronger than what she'd thought she could overcome.

She was right back there feeling it all again.

Only this time she knew how it would end.

"Jake!"

At first she thought she'd been imagining things, seeing things through the wall of flames and smoke. But his voice came through the fire, loud and clear.

"Emma! Back up as far as you can. I'm coming through."

He charged through the ring of fire encasing the stairwell, wrapped up in what looked like the living room drapes. He made it to her just as another large section of the ceiling fell, exposing more of the attic and the scary sight of the giant, melting hole in the roof, which was crumbling wider by the second.

"Look out!" Jake shoved her out of the way as a huge chunk of the roof caved and broke right through the ceiling. The fallen roof brought down everything with it, causing an inverted volcano of molten flames and debris burned to a crisp not five feet away from them.

They were now trapped up there with a solid ten feet of fire between them and the stairs. "Jake, what do we do? The kids are still up here—"

They both jumped back as another section of burning ceiling crashed down in front of them. The longer they waited, the more the hallways all around them were getting taken over by fire. Soon they'd be cocooned in flames from all sides.

"Are they together? The kids?"

"No. Megan's room is down to the right, and Peyton is down to the left. I couldn't get to either of them; the hallway that splits off to their rooms looks just like this one. Completely engulfed in flames."

"I have an idea. But we need to split up. You save one; I'll save the other. I'll be right behind you." He threw one of the wet drapery panels he'd used to get up here over her like a cloak. "This should protect you a little, but you have to keep moving. Cover yourself with it completely and run as fast as you can down the hallway." He pulled the wet fabric down so it covered nearly her entire face. "Try to stay low and breathe under this pocket to avoid inhaling smoke."

Another chunk of burning ceiling and scorched roof shingles fell onto the stairs, this time breaking through to the ground floor.

"We're out of time. Go, Emma. Run!"

And Emma ran.

She used a corner of the wet drapery panel to open the burning-hot doorknob and yanked a crying Megan to her, wrapping the wet fabric around them both. They sprinted as fast as they could back down the hall to the landing, never stopping, no matter what fell on them or around them.

But when they got there, all Emma could see was fire.

"Emma! This way!"

She tried to follow his voice to get her bearings, but her eyes could barely make anything remotely familiar.

There was fire everywhere. They couldn't move without walking into a blockade of flames. They weren't going to make it. She hugged Megan to her and crouched lower, inching them a few steps back and forth when a new chunk of fire fell near their feet.

Suddenly a hand shot out to grab her arm. "Follow me!"

Jake wrapped his wet drapery panel around them all and pushed them through a curtain of fire to the top of the stairwell, which now had a slim opening without any debris. Jake had managed to shove aside the blockade of fire by clearing out the collapsed roof and caved-in walls using the mattress from her bedroom. Which was now laid nearly parallel with the ground over the top half of the stairwell.

"Step up onto the mattress. And don't look down!"

So of course she looked down.

And nearly screamed.

The entire top half of the stairwell was now a big gaping hole under the mattress.

"Emma, you have to move. I can't carry you both. The mattress is wedged against the walls, so just go across it like a bridge down to the next landing. It's burning fast, though, so move. We have to get down the stairwell before the rest of the roof falls on us."

He basically dragged them across the fast-charring mattress until they were on the second landing, where another tunnel of flames awaited.

The bottom steps were a blaze of fire.

There was no way to get to the front door.

Jake didn't let them hesitate for even a second.

She felt his arm tighten around her waist and, suddenly, she and Megan were airborne alongside him.

The three of them landed in a heap in front of the staircase, just as it collapsed and got swallowed up in the fire. With the front door just steps away, Jake picked up Megan and held her on his hip while he yanked Emma to her feet. They sprinted the final few yards and punched through the front door onto the front yard a mere second before the front half of the roof came crashing down behind them.

Emma felt several neighbors helping her away from the burning house until they were a safe distance away. The cold grass felt almost painful against her skin, but her legs couldn't keep her upright. She fell to the ground and simply lay there, dragging oxygen in by the mouthful, ignoring the jagged shards of pain in her throat with every breath.

She could feel the edges of her vision blackening. The air in her lungs felt heavy, and every cough she couldn't contain was excruciating to let out, but she kept on breathing to keep from passing out.

There was a muscle cramp in seemingly every square inch of her body, and her skin was raw and sensitive to even the slightest breeze. People were shouting all around her, but she found she could hardly focus on anything. It was all a spinning mess of lights and noise and a throb in her head somehow beating at a different rate than her heartbeat.

The only thing that did register was Jake's voice. Just like in the fire, it calmed her as soon as she heard it, even if it wasn't directed at her this time.

"Shhh, Megan. You're going to be okay. You hear that? That's the ambulance coming to help you. I know everything is sore, sweetie. Just hang on."

When the meaning of his words began sinking in, Emma found the strength to lift her heavy eyelids to try to make sense of what she was hearing and seeing.

Megan. Crying in pain. Something about her left arm didn't look right. Her nightgown was burned through on her chest. Her neck was bleeding. And her cheek . . .

"Oh my God, Megan's been burned!" screamed a neighbor. "Someone, do something! Get some water!"

"No!" shouted Jake. "Stay back!" Instead of explaining his actions, he hovered over Megan, not touching her and preventing anyone else from touching her, as well.

"Ignore them," he soothed in that calming voice again. "Just stay with me, Megan. Let me know if you're feeling cold." He took the blanket a neighbor was holding out to them and draped it over her legs and stomach, and the unburned parts of her body.

"Jake?" whispered Emma, not wanting to distract him, not after hearing a neighbor say that Jake was doing everything exactly right.

Two ambulances screeched to a halt on the grass right beside them before he could answer her. The paramedics crowded around Megan seconds later.

When the paramedics tried to check her out, as well, Emma pushed them away.

Her scattered thoughts were starting to blend together, and her entire body felt as if it was slowly shutting down. But . . . there was something. Something she needed to ask Jake before it was too late.

She watched Jake crumble to the ground as soon as Megan got lifted into the ambulance. A pain-filled expression unlike any she'd ever seen descended on his face as he hunched over, arms covering his head in anguish.

That's when she knew.

"You left Peyton up there," Emma whispered brokenly. She watched Jake's eyes slam shut in grief. "Why, Jake?"

"You've heard all the details, Emma. I know you have. And you saw the roof, the stairs. I needed to clear a path through that tunnel of fire in the hallway at the top of the landing and find a way to get you guys over the top half of the staircase since the steps had become engulfed in flames. So after you went to get Megan, I ran to your room to grab your mattress. I'd only just barely bought us a few-second window when you returned with Megan. I *couldn't* save Peyton. There was just no time."

Emma processed the words as facts, but still she couldn't meet his gaze. "That's what the articles about the fire said, too. I read them all, you know. Each and every one. The ones that called you a hero, and talked about your first-aid certification as a junior lifeguard having been a help to Megan's burns. The ones that had firework-banning agendas painted you the worst, of course, but even they called your actions heroic."

He'd done so much quick thinking that night. Pulled in the lawn hose from outside as much as he could, partway up the stairs. He'd yanked the tall drapes from the front windows down so they could use them as cover. And he'd doused the curtains with water before running up to get to her.

"Why didn't you save him . . . after promising me you would?" she asked again. Needing to know.

"Sweetheart, you know all this. If I'd gone after Peyton like I'd promised, we would've been trapped, and we all would've died up there. There is no way the fire trucks could've gotten to us in time."

The articles had all reported the same thing.

By the time the first responders had gotten to their home in the far outskirts of Riverside, the house had practically imploded with fire.

Peyton's room on the second floor had collapsed completely, right before their eyes.

"But you *promised*, Jake." The barely audible statement sounded as if it were coming from the teen version of herself. Their parents and lawyers hadn't allowed any communication between their families, so in a way, sixteen-year-old Emma was still back there wanting to know why sixteen-year-old Jake hadn't kept his promise.

"I had to break my promise, sweetheart." Jake's voice was raw with fresh pain. "And I will hate myself for that for the rest of my life. But

I also know that I'd do it the same way all over again. To save you and Megan."

"But you promised," she repeated. Only this time, the twenty-nine-year-old Emma was the one asking the underlying question.

The real question she'd been asking all along.

"Do you need me to say it, Emma? If you do, I will. I'll say it."

Did she? Could she bear it?

Even though a part of her knew the answer to the latter was no, she also knew the answer to the former was yes. "You save one, and I'll save the other . . . why, Jake? Why did you tell me that when you knew you weren't going to save the other?"

He paused for a long few moments, silently giving her a chance to call the question back. When she didn't, his eyes ran over her face then, as if he were remembering every detail about her. One last time.

"I said that because they were your siblings, Emma. I couldn't make that choice." He exhaled raggedly. "I said it because I needed you to choose which of your siblings we were going to save that night."

Emma dropped to her knees, defeated now that the words were out there, unable to be kept hidden like they'd been all these years. Unable to be avoided. "You wanted me to choose . . . and I chose Megan."

"Yes, Emma. You chose Megan, and because of that we *saved* Megan. Had you not made a choice that night, you would have lost them both."

"So that's why you lied to me. You knew we couldn't save them both, so you lied so I would make a choice."

"Yes," he rasped, sounding tortured over the reminder. "I knew you wouldn't choose if you thought we could only save one . . . so I lied to you."

"*Of course* I wouldn't choose," she cried out, lashing out at him even though she knew it was wholly unwarranted. Unfair. "I didn't choose to save him that night, Jake. My own little brother."

Jake gripped her shoulders and reached down to tip her chin up to hold her gaze, not allowing the shame to keep that connection severed any longer. "We *couldn't* save both of them. You *know* that. I know you know that."

"I do." She shrugged helplessly. But it didn't matter. "I know it's not logical, but I've never been able to get past the fact that by asking me to choose, you basically asked me to sign a death sentence for one of them."

Anguished tears welled in her eyes. "And I did. I signed Peyton's life away. I chose Megan over him. Chose her life over his."

She shook her head at Jake sadly. "Do you still hear him in your nightmares? Peyton? I do. I hear him in mine all the time. Crying, screaming . . . dying all over again."

"Emma . . ."

She pulled away from him, and his shoulders fell.

"I am so sorry I made you choose, sweetheart. More sorry than I could ever put into words."

She didn't want him to apologize for that. Not for the choice he'd forced her to make then, or the one he'd forced her to make now.

Because there was another big choice here he was asking her to make.

And just like then, she had to decide.

For both of their sakes.

"Jake . . . the guilt, the anger, the sadness. The pain. I know it's not fair to you that you're tangled up in all of this for me. Even more so now that I know you weren't even the one who set the fire to begin with. Still. I just don't think I'll ever be able to detangle you from all of that." The tears she'd been holding for what felt like the past fourteen years finally broke free.

Jake dropped his forehead against hers and just held her in his arms.

When he finally spoke, his voice was as wrecked as it was resolute. "I can't take away the pain from that night, Emma, but I can stop it from hurting you again now. I couldn't make that choice for you that night, but I can make one for you now."

Her brain was screaming at her heart to stop this. Stop it before she lost him forever.

But she couldn't.

She shut her eyes and raged against the universe for being so unbelievably cruel.

For putting them in that situation fourteen years ago.

For putting them in this situation now.

When she finally found the strength to open her eyes, both her brain and her heart mourned what she saw before her.

Jake was gone.

Chapter Twenty-Four

What a difference fourteen years makes.

Her whole life, Emma had been the big sister who never shed a tear. The one who couldn't cry or complain because her baby sister had it ten times worse. Any problems she may have had would always pale in comparison to what Megan had to go through.

So she never allowed herself to cry.

The night Jake left, Megan had happened to stop by, and at the sight of Emma's tears, she did what Emma used to do whenever she used to catch Megan crying. She grabbed a comforter and threw it over them both like a tent. A force field against the world.

And like she'd remembered doing with Megan so many nights throughout their lives, they just stayed there under the comforter in silence. Stayed there until the tears finally slowed. Stayed there until finally Emma didn't need the force field to face the world again.

That was a week ago.

Jake was still in town working on the library, but somehow he'd found ways to ensure their paths never crossed. Knowing he was so close and yet still out of reach made her *almost* need a force field every day and every night.

Her heart was a mess over how much she missed him. How screwed up was that? For her to miss him like this while a part of her, the part stuck in her past, still had all this pain and resentment locked away inside.

So she turned her feelings off. To get through the days and nights. Really, life felt numb without him anyhow.

"Jake looks just as bad as you do," announced Megan, joining her in the kitchen.

For the past week, Emma had let her other workers man the front of the bakery while she kept hidden in the back, just trying not to bum out everyone she came in contact with.

"Are you trying to make me feel better?" asked Emma. "Because that just makes me feel a thousand times worse. I don't want Jake to be unhappy."

"You just don't want to be happy with him?"

Youch. Looked like the force field was gone, and Megan was no longer coddling her.

"It's not that simple."

"But it could be. You could just want to be happy with Jake, and then go out and be freaking happy."

Emma sighed. "How do you do that, Meg?" She really wanted to know. "How do you just *be?* How have you been able to look at Jake nearly every day and not—"

"Hate him?" finished Megan quietly.

Yes. That.

Emma had not told her about the call she'd overheard, or that Jake hadn't been the one to launch the firework that had burned down their house. Jake had asked her not to, and Emma hadn't wanted to bring back bad memories for Megan.

So when Megan replied plainly, "I don't blame Jake for my injuries," Emma knew that wasn't because she knew the truth. But rather because Megan was just being Megan.

Back when Megan had been barely eleven, and a woman at the bus stop had offered her sympathy for the "awful thing" that had happened to her, Emma remembered how Megan had said there was no blame to be had because the fire had been an accident.

At the time Emma had thought her sister had just been giving the woman a line. The kind you say when the person you're talking to wouldn't understand anything else. But as the years went by, more and more she'd come to the realization that Megan truly believed that there wasn't anyone to blame for the fire, anyone to hate for the pain she'd suffered.

"Jake didn't burn my body; the fire did," Megan continued, as if it was the most obvious line of thinking. "He didn't pull the trigger of a gun, or get behind the wheel drunk. So to answer your question on how it is that I don't hate him, the answer is easy. I don't hate him because I like him."

Sometimes having a sister this grounded made her feel afloat. As though she wasn't as evolved or actualized. "Okay, well you like him now. But what about before you got to know him here in Juniper Hills? Didn't you hate him then?"

"No." She shrugged. "How could I? I didn't even know him then. How can I hate someone I don't know?"

As simple as that.

It was a little maddening. But also humbling and inspiring at the same time.

"Emma, I think you're asking the wrong person these questions. I know exactly what my feelings are where Jake is concerned. Can you say the same?"

Emma let out a heavy sigh. "I thought you were only going to be the big sister that one day under the force field."

"Well, clearly I've surpassed you in sisterly wisdom, so there's a good chance this evolutionary change might be permanent," teased Megan lightly.

Emma looked at her sister with no small amount of pride. "How about we take turns?"

"Deal." Then after studying Emma for a beat, she asked, "Can today be my turn?"

Was she ready for Megan's brand of reality today? Not really. "Sure," she replied anyway, knowing there wouldn't ever be a good time to face how much she was screwing up her life.

"Do you love him?"

"Yes." Emma didn't even have to think about that one. Didn't hesitate one bit before she answered. She'd figured out her feelings about Jake a long time ago.

What she didn't know was whether love was enough to overcome her demons about their past.

∞

"It's time you find out whether love *is* enough, darn it," demanded Megan the next day when she stomped into the bakery.

Emma stared in shock at the roaring lioness before her, who looked and sounded just like her sister but couldn't possibly be. "Megan?" She almost poked the magnificently worked-up creature to make sure she wasn't a figment of her wildly creative imagination.

The sister look-alike was not to be deterred. "Look, tomorrow is Jake's birthday. Did you know that?"

Emma felt the blow land squarely on her solar plexus. She'd known Jake was born in May, but he'd never told her the exact date. Purposely changed the subject when she'd slyly try to get it out of him.

He'd always said he wasn't a big birthday person, at least when it came to his own. And she knew his mom had a lot to do with that.

"No, I didn't. Jake said he doesn't celebrate his birthday. Doesn't even let his brother and sister make a fuss."

"From what I can tell, he doesn't," agreed Megan. "But he's been a great friend, and he's doing an outstanding job on the library. So I'm going to drop off a birthday gift for him tomorrow anyway."

When Emma stood there mutely, unsure of how to respond, Megan sighed. "Look, I know you're hurting, and I know you're still working through stuff and looking for answers. But this is Jake's birthday we're talking about here. Are you going to show up for his birthday like you never fail to do for every senior citizen who doesn't have family visiting them at the local care home anymore? Or are you going to be a stubborn butthead?"

Yes, this was definitely a doppelgänger standing before her. The real Megan would never call her a butthead.

The Megan doppelgänger drilled her with a look. "I'll be here at eleven sharp tomorrow morning with the car. If you decide you're not going to be a butthead, be ready and waiting for me tomorrow. Janet can cover the bakery for a few hours."

And then she was gone.

The Megan doppelgänger was scary.

But also very, very wise.

Frankly, Emma wasn't sure whether she was going to be a butthead tomorrow or not. All she did know was that right there, right then, she couldn't stop thinking about a story Jake had once told her.

"Chocolate strawberry shortcake with whipped cream," he'd answered immediately when she'd asked what his favorite cake was. He'd had this boyishly happy look on his face when he'd said it, too.

For good reason. It was the cake his mom used to make for him every year for his birthday.

"My first year in juvie, I'd hoped and prayed that she'd bring that cake. Because the lucky ones did. The ones who had family who loved and cared and remembered, who would bring a birthday cake for their birthday." He hadn't been able to meet her eyes as he told her how much it hurt that she never came either year. "That first year on my birthday, I waited for her all day and all night. I wanted that cake so badly. Because it was my only source of hope."

If his mom couldn't bring herself to come to wish him a happy birthday, he figured there really was no repairing things between them.

He'd been right.

Jake told Emma that his mother had never spoken to him since, and he'd likewise never had a birthday cake since.

Emma had nearly bawled her eyes out by the end of the story.

And she nearly cried again today realizing that she hadn't told him why that story had affected her so badly. Not because she'd been hiding it from him, but because she'd been hiding the truth from herself.

Not even Megan knew that their stepmom had flat out told Emma that she'd never forgive her for her son's death.

"I trusted you to take care of him that night. Not just a random babysitter, but you, his big sister. And you let us both down. My son's dead because you didn't protect him like you said you would. And I'll never forgive you for that, Emma. Ever."

Later she'd also told Emma that their marriage failing was also her fault.

Emma at sixteen had been utterly heartbroken after hearing that. Had believed her stepmom. Had blamed herself entirely for it all.

Emma at twenty-nine understood just how cruel and wrong her stepmom had been for saying those things to her. Understood that it wasn't she who'd let her stepmom down, but the other way around.

"I should've told Jake that," she whispered to the empty bakery. Of course, she'd comforted Jake and told her how awful it was that his mom hadn't cared enough to celebrate his birthday. But she hadn't told him her story. Hadn't showed him that they were kindred spirits in that sense.

Now in hindsight, as she began suddenly dicing up strawberries like a freaking Cuisinart—and rinsing her tears off them so they wouldn't ruin the whipped-cream frosting—she realized that what made them kindred spirits wasn't their parallel experiences, and what she was feeling at the moment wasn't sympathy over their shared pain. It wasn't even anger or disappointment at their mothers. No. Rather, she felt an overwhelming sense of *determination*.

To show both their moms that they'd both turned out just great, despite not having the maternal support they should've had.

To no longer hide things from Jake, from her past, from herself.

And to bake that very cake for him for every single one of his birthdays to come.

Chapter Twenty-Five

The next day Megan stopped the car in the last possible place Emma expected.

"Megan, what are we doing here?"

"I told you—we're here to see Jake."

Here?

Emma reached into the car for the box with the cake she'd worked on all night and fell in step next to Megan.

They walked through the cemetery where their stepbrother, Peyton, had been laid to rest. They'd just been there the week prior to leave flowers on his headstone for Peyton's birthday.

Was that when Jake had first learned about the cemetery?

"Did he ask you where Peyton was buried, or did you tell him?"

Megan shook her head and whispered in the same hushed tones as Emma. "Neither. He already knew." They walked over to the section of the large cemetery where Peyton was buried, but Megan stopped them a few rows back. "Look."

Emma gasped.

Right in front of Peyton's headstone, they saw a picnic blanket laid out, along with a little portable DVD player, two colorful wrapped presents, and a huge spread of food containers, which were all still closed . . . because Jake was sharing a bowl of popcorn with Peyton first.

Hand covering her mouth, Emma edged one more row closer, but then quickly hid behind a tree when she saw Jake return to the picnic blanket.

The fun Disney movie playing on the DVD player was just coming to an end when Jake began critiquing the movie as if Peyton himself were sitting right there.

"So what'd you think, buddy? Thumbs up or thumbs down? For me, I'm split. I don't know if it's because you and I have been waiting to watch this since Christmas or what, but I don't know that it lived up to the hype."

He leaned over to pop the DVD out, then slid another one in.

"Okay, now it's my movie pick. This one is that martial arts flick I told you at Christmas might be out in time for our birthdays. Lucky for us they released it just this past weekend, so I scooped it up. Figure this one would be good for us to watch with lunch." Jake began whistling as he forwarded through the DVD previews and pressed "Play."

He then proceeded to open up the containers, revealing what looked like every item on the kids' menu at most diners, explaining proudly that he'd made each one from scratch this year.

"He's been coming every year," explained Megan. "Since he got out of juvie, apparently."

In shock over that news, Emma simply listened to Jake then begin pointing out a few of his favorite and then not-so-favorite scenes. There was an affectionate ease in his voice that made it clear that somewhere along the line in the past fourteen years, her deceased stepbrother had genuinely become one of Jake's best buds.

"How do you know all this?" whispered Emma.

"I came over here late on Christmas Day last year to leave a poinsettia plant. Remember? We'd come in the morning like we always do, but I'd forgotten the plant. So I came back after you were in the bakery getting ready for all the party pickups the following day."

The rest of Megan's details were a blur. All Emma could think about was that Jake had been here doing this for *years*.

They both ducked back behind the tree more when they saw Jake get up and circle around Peyton's headstone.

"When I first saw a little toy on top of the headstone," murmured Megan as they crouched down, "I tracked down the groundskeeper to find out all the info."

Emma couldn't believe Megan had kept this staggering discovery to herself this entire time. "Why didn't you tell me any of this sooner?"

Megan shrugged. "I figured it was his secret to keep, not mine to tell."

Damn the woman with all her logical moral and philosophical thinking.

"Now stop talking and listen," ordered Megan.

Oh, she'd been listening, all right.

Just the past few minutes alone were leaving Emma a big ol' weeping mess. Every new thing she heard him say to her little brother threatened to take her knees out from under her, none more than when she heard him officially start the birthday festivities.

"Happy birthday to us, buddy."

Jake finished his official toast to kick off the celebration and grinned proudly at the birthday spread he'd finally finished laying out in front of Peyton's headstone. It was definitely bigger than their usual celebration.

And undoubtedly more edible, as well.

"I know, I know. You're thinking I won the lottery or something, right?" He chuckled. "I guess I went a little overboard this year. But can you believe it? I've got jobs and contracts coming out of my ears for once. And even more amazing, I actually learned to cook."

As he finished opening the last of the Tupperware containers, Jake sat back on his heels and looked at the lavish meal he'd prepared for them this year. "Oh! Almost forgot."

He pulled out Peyton's juice box and put the present he'd wrapped for Peyton front and center on the picnic blanket.

"Here you go, buddy. I know how you like the fruit punches. This one's new. I tried it, and it's fancier than the stuff we normally drink, but I figured what the hey. We should get to splurge on our birthdays, right?" Smiling at the headstone affectionately, he placed the juice box down and then proceeded to open the present he'd wrapped for Peyton that morning.

This, too, was bigger than what he normally got—he tried not to go overboard with the presents because he didn't like Kenny the grounds-keeper having too much to clean up after the wild joint-birthday party Jake threw for Peyton every year. Since Peyton's birthday was a week prior to his own, Jake had begun throwing these parties the second year after he got out of juvie. He liked sharing his own big day with the little guy. Sure, his siblings remembered his birthday, but it wasn't the same as when you were a kid. With the party and the hoopla.

He always made sure to make a big hoopla.

Balling up all the pieces of opened wrapping paper, Jake plopped the big new Transformer on top of the headstone. "I found you a cool Transformer, buddy. I know you have almost all of them already, but this one even I've never had. I found it online. Pretty awesome, huh?" He settled back onto the picnic blanket. "You go on and play with that while I sit here and start digging into our breakfast. If you haven't noticed, it is actually edible this year, thanks to your sister. She's been giving me cooking lessons, you know."

At the mention of Emma, Jake felt his heart ache like it always did.

The past week had been rough. Every day, he'd wanted to go see her, but every day he'd stopped himself. She needed time. And space.

Even though giving her both was slowly killing him, he knew it was important.

He took a few bites of the homemade mac and cheese he'd been daring enough to try his hand at that morning. Surprisingly, not bad. He held up his fork to toast Peyton. "This is pretty good. I don't think I'll be doing any of that instant stuff for us from now on."

Of all the things he'd made, the pasta made him think of Emma the most, since it was one of the first things she'd taught him how to not ruin. Sighing, he put the fork down and gazed at his own unopened present. "Peyton, my man. I know it'll probably shock you to hear this, but your sister and I started dating this year. Crazy, right?" He unwrapped the slim box and showed Peyton what was inside. "That's right. Airline tickets. Two of 'em. And this one's got your sister's name on it. She mentioned how she'd never been out of Kansas, and how she'd always wanted to go to the beach. So I booked us open-ended tickets to California. I know, I know. I probably should've sprung for Hawaii or something, but those were crazy expensive. Maybe next year."

At least he hoped there was a next year.

"Man, I love her. I know you heard me say that a long time ago, back when I first got out of juvie, but this time it's more. I think she loves me back. Even when I'm driving her crazy." He chuckled. "And she drives me crazy right back. She's still stubborn as hell. You remember I'm sure."

Fiddling with the pasta dish she'd taught him to make in their last cooking lesson, he murmured, more to himself than Peyton, "I love everything about her. I just . . . wish she felt the same way about me, you know?" Exhaling heavily, he caught Peyton up on all that had been going on. "But with all the stuff that happened with the fire—you remember—it's just complicated. For her, the past is making a future for us impossible. But I'm not giving up. No way, no how. Fair warning, before I head out today, you need to help me think of a way to win her back, okay? I don't care how crazy the idea is. I'm getting her back, man—"

"And that's all there is to it?"

Jake froze when he heard the softly spoken statement. Hoping to hell he hadn't just imagined it, he turned around slowly.

And saw her.

"Emma."

Chapter Twenty-Six

Emma watched Jake turn around in surprise as she approached the picnic blanket and set the cake box down. If she didn't, given how hard she was shaking, she'd probably drop the whole thing.

"Do you know that you always used to say that to me back when we were teens?" She started at the beginning. "You'd teach me how to do something like play poker or fix my sister's bike. Every time you'd always make it seem so simple, so doable. Then when you were done with your lesson, you'd just grin at me and say in this easy-breezy voice, 'That's all there is to it.' And you'd always make me believe it *was* that simple and that doable."

"It usually was," he reasoned with a matter-of-fact shrug.

"For *you*, maybe."

Understanding bloomed across his expression. "But not for you?"

She shook her head. "No." She pointed her finger between the two of them. "Like this, you and me. Everything seemed so complicated, nearly impossible to me. From the very beginning. And it drove me crazy because I wanted to believe it was simple and doable. Believe it the way you did."

"But you didn't." A statement, not a question.

"I *couldn't*. Not the way you did. I tried, though—you have to believe me. My suggesting we start from scratch and pretend like we didn't have a past? I thought that's what I was doing. Channeling my inner Jake, making everything simple."

"That's not—"

She raised a hand to stop him. "Let me finish. It took me a while to figure out that you weren't emphasizing how simple everything was, but rather the other part. On the doable part. Am I right?"

He nodded gently.

"See, I didn't get that until yesterday. When Megan here came over to yell at me."

Jake's eyes widened in impressed amusement.

"I'd been spending so much time trying to figure out if it could be as *simple* as love overcoming all our obstacles. Yesterday I came to the conclusion that it wasn't. Zero simplicity when it comes to Jake and Emma."

His eyes darkened sharply. Whether it was from her talking about love or saying it in context with their names, she wasn't sure. But she drew strength from all the unfiltered energy and emotion his gaze lent her. "I finally figured out last night that it wasn't that simple, but it *was* doable. I just . . . had to . . . do it."

God, she sounded like a sports apparel commercial.

Jake's lips twitched to the side, but he remained silent.

"That's when I rewound and took another look at everything you've ever taught me. Fourteen years ago, and more important, over the past few weeks. Nothing you were explaining was simple at all. But they *were* doable." She gulped back the wave of emotions spilling out of her heart and up her windpipe. "Just like us. We're not simple, but we're doable."

Jesus, now she just sounded lame.

But apparently Jake didn't think so. He gave her a slow smile that made her knees weak. "So . . . you think we're *doable*?"

"That sounds so . . . inadequate. Criminy, I'm messing this up. I rehearsed it in my head all night, too, I swear." She shut her eyes and tipped her head back, mentally berating herself.

Jake slid a warm hand through her hair and pressed a soft kiss to each of her closed eyelids. "I think you're doing great."

"No I'm not." She frowned. "I sound like an idiot."

"I beg to differ. You sound exactly like the woman I'm in love with."

Emma felt her heart triple in size and the tears start up all over again.

Yes, that. That's what she should've led with. Her. Being in love with him. So that's exactly what she did next.

Or at least tried to.

Between all the crying and hysterical pointing toward the picnic spread, she probably only said about two or three actual human words.

Jake, however, somehow seemed to understand it all perfectly. He yanked her fully into his arms. "I've missed you so damn much, sweetheart."

Why was he so good at the speaking-words thing? While she was reduced to hand gestures and four hiccups that sounded nothing like "I missed you, too."

Almost as if hearing her silent question, Megan explained helpfully. "This whole crying thing is new for Emma. Give her a minute. She'll calm down."

And with that, Megan plopped down on the picnic blanket and started chatting with Peyton the way Jake had been doing earlier.

The sight of this amazing picnic Jake had put together for Peyton finally managed to untangle her tongue. "Wh-why didn't you tell me you've been visiting Peyton all these years?"

Jake smiled over at Peyton's headstone. "You never wanted to talk about the past. I didn't want to dredge it all up for you."

"I'm sorry you felt like you couldn't share that part of your life with me."

His expression hardened again like quick-dry cement. "For god-sakes, Emma. Could you please stop apologizing to me. I just can't take it when you do. The *last* thing you should ever have to do is apologize to me. Not after all that's happened with us—"

"Wait, stop, Jake. Let me get this out first."

She took a deep breath and went back to replaying all the words she'd rehearsed last night. "I used to wonder if I'd ever be able to trust the universe again. When it's mean. And messy. And when it takes the people I love from me. When it hurts the people I love. Now I know."

She gazed up at him. "And that's all because of you. I know that I don't know all the answers. Not even some of the answers. But that's okay. I know I'm screwed up. For a person to love me, they have to love all of me. And I never thought anyone would. Anyone could. Until you came back into my life. What I said earlier about you shar-ing your life with me, I meant it. I don't want us to start from a clean slate. I want our messy, crazy slate. I want us to work through our past. Together. For however long it takes. Do you . . . do you still want that, too?"

"More than ever, sweetheart."

A whoosh of air left her lungs, just as the same determination she'd felt when baking Jake's birthday cake pumped through her veins. "Fair warning. You and me, it's not going to be neat, and it's not going to be pretty. Not by a long shot. I still have so much guilt churning inside me that I'm not sure if it's going to be a smooth road for us ahead. Is that okay? Do you even want to be with someone as screwed up as I am?"

"I want it all, Emma. Our past, our present, and definitely our future." He took in his own deep, loaded breath then. "And you're not the only one that's screwed up, sweetheart. I have just as much guilt that I still need to work through." He brushed his thumb over her cheek. "Is that okay with you?"

"More than okay."

She laid her head against his chest and pointed at the amazing birthday party Jake had thrown for her brother. "I still can't believe you did all this for all these years. You've probably been a better brother to him the past fourteen years than I was a sister to him while he was alive. I'm glad he has you—"

Megan shot up off the blanket. "That's it! I can't take it anymore. Emma, why in the world do you keep saying that? That you're not a good sister? Not just about Peyton, but when folks talk about me. Our whole lives after the fire, folks would say that I was lucky to have you as a sister, and you would shut them down. Why? Why don't you believe it? Why, for chrissakes, don't you think you're a good sister?"

Emma glanced at Jake, and he just squeezed her hand to offer her silent support.

If she was going to try to be straight with herself from now on and really work through things with Jake, she had to do so with Megan, as well.

"Megan, I've never told you this, but part of what's been hard for me is knowing that what happened to you, and to Peyton, was partly my fault. Mom blamed me for it, and she was partly right."

When *both* Megan and Jake took exception to that, she held up her hands. "Again, just let me explain first. I have all these feelings inside me that I haven't been able to get out for fourteen years. So let me just get them out the only way I know how."

From the beginning.

"I know Mom wasn't right to say the things she did. To blame Peyton's death and the divorce on me. But for a long time, I struggled with my part in all of it. I second-guessed every single decision I'd made that night. That whole summer, really. Everything from my decision to take third-year French during summer school, which was why I'd had my earphones on that night in the first place; I'd been listening to my oral-language lab CD when I fell asleep. Another thing I'd beat myself up for. For years I wondered if I'd just taken another class, or if I hadn't fallen asleep, maybe Peyton would still be alive, and you wouldn't have gotten burned."

Emma must have replayed that night a few thousand times in her mind. Even now she could hear all the fireworks that had been going off that night. It'd been day six of the ten-day time frame the town allowed for fireworks to celebrate the Fourth of July. There was still at least a half hour before the firework curfew would kick in, so after checking in on the kids, she'd turned the CD way up to tune out all the loud bangs and whirls and hisses coming from outside.

The next thing she knew, she was waking up from a deep sleep.

And her entire house was on fire.

"I kept telling myself, for at least the first few years, that if I'd just been awake or if I hadn't been studying for French, I would've discovered that a firework had started a fire on our roof. And that the house was all but collapsing from the top down." Sure, the fire report said the fire had spread quickly, but there would have been more than enough time to save the kids if she'd been awake.

"By the time I woke up, parts of the downstairs were catching on fire already, and when I looked up the staircase, all I could see was flames all around. So I ran upstairs and found the entire second floor hallway engulfed in flames. I got to you kids too late. And that's on me. Honestly, if Jake hadn't come when he had, we all probably would've died up there. Because I wouldn't have been able to choose which of you to save."

Late at night, around the exact same time as the fire, Emma's nightmares would replay the images for her all over again. Along with the screams—the scared screams of her baby sister and brother coming from their rooms. Those were at times more torturous than the memories of the terrifying fire itself.

"I've never forgiven myself for choosing to save you over Peyton. Never. And the thing is, *that* made me feel guilty, as well. Of course I never regretted saving you over him, but still, a part of me felt bad about saving you and not him. Does that make sense? What kind of sister feels badly for something like that?"

"The kind who was forced into an impossible situation," replied Megan gently. "You shouldn't feel guilty about that."

"Shouldn't I? Do you know that in those thousands of times I've replayed that night in my head, some of those times, I've wondered what would've happened if I'd chosen Peyton instead. Instead of you, Megan." Another knife wound of guilt sliced through her chest. "I'd wake up screaming and hate myself for even thinking it. Then I'd hate myself for trying to find solace in my decision. It was . . . an impossible cycle I couldn't stop."

Emma's eyes fell to the ground in shame as she explained the rest of it. "I analyzed it, you know. My decision to save you and leave Peyton to Jake. I'd mentally measured, countless times, if your room was closer than Peyton's—if that had led me to my decision. And I'd tried to remember if I'd been thinking that you were lighter and maybe easier for me to carry if it came down to that." The guilt crept into her veins again, as slow and potent as Novocain. "But there was no difference in distance. And I hadn't even thought about you being a tiny bit lighter than Peyton, either. Which made me wonder . . ."

She'd never told *anyone* this before. "It made me wonder if I'd chosen you because you were my biological sister, and Peyton was my stepbrother."

Megan hissed a gasp of disbelief. Meanwhile Jake looked ready to slay an invisible dragon.

They both started talking at the same time.

But their voices became white noise as she turned to Peyton's headstone. "I'm so sorry, Peyton. So sorry I wasn't a better sister to you."

Finally Megan's sharp voice managed to pierce the remorse pounding in her ears like the ocean. "Emma. Stop that. Right now. You did *not* make a choice between your biological sibling and your stepsibling."

"How do you know?" asked Emma raggedly. "How can you be sure that I didn't weigh your life just a little more heavily than his because you were related to me by blood? That I didn't sign his death sentence because he was my stepbrother who I hadn't known as long as I'd known you? How can you know when I don't know? I don't know if in that moment, I'd chosen you for that reason. But if I had, then what does that say about me as Peyton's big sister? When we'd all first become a family, I told myself that I wouldn't love him any differently. That I wouldn't treat him any differently. That he was just my little brother the way you were my little sister. But what if that night, when push came to shove, I proved myself full of crap?"

Suddenly she felt Jake let go of her and turn her into the waiting arms of Megan. "Emma, Peyton knew you loved him as much as you loved me." She felt Megan smile against her shoulder. "In fact, he used to tell me so all the time."

Emma pulled back. "What?"

"Oh yeah, *all* the time. Peyton never saw himself as your stepbrother. He saw himself as your brother. Period. And the two of us would bicker constantly over who was your favorite. Peyton always maintained that he was cuter and cooler, and thus your favorite by leaps and bounds."

Despite everything, Emma found herself laughing. She could actually hear Peyton saying something like that. "I'm glad for that. That he thought he was my favorite. But it doesn't change the fact that *I* might have been viewing him as my stepbrother that night when I chose you over him."

"For crying out loud, you can't torture yourself over a single split-second decision you made when the house was literally falling down all around you. Isn't it enough that you tried to go back in to save him?" demanded Megan.

Wait, what?

Emma stared at Megan, stunned. "What did you just say?"

"You tried to go back for him. If you really thought of him as 'just' a stepbrother, you wouldn't have risked your life to run *back* into a blazing ball of fire."

"Megan, I have no idea what you're talking about."

Megan turned to look at Jake in confusion. "She doesn't remember?"

"Apparently not," replied Jake quietly, his expression unreadable.

She didn't remember.

Maybe that was a good thing. Because Jake sure as hell did remember. Enough for the both of them. Jesus Christ, carrying Emma's unconscious body out of the house that second time was the one nightmare that hit him the hardest. He'd thought he'd lost her.

That he'd been carrying her out of that burning house so her parents could bury her.

"You were unconscious on the ground when I found you that second time," he began, as the memories flooded him from every direction. "I didn't even know you'd gone back in until I heard some random neighbor saying they saw you running toward the house."

Emma looked at him in utter disbelief. "You went into the burning house again to look for me?"

"Yes. Because I knew, I just knew you'd gone back in. And most of the firefighters were up on the roof, or on the second floor over on the side of the house where Peyton's room was to try to get to him. I knew if I didn't go after you, I'd lose you."

"Jake, I don't remember any of this."

"Like I said, you were unconscious. It was probably a combination of smoke inhalation and being traumatized."

"But you found me?"

"Almost too late. You were at the base of the stairs, probably trying to figure out how to get up there when there were no stairs left to climb. I found you crumpled on the ground, and just barely managed to pick you up maybe a second before a falling beam from the ceiling came down. It . . . it would've crushed you, Emma." His voice shook as he remembered how close that whoosh of fire had been. It had burned his shirt. And it had landed with a deafening thud so loud, his ears had rung for hours afterward. "When I saw you lying there, not moving, I thought I'd lost you. It was the scariest damn moment of my life, sweetheart."

He couldn't stop shaking as the flashbacks kept on coming.

Finally a pair of arms wrapped around his middle and calmed his sensory system down. "I can't believe I never knew any of this," Emma whispered against his chest.

"So you see," Megan said softly. "You were an incredible sister to Peyton—one who didn't think about her own life before running back into a house that was seconds from burning up in flames completely. You may have chosen me, but you *went back* for him. You've always been a great sister, Emma. To both me and Peyton."

With a deep sigh, Megan shook her head at them both. "You two are like two peas in a pod. You've both been torturing yourselves over what you weren't able to do, while failing to give yourselves credit for the extraordinary things you *did* do. Emma, you saved me and then you tried to save Peyton. Who cares if you had on a pair of earphones when the fire first broke out? You were our hero that night, just as much as Jake was." Megan turned to Jake. "And you. You not only saved Emma *twice*, but you've spent the last decade being an incredible big brother to Peyton with these birthday parties and everything.

"You two are perfect for each other. Which is why . . ." Megan reached into her purse and pulled out a bright-red bow—the kind with the sticky back you put on presents. She reached over and stuck the bow on Emma's head. "Happy birthday, Jake," she said simply before leaving the cemetery and driving off.

Chapter Twenty-Seven

Best birthday present ever.

Jake sat down on the picnic blanket and tucked a visibly dazed and shaken Emma beside him gently. Still seemingly reeling from the cataclysm of discoveries and self-revelations, Emma wordlessly pointed at the bakery box she'd been carrying earlier.

"For me?" he asked, smiling over the extracareful way she slid the box over for him to look at.

"Happy birthday."

Jake opened the box and stared down at the cake in quiet wonder. "Chocolate strawberry shortcake with whipped cream frosting."

Of course she'd remembered.

"I thought that was a tradition we could bring back." She gave him a trembling smile. "To celebrate every new year of this amazing life you're leading."

He stared at her for a moment, wondering how it was that she knew exactly why his mom stopping the birthday cake tradition had affected him so badly. It wasn't just because he felt as though she'd written him off as a son. Or because he'd waited that day in juvie, hoping as each hour passed that she'd come with the cake and a hug. Or because he'd waited the following year, as well.

No, more than anything else, he'd felt as if his mom was saying that his life didn't matter anymore. That it wasn't worth celebrating. It wasn't just that he was no longer worthy enough for her to bother baking him a cake, but no longer worthy, period. If your own mom doesn't care about each new year of your life, then who does?

While his dad may have cast him aside so he no longer existed as a Carmichael, what his mom had done was, in a way, so much more hurtful.

"I never thought I'd ever see this cake again."

Jake looked at the cake that, until now, had existed only in his pre-juvie memories. Until now, his pre-juvie life and post-juvie life had never really crossed paths. Until Emma. She was his past, his present, and now, finally, his future.

"Oh, shoot," she cursed quietly. "I don't have any candles."

He shrugged and wrapped an arm around her waist to pull her closer. "Wouldn't have any new things to wish for even if you did." Kissing her softly on the lips, he murmured, "See, who needs a candle?"

Her cheeks colored. "I've missed your freckles."

With a smiling head shake, she sighed. "What is it with you and my freckles?"

"I like 'em. And they like me, too."

"*What?*" She laughed.

"When you blush, your freckles come out to say hi. And you almost *always* blush when you see me."

"Do not."

"Do so. Your freckles don't lie." He raised one wicked eyebrow. "It's sort of like how around you, my—"

"Oh my *God*. Not in front of my brother!"

Chuckling, he pulled the cake out of the box and placed it on the ground carefully before dragging her into his arms. "I was going to say *heart*, you pervy hussy." He placed her palm over his chest so she could feel what she did to him. "Around you, my heart never stops racing, and it always feels like it's going to bust through my chest."

She threw her arms around his neck and leaned in for a kiss, pressing the entire length of her soft, curvy body against his.

Until he raised the white flag.

"Okay, okay, so maybe it's not *just* my heart that you can get stirred up." He felt her shoulders shake with laughter. "That's not exactly helping, sweetheart." He pulled her off his lap and down onto the picnic blanket. "I think maybe we ought to start eating cake so we stay out of trouble while your brother is chaperoning us."

"He probably is, you know," commented Emma as she handed him a fork and a giant slice of cake. "Peyton actually knew that I had a huge crush on you, and he always used to tell me that he'd kick your butt if you did wrong by me."

Jake beamed. Just when he thought he couldn't love the little guy any more. "I think that's earned Peyton the first slice of cake."

"No!"

Jake froze. "What?"

"That's your slice."

"Okay," he replied slowly as Emma quickly cut another slice for Peyton and then one for herself.

"Dig in," she said cheerfully.

She even went so far as to push the plate closer to him.

Was it just him, or was she being even stranger than usual?

Putting a pin in that for the time being, he slid his fork into the moist cake and took his first unbelievable bite.

Holy crap. "That's even better than my mom's."

Emma lit up like a Christmas tree. "Yeah? Okay, keep eating."

Back to the peculiar behavior again. But an intriguing variety for sure. He just gave her a smiling headshake and went in for another bite.

Only his fork clanged against something hard inside the cake. He slid his fork out and tried again. Again it bumped into something hard, seemingly metallic, in his slice.

A shy smile bloomed across Emma's face.

"Is this—" he began, too surprised and too at a loss for words to even finish his question.

He'd seen this very thing in a bunch of movies before. Never once did he imagine that *he* would be on the receiving end of it. Truth be told, he'd always thought the whole thing a little silly.

But it wasn't silly. In fact, it was romantic as hell.

"I've thought about this a lot," said Emma in a quiet, contemplative voice. "If I could turn back time, knowing everything I do now . . . about you taking the fall for a stranger who I still don't want to learn the identity of—just FYI—and about how our lives would play out, I'm pretty sure I'd do everything exactly the same way."

"Yeah?" he asked as he hooked his fork on the symbolic little gift Emma had made sure he'd find, the reason she'd been so adamant that he have *this* particular slice.

"Well, except for one thing," she amended, emotion-rich eyes watching his every reaction. "I'd make sure to visit you at juvie. *Especially* on your birthday."

Even though Jake had been adamant about his siblings not visiting him in juvie, if Emma had shown up, he would've seen her in a heartbeat.

"You told that mystery caller you were talking to on the phone that if the woman you wanted to spend the rest of your life with couldn't come to terms with your past, with the choices you'd made a part of your history fourteen years ago, if she couldn't accept that part of you, of who you were, then there was no possible future there."

Damn. She'd remembered it almost verbatim. He nodded, now seeing her gift, her loud-and-clear message to him in an even more meaningful light.

"So yes." Her gaze held his. "To show you that I'm that woman, the one you should spend the rest of your life with, I'd make absolutely certain to visit you at juvie on your birthday."

He pulled her closer. "With this cake?"

"Yup."

"With this very romantic, very meaningful *metal file* baked into it?"

She blushed shyly even as her voice grew bolder. "Definitely."

"God, I love you, woman."

Epilogue

Four months later

"I still don't understand why you won't tell me more about your older brother. It's bad enough you've kept him a secret all this time. The least you could do is answer a few questions about the man."

Jake sighed as his beautiful, bossy bride took the lead on the dance floor and tried to squeeze classified info out of him like a sexy spy on a mission.

"Why is he the only one that kept the Carmichael name? And how is it that you went from barely speaking to the guy to him becoming your best man? And holy crap, is he hitting on my sister?"

That last one caught Jake's attention, as well. When he looked over to where Megan was standing, sure enough, there was Carter. *Huh.*

Yeah, he wasn't touching that one with a ten-foot pole. Those two were consenting adults. They were possibly the most ill-conceived match on the planet, but, then again, most would've said the same thing about his relationship with Emma. So again, he was giving that entire situation a wide berth.

"I'm sure he's just talking to her about her house," hazarded Jake, knowing that had to be at least partially true. He'd caught Carter jotting down various things that needed fixing at Megan's house. Jake had no doubt he'd be getting a nice covert to-do list when he and Emma came back from their honeymoon.

As far as he knew, Megan still didn't know that Carter was the man behind a lot of the financial help throughout her life. So that meant Carter would be expecting him to get creative on getting Megan to accept his "help."

Having Carter back in his life again was a lot of work.

But it was . . . nice.

When it looked as if Emma was getting ready to launch another wave of questions, he quickly diverted her attention to a more pressing, very real concern. "Sweetheart, are you *sure* I'm not going to poison all our guests?"

A doting smile overtook her features as she finally refocused all her attention back on him. "We've gone over this. Your last few practice runs turned out great. Everyone's going to love the wedding cake. You're stressed over nothing."

He gave the leaning five-tiered cake he'd baked and spackled with frosting that morning another dubious look before replying. "Don't play Miss Cool Cucumber. You're one to talk. I saw you continuously peeking up at the wedding arch you'd built like it was going to fall atop our heads."

"That's different." She sniffed, eyes shooting back over to the wedding arch in question now that he'd reminded her of it. They'd wrapped enough ivy and flowers around it so you almost couldn't notice the copious amounts of duct tape Emma had used to reinforce certain areas.

"Really? How so?"

"Easy. I'm a much better teacher than you."

He chuckled, then leaned in to whisper, "That's not what you said the other night when we—"

Emma whacked him before he could finish that dirty recap.

"Aand, there she goes, folks," called out Megan, shaking her head. "The first whack of their marriage. Glad to see that marriage hasn't changed them one bit."

The crowd laughed.

As did the bride and groom.

"She's transformed so much," murmured Emma proudly. "Six months ago, Megan would never have been able to host our wedding and reception in her backyard. But did you see her earlier? She was running the whole thing like a *boss*."

Jake couldn't agree more.

Their wedding had been perfect. With all their town friends in attendance and dressed to the nines, like the fifteen garden gnomes Megan had dressed in fancy little suits for the occasion.

Sans the tiny-pecker condoms.

Truth is, they no longer needed the condoms, seeing as how they'd decided to start trying for a baby the very night they'd gotten engaged. They knew better than most how important it was to live life to the fullest. And they were both ready. Business was booming, and the new home they'd moved into next door to Megan's had a little room perfect for a nursery.

With a crib waiting for them the day they'd moved in, adorned with a big red bow.

Courtesy of Megan, whom they'd asked not only to be their future baby's godmother but also to honor them with picking the baby's middle name.

Megan, being Megan, had decided to keep them in suspense from that day forward, giving them wacky hints of the names she was thinking of, each crazier than the last.

Now, sitting on the deck opening wedding gifts with their siblings, Jake and Emma found that Megan had spent the past month knitting the most intricate baby blanket they'd ever seen. And in the corner of it, embroidered in a gender-neutral green was her middle-name choice for the baby.

Peyton.

Looking over at his beautiful, emotional wife, Jake leaned in to suggest quietly, "I say we make her pick again."

At Emma's shocked, dismayed expression, he quickly added with a smile as he wrapped his arms around her, "Because I think that would be perfect as a first name, don't you?"

She gifted him with a stunning smile. "Peyton Rowan *would* be a strong name for a boy as rascally as his namesake."

He chuckled and kissed her on the cheek. "Or a beautiful name for a girl as adorable as her mom."

She deployed her freckles happily. "Peyton Rowan it is." Looking around at their family and friends all gushing over the beautiful blanket, she whispered in his ear, "Should we tell them already?"

Jake felt his heart nearly bust out of his chest again, same as it had three nights ago when Emma had first told him—in her cute, bossy way—that he needed to be in charge of finding their something old, something borrowed, and something blue, because FYI, she already had the "new" part taken care of.

Immediately he'd known just the thing to satisfy all three requirements.

After kissing the hell out of Emma, he'd hopped Megan's fence and "borrowed" the old blue yarn blob that had been serving as Gnomeo the garden gnome's beret since the night of her first barbecue.

Given the way everything had worked out for him and Emma, it seemed fitting that the blob got to reinvent itself a second time, as well.

Turned out all the blob needed was a simple wooden frame . . . to turn into a perfect fluffy little cradle, just big enough to nestle the ultrasound printout Emma had surprised him with that night. In more ways than one.

"I have a better question," he whispered back to his beautiful wife, his hand gently rubbing her tummy. "Have you decided which of my siblings you're going to ask to pick the *other* baby's name yet?"

Acknowledgments

To my amazing Montlake team and especially my stupendously brilliant and supportive dev editor, Lauren . . . thank you all for making this book a possibility. It's the book that's been in me to write for longer than even I realized. I might not have ever found it if not for you. So thank you for unearthing the story I didn't know I've been looking for, for believing that I could do it justice, and for turning it into the book it is today.

To all of my "friends in the biz" and kindred souls who give me that sense of belonging I've never felt until now . . . thank you for being you. You all are the smartest, savviest, most inspirational people I've had the privilege of calling my colleagues and friends. You're also the most supportive rocks who manage to both ground me and challenge me when I need it. I've never been prouder or more grateful to be a part of the unique family that is the romance author community.

To all of the authors whose books I inhale like there is no tomorrow . . . thank you for writing the hell out of these books. Each of you helps make this world we live in such a special place that's seemingly boundless in possibilities because of all you create and dare to dream. I wouldn't be the author I am today if I weren't still the voracious reader I've been my entire life. Rather than getting lost in a book, for me, reading has always been how I've found my way. Thus, you are each a part of the constellation I look to whenever I lose track of my true north. So thank you for always navigating me in the right direction, and lighting the way with your incredible talent.

To my husband, Mr. Violet Duke . . . thank you for being my everything. You are one of my favorite human beings on this planet, one of the few folks who can make me actually laugh out loud. You help me forget about meds, symptoms, and prognoses. And only you can get me to silly-smile even when you're driving me bonkers. Whenever you're near me, I feel stronger, happier, more inspired. Thank you for always making me believe I can do anything.

About the Author

New York Times and *USA Today* best-selling author Violet Duke is a former English professor ecstatic to now be on the other side of the page. She enjoys writing emotion-rich stories with fun, everyday characters and sweet, sexy matchups. Since her acclaimed debut series in 2013, more than a million readers have put Violet's contemporary romances on the *USA Today* bestseller list sixteen times, the *New York Times* bestseller list three times, and the Top 10 charts across the major e-retailers, both in the United States and internationally. Born and raised in Hawaii, Violet continues to live the no-shoes island way with her nutty kids and crazy husband, her most devoted fan. Learn about Violet's new releases at www.VioletDuke.com.